M000280168

THE PILOT

Fighter Planes and Paris

ED COBLEIGH

ISBN 0692392068
All enquiries are directed to Check Six Books, 3750 Sky Ridge Drive, Paso Robles, CA, 93446
Cover design by Bespoke Book Covers Ltd, UK
Edited by Irene Chambers, It's About Time Virtual Assistance
ALSO BY ED COBLEIGH
War for the Hell of It, a Fighter Pilot's View of Vietnam
ISBN 13: 9780692392065
Library of Congress Control Number: 2015902921
Check Six Books, Paso Robles, CA

DEDICATION

To Heidi
She tolerates my tales with good humor and grace.

THE PILOT

Fighter Planes and Paris

ED COBLEIGH

CHECK SIX BOOKS

Paso Robles

TABLE OF CONTENTS

Chapter One: The Latin Quarter, Paris, **April 2014** _____ 1

Chapter Two: Southern Iraq, **January 1994** _____ 11

Chapter Three: King Khalid Air Base, Saudi Arabia, **January 1994** _____ 23

Chapter Four: 4th/7th Arrondissements, Paris, **April 2014** _____ 32

Chapter Five: Northwest Thailand/Southern Laos **June 1971** _____ 43

Chapter Six: Ubon Ratchathani, Thailand, **June 1971** _____ 54

Chapter Seven: Le Bourget Airfield, Paris, **April 2014** _____ 63

Chapter Eight: Ramstein Air Base, Germany, **December 1961** _____ 74

Chapter Nine: Pigeon Forge, East Tennessee, **June 1961** _____ 85

Chapter Ten: 4th Arrondissement, Paris, **April 2014** _____ 94

Chapter Eleven: MiG Alley, North Korea, **February 1952** _____ 102

Chapter Twelve: La Closerie Des Lilas, Montparnasse,
           Paris, **April 2014** _____ 114

Chapter Thirteen: Hornchurch Aerodrome, England, **August 1940** _____ 124

Chapter Fourteen: Royal Air Force Club, Piccadilly,
           London, **September 1940** _____ 137

Chapter Fifteen: American Embassy, Place de la Concorde,
           Paris, **April 2014** _____ 148

Chapter Sixteen: L'Ile Saint-Louis, Paris, **May 2014** _____ 159

Chapter Seventeen: The Western Front, France, **March 1918** _____ 170

Chapter Eighteen: Le Coup Chou Restaurant, 5th Arrondissement,
Paris, **November 1918** _____ 181
Chapter Nineteen: Fouquet's Café, Champs-Elysées, Paris, **May 2014** ___ 189
Chapter Twenty: The Eurostar, Northwest France, **May 2014**_____ 197

**"THE FARTHER BACKWARD YOU CAN LOOK,
THE FARTHER FORWARD YOU ARE LIKELY TO SEE."**

--Sir Winston Churchill

CHAPTER 1

THE LATIN QUARTER

Paris

April 2014: The Pilot didn't fear the new jet or think it could kill him, for he had flown worse fighter planes, some much worse, and yet he was still alive. Many cold, miserable hours in the Sopwith Camel were recorded in his mental logbook, marking his flights in that primitive biplane, an aircraft which murdered nearly as many of its own pilots during the Great War as it did the men it was designed to kill. The stiletto-shaped F-104 Starfighter, another airborne challenge he had mastered, showed serious speed but struggled to maneuver on stubby, downward-slanted wings. It was a difficult jet to keep in the air. If those two treacherous aircraft hadn't done him in, the latest model fighter, the F-35, wouldn't either. No, the new jet, even with its reported flaws, didn't worry him.

Long ago he banished the fear of airborne death to a remote region of his brain, imprisoned where it wasn't allowed to impact his thinking or influence his decisions, however dangerous the immediate situation. Fighter pilots firmly believe in their personal immortality, with a blind faith in invincibility being a critical requirement for the job. This attribute the Pilot exhibited in abundance, even to himself. He liked to think that he wasn't afraid of much, except maybe of being alone, a fear he didn't admit to himself until a few shots of bourbon or glasses of wine worked their magic. So what was stopping him? Why wasn't he ready to sign up for the F-35?

What pilot wouldn't want to fly the planet's hottest fighter plane? Why was the offered choice to do so, or not, so difficult? The Pilot prided himself on making the fast decisions demanded by air combat, but the opportunity in front of him presented a different type of problem--too much time to think about possible consequences before deciding which course to take.

Often rife with a myriad of lethal possibilities, war in the air efficiently sorts the quick from the dead, rewarding fast, good decisions and imposing fatal consequences for bad or tardy ones. The Pilot had seen both types of choices made, witnessing victories as well as deaths, some of each richly deserved, others tragic. Now he faced a decision affording the supposed luxury of time, one allowing careful weighing of alternatives. The personal ramifications of his actions would be as significant as any he made while airborne; the stakes were that high.

An untested fighter plane could be dangerous, unreliable, ill-suited for its mission, and perhaps poorly designed. Only the crucible of combat could test the mettle--or the metal--of the F-35, and that hadn't happened yet. The Pentagon claimed the aircraft was almost ready for combat, but was it? The physical risk inherent in flying a new bird wasn't stopping him from pulling his decision trigger. No, the problem was more complex than mere mortality. If he chose to fly the F-35, would the necessary ethical compromises cost him his manhood while leaving him very much alive? This was another possible outcome to be considered, evaluated, and discounted or hoisted aboard. He had faced the specter of sudden death many times, staring down the Grim Reaper again and again, but he was never forced to give up his core identity--fighter pilot, lone-wolf fighter pilot. The F-35 threatened to change all that. Its advanced technology and intrusive electronics would dictate tactics, constrain actions, and allow command interference, taking the control stick out of the hand of its pilot and giving it to the software programmer. The Pilot didn't worry that the aircraft would fail but that it would succeed. Preliminary accounts were clear--the F-35 flew on the strength of its software, not on the thrust of its engine, the lift of its wing, or the lethality of its weapons. Flying the new jet would require the Pilot to take a new approach to air combat with him into the future, but could he make that adjustment?

Important crossroads in life usually go unrecognized until a path forward has been chosen and travel has begun, or has nearly ended. Crucial junctions are often visible only by looking backward, viewing the past with today's knowledge of the outcome in hand. This nexus was different, identifiable, distinct. The Pilot could clearly see his choice would have profound effects on his future or even determine if he had a future. The US Air Force (USAF) had given him three weeks to decide. Now the clock was ticking.

Crucial decisions are profoundly influenced by the places where they are made. Physical surroundings weigh heavily on a choice, setting artificial boundaries, limiting the number of visible options, and subtly steering the mental development process. A liberal, even libertine, great city's many carnal delights constantly tempt, offering alternate pleasure paths available for the taking.

Paris is such a city.

The French assert that a vineyard's total environment, its terroir, intensely affects a wine's final quality in the bottle. In the same way, the character of a city (particularly the French capital city with so much to offer) prejudices any lasting decision taken there with its distinctive outlook on life and its strong opinions on how life should be led.

The Pilot believed living in Paris would help him make his life-changing, possibly life-threatening, decision. Serious consideration of the future came readily to him in that city, a place so conscious of its storied history. The pervasive Parisian ambiance promoted reflection on the past, alternative futures, and the effects today's decisions have on the unformed yet-to-be. Paris's intense terroir forced him to acknowledge the way the past shapes our vision of the future and, once in place, the present alters our memories of the past. He observed this ongoing process all around him as he explored the city's older sections. The jumbled mélange of the ancient and the modern showed him how the present world's form was wrought by decisions made earlier, sometimes much earlier.

Everywhere in Paris he saw iconic structures built in the middle ages juxtaposed with soulless modern construction. Walking to work, he passed the jarring glass pyramids jutting from the Louvre's ancient, stone-paved courtyard. He lived not far from the absurd inside-out Georges Pompidou modern art museum, disconcertedly inserted into Paris's oldest intact neighborhood, the Marais. He often strolled the tree-lined Champs-Elysées, where Napoleon's triumphant army marched and later German storm troopers swaggered. All this living, constantly evolving history illustrated that while some concepts endure, others are rejected or modified, and no one can predict which will prevail and which will be left behind.

Paris evolved over the centuries, yet it remained much the same. Not like Rome, that eternal and eternally run-down city, or the City of London, where structural change is often viewed the way exposed female skin was by spinster Victorian aunts. The tension between progress and status quo, between the newly minted and the ancient, between what has been and what has been foretold mirrored the Pilot's personal dilemma. The French city's approachability and reasonable scale allowed difficult thought processes to come easier to him while he roamed its streets, thinking, considering. Now he must decide which path into his future he would select.

An officer of the US Air Force, he was stationed at the US embassy in Paris as the senior air attaché. In the rarefied world of international diplomacy, he wore his blue uniform only when required, usually at official functions.

In his early forties, the Pilot was of above-average height, well put together but not athletic, around two hundred pounds. He kept his dark hair trimmed short in a military style. Women considered his face attractive, set off by a hawk's nose and wide-set green eyes which often stared off into the middle distance. His natural self-confidence, expressed by his body language and reflected in his walk, set him apart from other, lesser men. Walking quickly, with long strides, he had a confident pace, purpose-driven. He moved with easy, natural coordination without wasted movement. In another time or another life, instead of a fighter pilot, he could have been a shortstop on the baseball diamond or a gunfighter in the Old West--two other professions where the penalties for failure are both highly visible and immediate. He projected the air of someone who has seen the bright lights and heard the loud noises, who has prevailed over dangers experienced by few.

He found out early in life that women were turned on by his confident aura, but his cocky attitude often presented a challenge to other men, particularly men internally insecure with their social status. In bars around the world, the Pilot was a man who provoked invitations for a marathon drinking contest, a pool table shoot-out, or a fistfight--gauntlets he picked up too often for his own good.

This afternoon, a Friday, found the Pilot idle, at loose ends with no scripted cocktail parties to attend at the US embassy, no visiting VIPs to escort around Paris, and no junketing members of Congress to patronize. The French work-week is thirty-five hours and ended today at noon. He left his office shortly after one o'clock asking himself, *Am I going native?* No matter. An open afternoon left him ample time for thought.

He recalled how French intellectual Jean-Paul Sartre once, perhaps only once, explained a concept clearly and accurately. His idea resonated with the Pilot's immediate status. A denizen of the Left Bank, Sartre wrote that midaft-ernoon is the most awkward time, too early to abandon an earlier project and too late to start a different task. Fortunately, today the Pilot's intended gig re-quired nothing more than Cognac, coffee, and contemplation; no need to aban-don those or to begin anything else. The three Cs could comfortably consume the afternoon.

He sat under the red awning of the tourist trap bistro on the corner of Boulevard Saint Michel and Quai Montebello, on Sartre's beloved Left Bank. The manila file lying on the table in front of him contained a letter presenting his problem. For the fourth time since its reception this morning at the embassy, he opened the file, unfolded the official message, and read it.

The Pentagon ordered him to report back to the States for duty and detailed his next assignment. What random spin of the personnel division's roulette wheel had landed his ball in this coveted slot? Flying the F-35! What a great job! *Well maybe*, he almost said out loud.

Half the fighter pilots in the US Air Force and all the jocks in the US Navy would give one of their own balls for a chance like this. Only the USAF's F-22 Raptor occupied a higher step on the fighter aviation ziggurat than the F-35; it was touted to be that good. But the orders in front of him remained unexecuted; he had three weeks to report, or not. Meanwhile, he considered his other options.

I've got my time in. I could retire with honor, move on with my life as a civilian, maybe even find a woman to live with and to love. Or, I could strap myself into the new jet, wring the bugs out of it, and with any luck, see some more combat. What is the career equivalent of Sartre's midafternoon quandary? I haven't finished the air attaché assignment in Paris; I could stay here. Was it too late in life to take on a new fighter plane? It had been years since he last flew a combat mission. He missed the physical and mental challenges, the danger-driven rush, the sweaty palms, the six-G doughnut in the pit of his stomach at the start of an engagement. Adrenaline is highly addictive; the Pilot was hooked deep and had been for a long time. Could the F-35 deliver that high? Would the ethical price paid be worth the emotional return? Still undecided, the Pilot returned the disruptive letter to the folder and tossed it back on the table with a dismissive flick of his wrist.

He looked back out at the street corner, crowded with people passing as they crossed the River Seine, and watched as they trooped into the Latin Quarter. A constant stream of humanity flowed by in the pale midafternoon sun. Inside, a Gallic waiter properly attired in a black coat and white apron appeared, standing quietly beside the Pilot's tiny, round table, and also looked out, not at the Pilot. The Pilot took the server's refusal to speak as a challenge; the first man to talk would instantly put himself in thrall to the other, emotionally dependent on an appropriate reply, a step lower in the masculine pecking order. He called the Frenchman's bluff by also remaining silent.

At last the waiter conceded and spoke, "Avez-vous choisi?" (Have you chosen what you want?)

Without looking away from the window, the Pilot replied, "Un café Américain et un Cognac, non, pas de Cognac, Je prendai un Armagnac," not adding the customary "S'il vous plaît." He curtly ordered a watered-down espresso with milk and an Armagnac brandy without saying "please" in French. One must show steely resolve, not genteel manners, when dealing with Parisian waiters long accustomed to treating foreign customers brusquely. His accent and his order of American-style coffee would instantly and erroneously label him as a tourist. The waiter would wonder why a visiting American would drink Armagnac in the middle of the afternoon.

From the look on his face, the waiter knew he had lost this engagement. He frowned, a wasted gesture unobserved by the forward-facing Pilot. The server spun abruptly on his heel and flounced off toward the bar without acknowledging the request.

After three cycles of the traffic lights on the intersection outside, the waiter at last returned, set the coffee and a small snifter of amber brandy on the Pilot's plastic table along with a paper check written in some sort of unbreakable restaurant code, and again vanished without a sound. The Pilot reflected, *Why should the server be friendly? He doesn't work for tips; service is included in most watering holes in France. But most Americans tip for service routinely; even faux hospitality would pay off for him. I guess it's hard for some people to act in their own best interests.*

How could he avoid adopting the surly server's counterproductive attitude? Which path forward would be in his best interests? What precisely were his best interests? What was it about the F-35 that was so worrisome? All the official accounts piped to the US embassy were laudatory, maybe overly, suspiciously so. He had to wonder if the message traffic was a sales job. The jet was touted to feature the last word in electronics--total connectivity, all the time. One need never fly alone; help was always just a bleep away. Was that a good idea? A single-seat fighter pilot was used to relying on his eyesight, reflexes, courage, and skill. Would the F-35's electronic magic aid or hinder him? *It is, Watson, a two pipe, or two snifter problem*, he concluded, taking his first sip of the Armagnac.

The foot traffic in front of the terrace fascinated the Pilot as always in Paris when the weather allowed outdoor people-watching. For April the weather was spectacular, sunny, and not too cool. Normally, April in Paris is dismal--rainy, windy, and cold. Folkloric legend states that whoever wrote the old standard show tune "April in Paris" was once asked, "Why feature April, the cruelest month?" The rationale given back was that May or June didn't rhyme, a triumph of poetry over precipitation.

As he alternately sipped Armagnac and coffee, the Pilot noticed how the stream of humanity crossing the bridge on his right and passing before him flowed ceaselessly like the Seine's swift waters under the arched stone span. The types of people in motion on the sidewalk constantly varied; each was an individual both immersed in and making up the stream. The human rivulet in front of him had been running continually during the last fifteen hundred years of

Parisian history. Students at the Sorbonne University were always here, but always mingled with others. From the priests, peasants, and pilgrims of medieval times; to the *sans-culottes* (those blood-stained revolutionaries) and the emerging bourgeoisie of the 1790s; to the soldiers, civil servants, and survivors of two World Wars; all had passed by this corner. Their spirits were passing by now among the living, and their descendants would troop past this intersection in the future. The French have a phrase for it: "Plus ça change...Plus c'est la même chose." (The more it changes, the more it is the same.) The peopled stream itself was constant, but the types of individuals in it changed slowly over the centuries, as well as varying minute by minute.

He ruminated further, considering the truism that not all change was for the best. Sometimes a change hailed as progress was actually a wrong turn, a corruption of freedoms fought for and won in the past. When was change for the better and when not? Technological change pushed our society into the future. Did change driven by advanced technology tend to empower us, or did it want to enslave us? The F-35 was the embodiment of technical advances, but did it represent progress or a threat?

Aye, but there's the rub, he thought, surprising himself with a quote from Shakespeare. The Pilot wasn't a big fan of the Bard. For him, Shakespeare's works featured far too many hackneyed clichés. It seemed that a time-worn phrase or overly familiar scene resided on every page. But he had to admit that Hamlet's indecision resonated with his own.

When to embrace technological change, and how fast to do it? An example of what not to do drove by the front of the bistro. The cavalcade of cars vying for position on the congested street was mainly French-built. French cars sold in large numbers only in France, much less so elsewhere. French automotive styling, always different, resonated poorly with the rest of the world. The French automobile sales gap mirrored a similar lack of global interest in French fighter planes. Sitting near the religious center of France, across the river from Notre Dame Cathedral, while contemplating the most secular of devices, fighter aircraft, didn't seem odd to the Pilot. He thought about fighters a lot. Bankers walked the streets inventing money schemes; chefs mentally create their next culinary coup; fashionistas obsessed over haute couture. Fighter pilots preferred to think only about fighter planes and flying. If only it were that simple again with nothing but airborne problems. At various times, life had been uncomplicated and clear for the Pilot--eat, sleep, drink, fly, fight, live another day, and occasionally get laid. That was a first-rate life, flying fighters back then. *Back then* included when the French knew how to sell fighters.

At times French fighters had been first-rate. The SPAD XIIIs and Nieuport 28 biplanes of World War I were world-class machines. Late in the conflict, their pilots gave the German Albatrosses all they could handle and more. Even the US Army Air Service bought French planes in quantity. In the 1960s, Dassault's single-engine Mirage jets were competitive with anyone's fighters. But a lack of investment in stealth technology, and the vain inability to cooperate and trade data with allies as equals, caused the French and their designs to be left behind. They hadn't changed fast enough to stay relevant.

Dassault's current Rafale twin-engined fighter appealed to the Pilot's eyes on an aesthetic level with its sensuous curves, perfect proportions, and clean lines; he thought it was supremely beautiful and probably a delight to fly, like the Mirages. But it was rolling only slowly off the production line in Saint Cloud outside Paris. It was new but at least a generation behind its American competitors; its technology was supposedly inferior to the cutting edge capabilities of the F-35. He remembered a quote by Marcel Dassault, the old man, founder of the eponymous aircraft manufacturer: "If it looks right; it probably is right." The Rafale certainly looked right to pilots, but it didn't look right to radar. Those sensuous curves were easily detectable by radar beams, unlike the F-35's sharp angles and slab sides. The US intelligence reports were adamant: those carefully calculated contours made the American jet electronically invisible. The Pilot thought the American design was too high-tech and its shape bordered on ugly. He knew the Rafale wasn't stealthy and thus wasn't right for the dogfights of the future. It also didn't play well with others, lacking the electronic connectivity between aircraft that allowed US fighters continually to share information on an airborne form of the internet. Like French cars, French fighter planes sold only in France. There was a lesson here somewhere, he thought, if only he could tease it out.

French distilled spirits sold successfully world-wide but probably not the stuff lurking in the snifter on his table. The harsh Armagnac bit his tongue with

the heat of too much raw alcohol and too much youth. During aging in the man-
dated black oak barrels, evaporation through the bent wooden staves is called
"The Angels' Share." The angels must have inhaled more than their vaporous
fair share from this plonk and left the Devil's portion behind in the cask for human consumption. He realized Armagnac can be quirky, but this stuff sloshed
way outside the envelope of acceptability. And he should have asked for a specific label instead of leaving the selection to the tender mercies of the waiter whom
he had challenged and defeated in a stare-down. *Score one for the house*, he thought.

In an attempt, probably in vain, to render the revolting stuff potable, the
Pilot poured the remaining Armagnac from the small globular glass into his
half-empty coffee cup, stirring it in. Flavoring oils floated to the surface in iridescent swirls as the milked coffee turned a lighter shade of brown. The rotating
liquid's unique tint appeared oddly familiar. In his deep memory, or perhaps in
the memory of someone very much like him, the fast-flowing, earthy color was
eerily recognizable, as if he had seen that pattern of hues in rapid movement
before. But where and when?

Most of one's memories are the results of direct experience, deposited in
our minds during our lives, departing when we do. Some memories are passed
between fighter squadron mates, in the crew room, over a bourbon and water at
the Officers' Mess, in the alert hut while waiting for a scramble call, or in books
written by pilots who have been there, done that, and won the medals. These
and other memories live on after us, and are handed down--fraternal, indelible,
shared between unrelated strangers across the skies of time.

The coffee's distinctive color was one of those memories, awakening a half-
forgotten scene from someone's past. Somewhere in the Pilot's consciousness,
drowning out the din of passing traffic and the clatter of dishes nearby, an unseen jet engine roared, echoing off hard-packed sand the color of watered coffee,
its noise unheard by anyone else in the café, but real all the same.

CHAPTER 2

SOUTHERN IRAQ

January 1994: The desert passing under the north-bound F-16 resembled the color of weak coffee with milk (café au lait). Two hundred feet beneath the jet's belly, the parched landscape screamed by at 480 knots (550 miles per hour). Objects were only fleetingly visible a quarter mile in front of the fighter's parrot's beak nose or a few hundred yards off each wingtip. Down on each side of the cockpit, closer in, nothing was recognizable; everything blended into an undulating burnt-ochre smear. The fighter's single jet engine screamed, converting kerosene to speed and noise and thrusting the F-16 tirelessly forward, barely above the desolate sand.

Iraq's gritty southern desert, forever coated with wind-blown dust, offered few landmarks for visual navigation. The few featureless villages apparently sprinkled at random around the countryside appeared all the same, as identical as the pencil-straight dirt roads connecting them. Blowing dust blurred the indistinct horizon, a blending of mud-colored sand and dirty sky. Overhead the jet's bubble canopy, straight above the Pilot's helmet, the cloudless sky should have burned blue, but it too was tinged with brown, tainted by the omnipresent, dirty haze.

Traveling at the speed of heat, the F-16 roared on over the barren scene, the engine's roar reverberating off the hard-packed surface. Outside, the jet's sonic blast would be painfully intense, but in the cockpit, the Pilot's soundproofed flight helmet with its liquid-isolated earphones kept the sound level low, almost quiet, silent inside his head. At this speed, the engine's thunder was left behind for the few wandering souls on the surface to deal with.

This is high performance flying at its best, thought the Pilot. *This is what I signed up to do.* As he flew extremely low and blindingly fast, the margin for error was vanishingly small. With one moment of inattention, one reflexive twitch on the controls, or one altitude-losing turn, he and his F-16 would disappear together in a long, fiery explosion smeared across the desert floor. The wreck would flame for a minute or two and then burn out in a rising cloud of dirty, black smoke, leaving nothing recognizable indicating a human and aircraft had died there. He couldn't consider that possibility, only the tasks at hand: navigation, weapons systems management, the fuel state, monitoring the radio, watching for missile threats, keeping in formation on his flight leader, and preventing impact with the ground, not necessarily in that order.

He flew the ideal tool for the job, the F-16. Originally named the "Falcon," the plane's moniker was changed by a timid Air Force bureaucracy to the "Fighting Falcon" in response to a threatened lawsuit from the Dassault Company in France, which had already christened a civilian business jet as a "Falcon." Instead of using its official, safe handle, pilots always called the F-16 the "Viper" after the X-winged spaceship fighters in the *Star Wars* movies. Other detractors, perhaps envious, referred to it as the "Lawn Dart," a riff on its diminutive size, toy-like profile, and propensity early in the development program to crash, hitting the ground vertically, nose first.

The Viper's compact airframe sported revolutionary technology; the Pilot's hands and feet didn't directly move the controls. Since the dawn of aviation, aircraft had been flown by control sticks and rudder pedals, each translating through a range of motion. The further the stick was pushed, the more the ailerons, elevators, and rudder moved, and the more the aircraft tried to respond. The control stick always resided between the pilot's thighs. Not in the Viper. The stick was mounted on the right-hand console, where a pilot could brace his arm under high G loads, and far from the instrument panel, so as to not obscure the flat-screen displays. The stubby stick with its many buttons only moved a quarter inch in any direction and didn't move the fight controls directly at all; computers handled that task. The rudder pedals were similarly fixed solidly on the floor.

Like the famed Sopwith Camel of World War I, the Pilot's F-16 was aerodynamically unstable, even divergent, in the vertical, or pitch, axis. Unlike the Camel, most earlier airplanes had built-in stability, the various aerodynamic forces balanced out so the craft would fly hands-off for a time. Those planes wanted to fly straight and level until their pilots commanded them to turn, climb, or roll. Once the science of flight was well known, unstable aircraft like the Camel disappeared until the Viper took advantage of the maneuverability afforded by instability.

The Viper wanted to pitch up violently, only flying straight and level when directly ordered to do so. Three onboard computers interfaced between the Pilot's inputs and the aerodynamic control surfaces. The computers took their instructions from subtle pressures applied to the fixed controls by the Pilot. Without the computers' constant, split-second adjustments, the aircraft would start a vertical climb, over-stressing and tearing apart the airframe before the remaining wreckage tumbled end over end.

The Pilot felt the F-16 spliced directly into his central nervous system. Relieved of the necessity to physically move the flight controls, he was required just to press lightly with his gloved hands and flight boots. Only the throttle moved, sliding through its eight-inch range of motion. He barely thought of moving the aircraft; it instantaneously responded to his command. The inherent aerodynamic instability gave Viper lightning reflexes; it desperately wanted to dart, turn, and roll, but its computers held it straight and level until the Pilot desired otherwise.

The radar altimeter read 180 feet above the sand. Without any conscious thought process by the Pilot, the jet climbed back to 200 feet. His flight leader had moved out on his left, a little over a half mile away, when he noticed this. His jet slid back into formation, seemingly without being asked. The Pilot, the computers, the engine, and the airframe had formed a seamless team, each keeping the other members alive.

Important information required by the Pilot was projected on a small plate of glass directly in his view as he looked out over the nose. The data appeared superimposed, floating ethereally on the blurred desert scene ahead, projected there by the Head Up Display (HUD). Now the HUD told him ten seconds to go until the next navigation waypoint, the map coordinates where he and his flight leader planned to separate and individually attack the target. Half way to the horizon directly ahead, he spotted the the Initial Point (IP), an intersection of two desert dirt roads, coming up fast. The two F-16s flashed over the cross-roads. Time to get serious.

"Viper Flight, IP," his flight leader's disembodied voice sounded inside his head, heard over the radio.

The Pilot clicked his radio transmit button on the throttle twice without speaking, acknowledging that he heard the IP call. He turned right forty-five degrees, careful not to lose altitude during the shallow-banked turn, and looked over his shoulder. His flight leader's jet was departing ninety degrees left, behind his F-16's wing line. He quickly lost sight of Viper Leader on the hazy horizon; he penetrated the target area alone. Now came the mission's hardest, most dangerous phase--an attack on a Surface-to-Air Missile (or SAM) site, among the most hazardous tasks a fighter pilot can attempt. Both pilots of Viper Flight were now on their own until they converged over the target to shoot it out with the SAM site in a desert duel to the death. With his flight leader no longer a visual presence, only a remote voice on the radio, he surprised himself by wondering if he would ever see her again.

They would soon kick open the Iraqi version of the Long Branch Saloon's swinging doors. Survival in the imminent bar fight was seriously in doubt for the two pilots of Viper Flight.

A SAM site attack rivals an old west Dodge City shoot-out in danger. Instead of Colt revolvers, the weapons of choice are guided missiles for both sides. A SAM site's mission is shooting down aircraft and killing pilots. So pilots love striking SAM sites, preventing losses of their own kind. No exception, the Pilot lived to kill SAM sites, and he was good at it. The rewarding mission was difficult and could be hazardous to one's health, factors that increased the SAM killer's status in the squadron. When successful, they protected others' lives, and everyone knew it.

SAMs have a maximum range beyond which they cannot fly. The site itself has a minimum range inside which the missiles cannot be guided. Drawn on a navigation chart, these limitations form two concentric rings centered on the site, one much larger than the other. The resulting depiction forms what the squadron's gallows humorist labeled "The Doughnut of Death." The secret to silencing a SAM site while surviving the attack is transiting the death doughnut at extremely low altitude, below radar coverage, then mounting a direct attack on the site from inside the minimum range circle. The SAM site's operators know the doughnut's extent better than anyone and have no death wish. So a SAM site usually defends itself inside the minimum range circle with anti-aircraft guns; short-range, man-portable, anti-aircraft missiles; and small-caliber, automatic weapons.

Passing through the doughnut, the Pilot and his flight leader must now find the site, attack it, avoid the short-range defenses, and get out of Dodge City alive. Precision flying would be the key to survival and success; the timing had to be perfect.

He kept the Viper down on the deck, low and fast, as he followed the navigation guidance on the HUD and woke up his own guided weapons. The F-16 carried a Maverick missile under each of its stubby wings. Each missile packed a three hundred pound warhead optimized for maximum blast effects. Detonation would hurl a steel storm of jagged fragments into anything within its lethal radius. Behind each Maverick's glass nose dome, a tiny camera stared out along the F-16's projected line of flight. The cameras captured images of the scene ahead and projected those images electronically on a small screen in front of the Pilot. He saw what the missiles saw, as if peering through their Cyclops eyes. The image from the right missile was as clear as the picture from the left. One Maverick would be the primary weapon with the other held in reserve.

Great, thought the Pilot. *Both Mavericks are players. Now all I have to do is get in, let them do their thing, and get out alive.* The missiles' *thing* was killing the SAM site operators. It wasn't productive destroying the big missiles on their launchers; there would be too many, with a stock of replacement SAMs stored nearby. Near the site's center lurked the guidance radar and control van, a trailer where the operators sat as they commanded their missiles. The radar van was more expensive and harder to replace than the missile launchers, but spares were available. The human operators represented far more value; they trained for years to ply their deadly trade. Skilled SAM operators were rare in Iraq, and the Pilot hoped to make them even rarer. The planned assassination hinged on the element of surprise. If the operators suspected their site was under attack from inside minimum range, they might bolt, disappearing into a nearby bunker. They were also known to jump into a waiting pickup truck and flee across the open desert in panic. Destroying the control van would tally a mission accomplished; killing the site's masters would be far more rewarding. He would have but one chance at it.

The HUD said five seconds until the pull-up point; he spotted the landmark approaching rapidly, a dog-leg concrete bridge crossing a muddy irrigation canal. He flashed over the pull-up point and applied gentle back pressure to the fixed control stick. The jet responded instantly with five Gs. The F-16 changed course like a good cutting horse, anticipating the next move. The Pilot's two hundred pound frame now weighed a thousand pounds; the five Gs pushed him down into the ejection seat. He tightened his neck muscles and fought to keep his head erect. His left hand pushed the throttle through the detent notch into afterburner range. The afterburner sprayed raw fuel into the jet engine's exhaust just past the red-hot turbine, tripled the fuel consumption, doubled the thrust output, and converted the F-16's aft end into an air-breathing rocket. A satisfying shove in the back from the extra thrust told the Pilot the 'burner had lit as the Viper accelerated in a thirty-degree climb. His thumb tightened on the mike button, but before he transmitted, Viper Lead came on the radio.

"Viper Lead's up." Her voice projected calmness, her tone matter-of-fact, no different from calling, "Eight ball in the side pocket," instead of announcing a fight to the death with a waiting SAM site. She portrayed quiet competence in the air with her transmissions. No matter how stressful the situation, radio messages must reek with detachment, a point of pride among fighter pilots. An effective flight leader exudes confidence--confidence he or she will make the right decisions, get the flight to the target, accomplish the mission, and get everybody safely home again.

"Two's up," he replied on the radio, his voice dripping with boredom.

He thought, *You want cool? Check this out.* Not readily apparent in his laconic reply was his relief at knowing she accomplished her pull-up and was now in for the kill. Their plan called for simultaneous attacks from opposite sides of the compass, the Pilot from the east, his flight lead from the west. Their separation would divide the point defenses' attention and give the Bad Guys two lethal problems at once. The quick dual attacks would also reduce the operators' time to take cover and cut the Iraqis' chances to live and fight some other day.

The altitude readout on the HUD wound up: two thousand feet, three thousand feet, four thousand feet. He looked out in front of the left wingtip's leading edge for the SAM site. There it was, matching the photos taken this morning by the spy satellite. Single-track dirt roads bladed into the café au lait sand connected the missile launchers with each other and the control van/radar unit in the site's approximate center. Berms of sand scooped from the desert surrounded the radar van on all sides, protecting it from near misses. He couldn't precisely identify the van with brown camouflage netting draped all over it. He saw only its general location inside the berms, centered by the encircling missiles clearly visible on their erect launchers. He caught a glint of movement from the rotating search-and-track radar antenna mounted on the van's roof. The site was active and searching, searching for him and Viper Lead. Good, the high-value targets, the human operators, were home and open for the business of shooting down him and his wingman. The bartender stopped polishing glasses, the saloon piano fell silent, and the Bad Guys loosened the Colts in their holsters for the coming showdown.

Five thousand feet on the HUD, time to step inside from Dodge City's Main Street and get this shoot-out done. Could he and his leader launch their missiles to the control van before the operators fled and, more importantly, before the local defenses tagged Viper Flight? He willed the jet to roll left 135 degrees, looking for the target. The G loading told his body that gravity, and thus Mother Earth, was always oriented down toward the jet's belly. It appeared to the Pilot's vision as if he rotated the brown earth to a position overhead, not that the F-16 rolled inverted. He pulled the nose down with four Gs until the aiming index on the HUD pointed at the SAM site's approximate center.

At the apex of his pop-up, he toggled off flares and chaff and pulled the throttle back out of afterburner. Ejected from the aircraft and rapidly left behind, the flares were burning magnesium shards, white and red points of light hotter and more distinct than the jet's exhaust, to decoy heat-seeking missiles. The chaff cartridges fired shotgun shells of shredded, aluminum-coated plastic into his wake. The chaff's bright radar return would bloom and confuse any missile guidance radar, he hoped.

He banked and ruddered the diving jet until the HUD's aiming index, the "death dot," covered the center of the SAM site. Without moving his head, he looked down at the cockpit display. The van stood out on the black-and-white TV like a dog's balls. The missile's camera didn't operate in normal light, or the van would be invisible under its sagging tent of brown netting. The Maverick peered in the infrared spectrum and produced a TV-like image from differences in heat emitted by the target area. Relatively cooler areas were darker; hotter objects showed whiter on the instrument panel display. The van, easily the hottest object on the screen, glowed shimmering white, the nets transparent to the radiant heat produced by the diesel generators, electronics, and air conditioners.

With the F-16 hurtling downhill in the dive, the target grew bigger and bigger in the cockpit display and the HUD's real world scene. Not much time left. The Pilot fingered a control tab on the front of the throttle and locked the missile onto the malignantly glowing radar van. The aiming dots displayed on the cockpit TV grabbed the van, shrinking around its white-hot outline; the missile knew its target. His right thumb pressed and held down the red ordnance release button on the top of the aircraft control stick. *This better work*, he thought. *I'm not hanging my ass out for nothing.*

The Maverick hesitated for a second's eternity, long enough for the Pilot to wonder if it was functional, then left in a hurried whoosh. A thick-white, dense smoke trail from its solid rocket motor pointed back at the F-16. If the Bad Guys hadn't seen him yet, they would now; the rocket's exhaust marked his location in the hazy sky. The missile climbed for a short time after clearing the launch rail. Then he saw it nose over toward the target. Programmed to attack vertically, the steep terminal dive increased its accuracy and would concentrate the warhead's fiery blast inside the bulldozed berms.

Inside his helmet an inner voice said, *Tonto, our work here is done; time to ride the hell out of Dodge City.* On reflexes alone, he rotated the world on end once again and pulled the nose farther down toward the desert. As the jet rolled, he caught a glimpse of another Maverick smoke trail arching downward toward the site from the west. If the missiles guided, and they gave every indication of doing just that, each would have a ninety percent chance of impacting within three feet of the targeted van. No need for a re-attack with the spare Maverick.

As the desolate desert rushed up to meet the diving Viper, the airplane seemed to pull itself out of the descent without conscious effort on the Pilot's part. He leveled off back down at two hundred feet and turned toward the planned join-up area. Viper Lead had selected the rendezvous point--a ragged cluster of dusty buildings, the closest village south of the target. She wanted the Iraqis to see who torched the local SAM site.

He couldn't resist a slight left turn, looking back over his shoulder at the site, now behind a small rise and disappearing quickly behind the F-16's tail. He violated the ground attack pilot's cardinal rule--never linger and admire your work--but few jocks could exit stage right without a wee peek. A greasy-black mini-mushroom cloud rose from behind the low hill. Only volatile petroleum burned with such a fast-rising smoke signature; at least one Maverick must have hit near the van and touched off its diesel fuel tank. A U-2 reconnaissance plane would be high overhead later in the afternoon, photographing the site from the stratosphere's upper boundary. Its high-resolution cameras would record the destruction and hopefully confirm the likelihood of the operators achieving martyrdom.

As the designated village disappeared under the nose, the Pilot started a right 360-degree turn, waiting for her, another no-no in Indian Country. One compartment of his mind mused, *Rendez-vous means "meeting you" in French, like two lovers finding each other on the Champs-Elysées. It's a strange word to use for a join-up of combat fighter jets over enemy territory.*

The radio came alive. "Viper Two, got you in sight. Come back left," he heard her say.

Late by seconds at the rendezvous, she must have also stuck around, checking out the missiles' impacts. *You're a naughty, naughty girl*, he thought, *but how naughty?*

Back in formation, they exited the target area, staying at low level longer than tactically necessary for the fun of doing so until the Persian Gulf's aquamarine water came into view ahead. Viper Flight roared over the beach, out of SAM range at last, and pointed their noses up into a less threatening, even sheltering, sky. The malevolent desert of Iraq became a shimmering blur lost in the heat wake behind their Vipers' tailpipes. A post-strike aerial refueling and a boring medium altitude cruise back to their temporary base in Saudi Arabia would finish the day's work.

He had time to come down gradually from his adrenaline high on the routine flight home. The lack of action gave him the opportunity to think, *Damn, that was exciting! We actually pulled it off.* In the cockpit, he slowly relaxed, the tension flowing from his body through the flight controls to the outside of the jet, into the ether, unseen and unfelt. Like all fighter pilots, the Pilot thought it wise to downplay the extent of the risks he incurred, even when talking to himself. Of all the myriad of things which could have gone wrong, none did. He didn't hit the ground, splattering himself and his jet across several acres of desert. Neither one of them got nailed by a SAM in the pop-up. The Mavericks worked perfectly; the Vipers didn't have to circle in range of the Bad Guys' guns for a re-attack. Neither jock got a heat-seeking missile rammed up a tailpipe on egress. He had to admit to himself he got off on hacking such a difficult mission.

A long, over-water flight in a single-seat aircraft lends itself to introspective reflection. All the Pilot had to do was fly extended formation, monitor the gages, and continue to think.

He asked, *Why do I enjoy it so much?* He and his fight lead had just flown a mission only a tiny percentage of the world's pilots could even consider. Maybe that was why he loved it--taking pride in doing a difficult, dangerous job few aviators would willingly put on their things-to-do list. They had to fly very low and very fast, but with precision, each arriving over the SAM site at exactly the same time, to the second, while making well over 550 miles per hour over the ground. Yet they had done it, and he was proud of their success. He remembered the ancient Greeks found excessive pride unforgiveable, a cardinal sin. But Greeks of the classical era also earned renown as great warriors. How did that work? Could you be a humble, great warrior? Does the strong ego required to be proficient at killing other humans in a war-time duel preclude the introspection needed to be humble?

Maybe the way the Greeks fought, up close and personal, kept them mentally grounded. It would be a difficult thing to hack someone to death with a short, dull sword. To parry a thrust, make your move, and then, while covered with your enemy's spurting blood, watch the light in his eyes go out. No, the sanitary, air-conditioned cocoon of a modern fighter's cockpit lent itself to detached killing and thus facilitated taking pride in doing so cleanly and efficiently.

Was the rush of soul-corrupting pride he experienced worth the six or seven lives they snuffed today? Certainly the deaths were justified by the Allied lives they probably saved by silencing the SAM site. How many more dangerous, high-payoff sorties could he pull off? Would he get drained by repeated adrenaline overloads, get ragged, or get twitched with the risk? Or would he get jaded, overconfident, and bust his ass through an excess of hubris? Maybe he could keep on flying by submerging such questions into mental deep storage.

He watched Viper Lead as she took on fuel, her F-16 hanging motionless behind the airborne tanker. She had led a hell of a mission, taking them into the Valley of the Shadow of Death, smoking the Bad Guys, and bringing them home. They had worked together as a tight team, call sign Viper Flight. Why was he able to get in synch with her tactically but not personally, despite his numerous tries over the past few weeks? As a fighter pilot, he knew her well; as a woman, not so much. He tried to think of a way to remedy an uncomfortable situation and generate a feeling of intimacy between them. He was frustrated, unable to come up with any plan having a chance of touching her emotionally and leading to a physical touch. This was a different sort of challenge--one not to be avoided but welcomed.

The Pilot released the side clasp from his oxygen mask, letting it hang loose in front of his face while he poured out the tablespoon of sweat generated by the stress of combat and collected by the mask. Facing him was a narrow V of folded rubber, soft and wet. Hidden in the dark triangle, near the point of the V, nestled a tiny round microphone. Surrounding the welcoming cavity was the hard-back structure supporting the mask. He glanced down at the still-warm mask before he re-attached it across his face.

How long has it been since I've been with a woman? the thought burst into his mind without warning. *Is sheer horniness why I'm so attracted to the woman flying Viper Lead?*

No, that's not it. The other women in the squadron, some hot and some not, have nowhere near her allure. Perhaps it's her air of mystery, un-obtainability, remoteness, coupled with extreme competence. Maybe it's lust for the out-of-reach. Whatever hold she had on him wasn't going away anytime soon.

She was probably great in the sack, but there had been other proficient lovers in his life. Sex was like Tennessee sour mash whiskey--the worst he ever had was wonderful. *Maybe if I could get her in bed, I could discover why she turns me on,* he thought. Sex promotes intimacy, but how do you have sex without intimacy, a connection first with someone you care for? Someone you care for! Where did that come from?

The tanker gently rolled into a shallow bank, starting a turn at the end of its racetrack pattern, taking Viper Flight with it. Viper Lead, still taking on fuel, remained hanging on the boom. The angle of bank brought the mid-morning sun low on his right canopy rail, flooding the cockpit with its rays. To keep formation on the coupled pair, Viper Lead and the KC-135 tanker, he had to look directly into the blinding glare. The Pilot added a few ounces of back pressure on the control stick, and as the nose came up into a climb, he rolled the jet right, over the tanker. Inverted, he saw the tanker fill his canopy as it passed right to left, seemingly on top of his jet. He let the nose fall as he completed the barrel roll and stopped the F-16 level with the tanker's opposite wing. Not the safest of maneuvers, rolling over an aircraft carrying one hundred thousand pounds of jet fuel. Viper Lead would probably have a few choice words for him during the post-mission debrief. Perhaps his irresponsible stunt to avoid harsh illumination would provide an opening. Male hummingbirds put on a death-defying, aerobatic flying display to win a mate. Would such a move work with her? The Pilot had read that the life of a male hummingbird consisted solely of flying, fighting, feeding (drinking), and fornicating. *How do I get a gig like that,* he thought. *Maybe if I lead an exemplary life as a fighter pilot, whatever that entails, I'll get reincarnated as a hummingbird.*

Now up-sun from the tanker, the F-16's cockpit was in deep shadow, along with his thoughts. *Someday there will be the right woman for me. I haven't found her yet.* Was his flight leader a candidate? *Who the hell knows,* he concluded as they dropped off the tanker and pointed their Vipers' noses toward Saudi Arabia.

CHAPTER 3

KING KHALID AIR BASE

Saudi Arabia

January 1994: The night after they killed the SAM site operators, she came to him. He was in his "Officers' Quarters," a pretentious name for a tiny, windowless room barely large enough for two hard, narrow bunks, a desk, and a locker. His roommate was out night flying; she would have known that from the flight schedule.

A firm knock rattled the door, interrupting his perusal of some trivial paperwork.

She stood outside the open door but back from it, shifting her weight from one leg to the other. Her flight suit displayed only her name tag, the squadron patches removed from their Velcro mounts as if in preparation for a combat mission.

"Hi, what's up?" the Pilot said, leaning on the doorframe. Probably some last minute change to tomorrow's flying schedule or worse, more paperwork.

She looked him in the eye, unwavering, as usual. "I've found something you might be interested in," she said. She hesitated a moment, silent. "May I come in; is this a bad time?" This was a first; she had never been alone with him in his room. Whatever she was wanting promised to be a bigger deal than a delayed briefing time or more forms to fill out.

"Sure, step into my palatial suite. Sorry, it's the butler's night off; the place is a mess."

She glanced left and right down the empty hall, quickly stepped inside, and shut the cheap, flimsy door behind her. He heard the lock click; she had turned it behind her back. Not what he expected tonight.

She reached into the deep, right-leg pocket of her flight suit and brought out a handful of miniature bottles of alcohol, the kind sold on civilian airlines but prohibited on the USAF transports bringing the squadron's personnel to the desert.

"Holy Shit! If they catch us with these, we'll get grounded. Where did you score them?"

In deference to the prickly, Islamic sensibilities of the Saudi royalty and their medieval-minded mullahs, the USAF strictly forbade alcohol consumption on American bases in the region. The Saudis were clear: it was acceptable for infidels to risk their lives defending the Kingdom and the Two Holy Places from Saddam Hussein, as long as they didn't pour themselves a few beers afterward; it was admirable for American women to fly combat in supersonic jets, provided they kept their heads and arms modestly covered and didn't drive while on the ground; and it was all right to defend one sect of Islam against another sect, if the defenders didn't display any symbols of their own beliefs, like a Christmas Tree, while doing so. The Saudis desperately desired defense from both the invading Iraqis and invasive social progress, better known as life-as-practiced-in-the-modern-world. Still, she had somehow procured some alcohol, itself an Arabic word.

Using "we" instead of "you" in the grounding threat, he acknowledged that once the bootleg booze entered his room, he had involved himself in any covert game afoot. The possibility of disciplinary action wasn't as serious a threat as being grounded, the ultimate sanction for a fighter pilot--no flying, only paperwork.

"Where I scored these isn't as important as what we do with them."

She smirked at his surprise, her hands closing around the stash of bootleg booze. He caught the merest hint of a smile around the corners of her mouth.

"What'd you have in mind?"

"I believe a good flight leader always takes care of her men."

"The mark of a born leader. Have a seat, anywhere."

Facing the Pilot, she sat erect on his roommate's bunk, the only spot available other than on the bed next to him. He had found two plastic glasses and a room temperature bottle of water on the desk. She poured the contents of one miniature into each glass, and he topped them up half way with the water. Sitting on his bunk across from her, he raised his glass.

"To leadership."

They touched glasses with a plastic "dink" and each sipped a wee dram of the amber liquid. Her gaze had scarcely left him since she knocked at the door.

Her eyes set her off, separated her from other women. Large, and dark like her hair, they defined her personality and formed the basis for her attractiveness. In everyday life, her eyes were always focusing on something or someone and looking ahead, or were they looking back? She projected an air of knowledge and self-confidence beyond her years, the attitude showing in her eyes.

Confidence polished another facet of her considerable appeal. She was one of those women whose attractiveness flowed from her personality and not just from her physical attributes, obvious even through her baggy flight suit. Self-confidence is a fighter pilot's stock in trade. Most have it in abundance, often to but not beyond the point of overt arrogance. The pilots joked that the squadron's unofficial motto should be, "If you don't know who the world's greatest fighter pilot is, it's not you." Other, less self-assured men would have found her attitude a downer, even threatening, but it turned the Pilot on, a fact he tried to hide, mostly successfully, while in public. No sense in causing intra-squadron sexual problems.

Nearly all squadrons' pilots were married with spouses stateside or stationed somewhere else overseas in the Air Force. She had shut down the few bachelors. Despite her broadcast attractiveness, their approaches prompted no response. She projected an air of cold unavailability like a force field around her. Relationships with fellow pilots were always professionally correct. She laughed and kidded with the guys and other women in the squadron but only to a point. She never shared any of herself; any questions of a personal nature she deftly deflected. Equally vague was her history. Like all officers, she was a college graduate, but no one knew from where. She sometimes spoke of playing soccer in college but offered no details.

He found himself noticing how her flight suit clung to her hips--the slender hips of an athlete--how her chest filled out the camo-streaked uniform. Above average in height, trim and in shape, she displayed just enough curves to advertise her femininity but not enough to draw rapt attention. She had slim shoulders and a round bottom, visible even when viewed through a layer of fireproof, government-issue cloth. Her 120 pounds provoked some kidding; the guys claimed she held an unfair advantage in high-G maneuvers. They bitched that six Gs times 120 pounds totaled a lot less than six Gs times 200 pounds. She shook it off, kept her weight down, continued jogging, and could hold her own on the racket ball court.

Those eyes still drew him in. She had almost-black hair, and it framed her eyes, emphasizing their depth. When she first arrived on the squadron, she wore her hair in a style called a "page-boy" in earlier years. Her haircut at the time was perfectly tailored to fit under a flight helmet. Lately he noticed she let her hair grow until it brushed the top of her shoulders, in violation of USAF regulations, but no one in any position of authority ever complained.

Fighter pilots' shared bonds aren't forged through common interests or by common backgrounds, but by shared risk. Every flight, particularly in combat, requires each pilot to place his or her safety at times in others' hands. If a wingman or flight leader blows it big time, the results can be catastrophic for everyone. She flew well; she led flights in harm's way and brought them back alive, thus she gained acceptance, whatever mysteries attached themselves to her personal life or background. But now he saw her in a new light, alone with him under his room's stark fluorescent lights.

The amber liquid flowed out of the cheap glasses as they sipped. She leaned back on the bunk, her shoulders propped against the white wall. After weeks on the wagon, the whiskey mixed with tepid water resembled nectar of the gods, the whiskey gods of Lynchburg, Tennessee. The dark drink, even diluted, tasted of sour mash and sweet, toasted oak. It went down smoothly despite its warm temperature.

"It's been, like, forever since I've tasted bourbon," she said.

"Well, you'll have to wait even longer for some. It's not bourbon; Jack Daniels is Tennessee sour mash whiskey. It's usually not wise to correct one's flight leader, but hell, the distinction is important."

"What's the diff'?"

"Jack is filtered through charcoal after distillation; plain bourbon isn't. They just pour it in an oak barrel and trust the aging mellows it enough."

"Why doesn't it taste like charcoal? When I get charcoal blown over a steak on the grill, it's gross," she said.

"I'm clueless. Maybe it does. There's only one way to find out: gather more data."

She fished two more bottles from her pocket and offered the pair to him. Their hands met, and she maintained contact, fingertips to fingertips for a time, the exact interval between commitment and ignition of a Maverick's rocket motor. He twisted off the tops from the tiny, square, black bottles and refilled their glasses after their hands parted.

Before either could speak again, a jet engine's roar from the nearby runway interrupted their conversation. They didn't register the din from outside; constant repetition had long since faded the racket into the background noise, despite its high intensity. The afterburner's scream allowed him time to construct a new verbal gambit mentally. How could he bridge the gap that had always been between them?

"What's your plan after Operation Southern Watch is over?" he asked.

"I don't know. What about you?"

"Oh, I'll be flying something, somewhere, sometime."

This was getting them nowhere. He needed another approach if he wanted an emotional connection. She took another sip of her drink, obviously waiting for his next gambit; the move was his to make or screw up. He couldn't think of anything un-foolish to say.

"I still can't believe we pulled off the SAM suppression mission today; that's as gnarly as it gets," she said, taking the initiative.

He ran with it, sticking to the safe subject of combat flying and replying, "Not a mission you'd want to try every day. You or I would probably try again, but eventually, the odds might catch up to us. Do you feel sorry for the half-dozen hajjis we smoked? You know they would've gleefully killed us if they were quicker on the draw."

She thought for a while with dark, downcast eyes and her plastic cup pressed against her bottom lip. Her top lip quivered. "You're right. If the situation were reversed, they wouldn't give a shit about us."

"You're a girl-type person--"

"Your visual identification skills are impressive; I had no idea you'd noticed."

"How could I not? Do you ever think about what the Bad Guys would do to you if you ejected and were captured? Their own women are little better than slaves. They're not respecters of womankind. They'd love to get their hands on an American female pilot for information and recreation." He watched her closely for a reaction to his emotionally loaded question. Her face showed no emotion, but her glass twitched in her hand, the ripples in her drink almost spilling over the rim.

"That's why killing those bastards leaves me no regrets," she said after a moment.

"And makes me want to kill them for you. Evil must be confronted."

"My hero."

She hoisted her glass in a mock toast. He thought for a while; should he press on with the newly established connection or back off a notch? In for a penny, in for a pound. He continued, "It seems the Geneva Convention on prisoners of war only applies when we fight Europeans, like the Germans. The assholes we've fought in the last few wars totally ignore the rules. I admire your guts for risking what they'd love to do to you. But, enough of that cheery subject. What did the post-strike photos tell us?"

"The U-2's pictures show a smoking crater where the control van would've been, surrounded by burning camo nets and indications of an oil fire, but with no bunker nearby. So we must've incinerated the operators. They're probably enjoying their seventy-two virgins as we speak." She took a deep drink, emptied the plastic glass, and set it down on the bunk.

"The Dragon Lady comes through again," he said, referring to the U-2 spy plane by the pilots' nickname for their exotic bird. He poured some of his whiskey and water into her cup.

"What's with the Dragon Lady handle? Where does that come from?"

"She was a character in an old Milton Caniff comic strip, very attractive, with a tight silk dress slit to the hip, dark hair, and high heels. The Dragon Lady is cold, hard to understand, distant, but effective and always mysterious," he said.

The thunder of another afterburner takeoff rattled the walls. She let her arms slide to her sides, slouched against the wall, and kept her feet flat on the floor. For the first time, she looked away from him, staring up at the ceiling, her hair brushing across her shoulders.

"We're not talking about an airplane are we?" she asked.

"No."

"The 'Dragon Lady.' That's what the guys in the squadron call me, isn't it? Do you think I'm the Dragon Lady?"

A Gallic shrug rocked his shoulders, and he extended his arms, palms up. She looked up as if searching for the sky, avoiding his gaze, her hair flowing across her shoulders, down her back.

"No, you're not a cartoon person to me but a vibrant woman. I try to see through the cold to the warmth, maybe even to the fire inside you."

She looked down from the low ceiling into his eyes, hers glistening and tearing, soft even in the harsh, sterile light. "Are you trying to seduce me?" She crossed her arms over her chest, her fists clenched tightly.

"No, I'm not that subtle." He leaned back on his bunk. His glass was empty, the last of the miniatures drained dry.

"You're the only one who hasn't tried."

"Is that why you're here? If so, you can leave now. I'll escort you to your quarters."

"I live three doors down."

"No problem, the offer stands. Why did you knock on my door, come in, and mess with my mind?" He sat up straight, leaning toward her, eager to hear her next words.

"I'm here because I want to be and have for a long time; I thought you knew." She sat with her flight boots still on the floor. But as he watched, she crossed her left leg over her right. A woman's sexual pose, not an androgynous fighter pilot's move.

He looked across the narrow gap between the two bunks separating them. "This formation is unwieldy; I'd much rather have you on my wing than head-on." Had they bridged the emotional distance between them, aided by smooth-brewed alcohol and rough-cut honesty?

She laughed as she too sat up straight. "A flight lead is never out of formation, only her wingmen. But you do have a point."

She hesitated for an instant; her eyes focused on something not visible, as if making a decision, then stood and sat down next to him. As she did, he wrapped his arm around her and drew her close. She offered no resistance as he tilted her head to his and kissed her. His kiss was warmly received then passionately returned. Weeks and months of sexual tension began to melt in a few burning seconds.

At long last, he stood, took both her hands, and helped her to her feet. He slowly, slowly unzipped her flight suit from her neck down. She tilted her head back and let her hair hang free, looking up again at the ceiling. As the descending zipper unveiled her chest, he could see she was braless. As the zipper's deep V exposed more and more pale skin, passing her slim waist and below, it was obvious there was nothing under her flight suit but her.

He spread her unzipped flight suit off her slender shoulders and let it fall--her arms were straight at her sides, pressed against her thighs. It slipped to her waist and stopped, hung up on her bare hips and smooth, naked bottom. She raised her arms, and the crumpled uniform fell around her ankles. She stood nude before him without self-consciousness, her legs slightly apart.

He ran his hands along her hourglass sides and asked, "Do you always fly dressed, or should I say undressed, this way?"

"I'm not flying now."

"We'll have to see what we can do about that. But, really, do you fly with nothing on but a flight suit, or is this a special occasion?"

"I guess that will have to be my little secret," she answered as she helped him out of his flight suit.

They sat on his bunk, unlaced their combat boots, and pulled off the dusty suede lumps. He lay back on the thin mattress bunk, and she gently and slowly lay on top of him. He could feel her breasts pressed against his chest. He slid his hands down her sculpted back and cupped her round, nude cheeks with his palms, his fingertips lost in the folds of her bottom. She didn't resist when he pulled her closer and rose between her thighs.

After another deep kiss, he told her, "You know, this will alter your reputation in the squadron for being uninterested in sex."

She took a deep breath, her hair hanging down around her face, and stared down at him. "Not if you keep quiet."

"Well, I guess this will have to be *our* little secret."

CHAPTER 4

4TH/7TH ARRONDISSEMENTS

Paris

April 2014: When not restlessly roaming *les rues*, the streets of Paris, the Pilot holed up in a cramped apartment at the summit of four flights of stairs on the Island of Saint-Louis. He drew inspiration from the island's old buildings, classic structures exuding character and personality. Ile Saint-Louis reminded him of a small French village magically transported to the bustling center of Metropolitan Paris. Because it was quieter than the surrounding city, with minimum traffic and isolated on all sides by the Seine's flowing moat, he found it easy to walk from the island to all the sections of Paris he cared about and to his office at the US embassy. The small rooms verged on tiny and appeared shopworn, but the flat served him well as his pied-à-terre (sanctuary) in Paris.

The Parisian weather had returned to its normal state for April--miserable. Rain had fallen off and on all day, never pouring yet never stopping. The coming evening promised more of the same, at least until an Atlantic cold front blew through. The city was chilly, and a damp wind from the west drove gray, low-flying clouds along, their ragged undersides reflecting the city's lights in the gathering dusk. Central Paris is a low-rise city; tall buildings are prohibited near its historical center. With no man-made obstacles, the scudding clouds passed unhindered over Paris's centuries-old heart, their indistinct shapes dimly illuminated by the city in their passing.

Paris's timeless moniker as the "City of Light" was bestowed long ago in reference not only to visual illumination provided by the recently-invented street lamps but also to the city's central role in the Age of Enlightenment. During that past *époque,* thinking people shined the light of reason toward the dark clouds of superstition, illuminating the irrational beliefs they found hidden there. Results were mixed. The ancient fog of baseless emotion was briefly lifted, but then the clouds of ignorance blew back on the winds of time and are with us yet, weakened but no more dispersed than the bleak overcast oppressing the Parisian twilight.

Whether a destination was within walking distance or not, now was not the time to venture far on foot. The rain had cranked up its intensity as daylight faded and the cold front neared the city. As usual, the drenching downpour dissolved Paris's infamous water-soluble taxis; none would be available until the weather cleared. Buttoning the tan Burberry trench coat he called his "foreign correspondent's coat," the Pilot crossed the swiftly flowing Seine to the famous left bank (La Rive Gauche). He walked quickly, shoulders hunched against the rain and coat collar flipped up, along the Quai de la Tournelle toward the Saint Michel RER regional underground railway station. The next westbound train soon came; he got off at Les Invalides.

Walking in the failing light of a rainy Paris and wearing a trench coat developed for use in the Great War made him feel he had traveled back in time into a film noir from the 1940s. The city around him remained in color, but only just. As the night approached, his surroundings became increasingly dominated by shades of gray and black. Circles of pallid light cast half-heartedly on the wet pavement by dim street lamps punctuated the typewritten lines of the streets. He couldn't avoid anticipating a faux cinematic adventure tonight, probably involving shadowy spies, corrupt cops, a mysterious woman, and danger. On cue nearby a police siren wailed its Oooh-Aaah, Oooh-Aaah, an eerie wail unique to France.

Trying in vain not to get wetter or colder, the Pilot hurried briskly along the Boulevard des Invalides with his hands thrust deeply into the trench coat's pockets. Banks of lights illuminated the immense Les Invalides building on his right; the rain and mist swirled between the yellow flood lights and the stone facade. Once a hospital and rest home for soldiers maimed in countless French wars, hence the name, most of the building was converted into France's premier military museum. The architect of those wars, the Little General himself, lies in state behind the museum in the magnificent Tombe de Napoléon, the converted church capped with a gold copula.

The Pilot looked forward to dinner at restaurant L'Auberge D'Chez Eux on the corner of Avenue Lowendal across a small concrete park from Napoleon's tomb. He liked the overly cheerful ambiance; the joint was almost a parody of a country restaurant in France's southwest regions. Lace-curtained windows accented red-checkered table cloths and wooden-slatted chairs. Colorful mottos and flowers painted on the pale-yellow plaster walls added the final faux country touch. The forced charm strayed over into the realm of the cheesy, but the cassoulet was excellent, the portions generous, and the wine cellar beneath the restaurant well-stocked.

The people he passed on the street were oblivious to his hurried passage. Large cities discourage personal interaction between strangers, and Paris does this is better than most. Each random individual seemed lost in thought, hiding behind umbrellas and downcast expressions in the rain and the wind and the twilight, while hurrying home to the tiny apartments Parisians manage to call home.

To his right, the Eiffel Tower (La Tour Eiffel) dominated the murky skyline, as it does when seen from anywhere in Paris. This early evening, the tower's upper half was lost to view, hidden in the low overcast and mist. The tower appeared to reach forever skyward, its solid foundations anchored in the wet city and its peak obscured by the clouds--a tower of infinite height.

Ignoring the rain, he stopped outside Napoleon's tomb and took a long look at the imposing ornate structure hosting the Emperor's red quartzite sarcophagus. The Pilot asked himself if Napoleon, dying of cancer at age fifty-one on St. Helena Island in the remote South Atlantic, ever asked himself if it was all worth it, if his life had been a success. Countless battles won, the Empire established, crowned the Emperor of France in the nave of Notre Dame Cathedral, both the art of war and the French legal system revised, thousands of wagonloads of loot carried back to France, and Paris enriched--all were Bonaparte's supreme triumphs. But what about the bitter-cold retreat from the debacle of defeat in Russia, the dungeon on Elba, the final rout at Waterloo due in part to his hemorrhoids, and the final exile far away from his generals, his court, his wife, his mistresses, and his France? What of the hundreds of thousands of lives snuffed out in his wars? To which side did the scales of his life tip? Did he even think about which way they tilted?

What of France itself? Did it sell its national soul for a few decades of glory, *La Gloire*? Some looted treasures remain in Paris to this day, and the Napoleonic Code remains the basis of French law. But the French have won no major military campaigns without extensive Allied help since the crushing loss on Waterloo's killing fields in 1815, a losing streak longer than that of baseball's hapless Chicago Cubs. But still, Napoleon's era is remembered as a high point in France, and the downside is little spoken of.

The lights inside the restaurant projected outside, reflecting off the sidewalk's many puddles. The interior was radiant and inviting in the gathering gloom. Wafting out the front door as it swung open, the aromas of andouille sausage, roast duck, and foie gras dissipated into the damp air. The restaurant was warm, as promised. Inside, the Maître D'Hôtel helped the Pilot out of his dripping trench coat. Enough pondering life's mysteries, his impending career decision, and old black-and-white movies. Next on his agenda was nothing more than a good meal and a better bottle of wine.

He saw her sitting alone at a table for two against the window, looking out on the wet, deserted street. She was smartly, no elegantly, dressed in a black business suit and shiny-white silk blouse, both tailored tightly enough to show off her body's curves and yet severe enough to indicate she was a business or government professional. Somewhat tall with long legs fashionably bare, she wore black stiletto high heels. Her dark, flowing hair reached past her shoulders framing a classic French face featuring dark eyes, a sharply pert nose, high cheekbones, and slightly thin lips. On her table sat a tall flute of Kir Royal, crème de cassis and champagne, with tiny bubbles rising in long streams dancing over the red-and-white table cloth--an aperitif signaling refined, if expensive, taste. There was no cell phone visible, a good sign and an indication she wasn't tethered to her devices; she was available for personal interaction. She had not yet begun her dinner.

He dispatched the knowing host with a wink and a slight wave of his hand. The Pilot slowly stepped to her table and stood a respectful distance away, not hovering over her. He told himself not to smile, as much as he wanted to, and he wanted to a lot. In France, smiles are for friends, lovers, and family, never strangers--a cultural oddity causing the French to be unjustly labeled as unfriendly. No, the smiles would come later.

"Veuillez m'excuser de vous déranger" (Excuse me for bothering you), he said with as much gravity as he could muster. "Etes-vous seule? Je serais honoré de vous joindre." (Are you alone? I would be honored to join you.)

As he watched, waiting for her reply, she slowly raised her head and brushed her hair aside with a wave of her hand, as if erasing an errant thought from her mind. She uncrossed her smooth legs from under the table, pivoted toward him, her knees pressed tightly together in a short skirt, and responded in a way respectable French ladies over a certain age never do--looking a man not known to her directly in the eye. Her reaction to his question seemed to take forever, in slow motion, a scene that would replay in his memories many times in the future.

After contemplation, as if weighing the alternatives, she replied in excellent French-accented English without looking away, their gazes locked, "Do I know you?"

"Not yet," he said, also in English.

"You seem extremely confident, Monsieur."

"Yes, I'm told it is but one of my many faults."

She pressed her lips together stifling a smile, her dark eyes opening farther in amusement. He felt a connection leap between them, a link tenuous and new.

"So there are other faults. What are they?"

The Pilot casually pointed down to the vacant wooden chair across from her, careful not to touch it, respecting her space. "That would require some time to explain in detail."

"As you wish."

She solemnly nodded her permission to join her; he sat across the small table and introduced himself. She replied with her name, extending her right hand halfway across the table without waiting for him to make the first handshake move. He took her right hand in his left, slightly raised it above the checkered tablecloth, and dipped his head to meet it. He brushed his lips gently across the back of her hand and straightened back up, wisps of her perfume assaulting his olfactory senses.

"Enchanté" (Glad to meet you), he said, still not smiling.

"Enchantée."

A stronger hint of a suppressed smile of her own played again around her mouth, provoked by his hand-kissing ceremony, an action almost never taken by Americans and considered today to be overly formal, even quaint, by the French themselves. She was sufficiently attractive to warrant a long second look by any man with a pulse, and she made the most of her assets: her eyes, hair, legs, and slender height. But she wasn't breathtakingly beautiful enough to generate success on her good looks alone; she needed to try.

As they talked, she came across as self-assured; she exuded an upper-class confidence marking her as a member of the French elite, perhaps even a graduate of one of France's highly competitive, prestigious top universities. She was comfortable with who she was and proud of how she looked; that much was obvious to the Pilot's studied gaze. He couldn't stop looking at her, nor did he try to look away.

They discussed the menu and agreed to share hors d'oeuvres from the bounty on the rolling *chariot*, ordering their dinners from a knowing, old waiter who listened without hurrying them. The server had watched similar scenes play out many times. The Pilot selected his long-awaited cassoulet, a regional specialty from southern France. Drawing its name from the ceramic crock in which it is often cooked, good cassoulet should include pork belly, Tarbais beans, sausage, roast duck, and duck fat. In English-speaking countries, the dish is called "pork and beans." She ordered the *cuisse de canard confit* (roasted, preserved duck leg and thigh). After much examination of the wine list and discreet suggestions from the sommelier hovering over their table, they agreed on a Côte Rotie, a Syrah wine from the upper Rhone valley, hearty but fruit-forward. The bottle was expensive, a special occasion wine. His infatuation with the woman across from him swelled by the minute. If this wasn't a special occasion, what the hell was?

Throughout the meal, they chatted in French, discussing the weather, recent films, French politics, and books they had read, intended to read, or were planning to pretend they had read. Their respective professions and the world of work were taboo as always in France. It would have been extremely rude to inquire straightaway about the other's job, not unlike demanding annual income figures. They were careful to address each other with the *vous* second person plural/formal verb form. The *tu* form, the second person singular/familiar, is strictly reserved in French for family, close friends, pets, spouses, and lovers, none of which applied. Yet.

Underneath her impeccable manners, he sensed a steely resolve, an underlying sense of purpose. She presented the air of someone on an unnamed mission, dedicated. What was the quest she was so obviously on? Before he could explore the question with her, she turned the conversation toward the light.

Finally, her curiosity reigned, and she asked in English, "Your French is very good. [They both knew it wasn't.] You have a very unusual accent. Where did you learn?"

"In Southwest Louisianá, many people are fluent in French."

"I thought only older people speak Cajun French."

"Peut-être." (Perhaps.)

"Is it true the legal system in Louisiana is based on the Napoleonic Code?" The question surprised him, indicating a depth of knowledge of francophone America rare in the often insular world of France. Her query signified a first-rate international education.

"Yes, but the laws are written in impenetrable English by American lawyers."

The joke provoked a visible smile. They agreed to converse in English unless only a French word or phrase would do.

After a leisurely dinner, the plates were cleared, the empty wine bottle was removed, and they split the not-inconsiderable check. Despite the obvious rapport between them and the increasingly friendly conversation, the Pilot knew the next move belonged to him. Not unaccustomed to picking up unescorted ladies, for some reason he hesitated this time. The woman across from him was different--serious, with a hint of danger about her and steel beneath the lace. Danger for whom? The Pilot or the lady herself? Not for the first time, he accepted a challenge, one spiced with perils yet unknown. He looked into those dark eyes and took a deep breath. He had but one shot; he had to make it count.

"Tomorrow I'm visiting an art museum, filling a gap in my education. Would you be interested in assisting me?"

"Which museum did you have in mind?" She sat up straight in her chair and leaned forward as she uncrossed her legs under the table.

"La musée de l'Air et de l'Espace au Bourget." (The French national air museum at Le Bourget Airport just outside Paris.)

"I expected the Louvre or La musée d'Orsay; Americans favor those two. Curiously, I didn't know airplanes were objets d'art."

"Au contraire, they can be, seen in the correct light, from the proper angles. I suspect airplanes haven't been properly shown to you."

"Peut-être. And I suppose you would be the one to explain. Let us hope being a boring guide is not one of your dreaded many faults." She retrieved her phone from her purse and tapped it a few, quick times and returned it to her purse. "How were you planning to travel there? The RER?" He nodded yes, and she sealed the deal with a warm smile, her first. "There is a train arriving at 1030 hours. I can meet you at the Le Bourget station."

"Why don't I come by your residence and pick you up?" he ventured. "We could take the train together."

"No, that is impossible."

She stood, gathered her purse, and let the Pilot help her into her stylish long coat. Why was she so adamant about not revealing where she lived? Was she married? He hoped not. Married women weren't strictly off limits, particularly in libertine France, but chasing someone's wife would require him to evoke the fighter pilot's standard risk/reward trade-off. Would the possible rewards of a hazardous mission be worth chancing the certain risks? Aside from the potential problems presented by a pissed-off, cuckolded husband, there was always the greater danger of becoming too fond of an unobtainable woman. Something inside him hoped she was unencumbered, available without *des liaisons dangereux*, needless of deception, and open to a more permanent connection, perhaps even love.

The rain having stopped, he escorted her to the waiting taxi summoned by the Maître d'Hôtel. As she slid down in the back seat, her long coat gapped open and askew, presenting her body like an offering flower. Delighted, he saw that her business suit's short, snug skirt terminated several inches sooner than one would expect, almost as abbreviated as one would dream for. She looked out at him, not bothering to readjust her miniskirt, all the better to display those gorgeous nude legs, uncrossed, with the hem of her skirt stretched tightly, spanning her thighs. She waited until he wished her "Bonne nuit" (Good night), replied the same, then closed the car door before giving the driver her home address.

Stepping away from the now-vacant curb, alone once again in the wet night, he confronted two choices: he could walk to his right toward the Latin Quarter and his flat on the island or turn left in the direction of the Eiffel Tower. The tower's spire had emerged from the overcast and mist, standing erect and proud in the night. In the other direction, his apartment now seemed to him to be achingly empty instead of merely shabby and small. A quote from philosopher/catcher Yogi Berra popped unannounced into his head: "When you come to a fork in the road, take it." The Pilot silently agreed with Yogi and turned left.

The weather front had moved through during dinner; the dark sky was rapidly clearing. The freshening wind dispersed the lowest clouds, and isolated stars appeared, bright enough to compete with the glow from the City of Light.

He was too amped up to sleep, even considering the half bottle of Côte Rotie consumed. A night walk would clear his head and, if long enough, relax him. He passed L' Ecole Militaire, the French senior military academy, and stepped into the Champs de Mars, the lengthy, empty, green park separating the war college and the Eiffel Tower.

The Field of Mars, the god of war. The pastoral expanse stretched flat, desolate, and windswept in the night from the military school to the tower, like a deserted no-man's land, an abandoned killing ground. The generals who almost lost World War I attended that school, marched on the Field of Mars, and learned how to stage human-sea attacks there. They were long gone now, along with the men they mindlessly consigned to an early, futile death. The emptiness of war was expressed now as a field of grass reaching the base of the tower. The wind was stronger now and colder, feeling as if it had come from some long-ago, frozen battlefield, carrying with it the souls of young men.

Overlooking the military college at the other end of the Field of Mars, the tower had been erected for a peaceful world's fair twenty-five years before the Great War erupted. The irony was not lost on the Pilot as he stopped halfway across the park. Had the future martinets of La Grande Armée attended the fair? Had the arrogant Prussian militarists who attacked France to punish Serbia been there as well? Probably not.

Transit of the Champs de Mars required a long walk. The immense tower, illuminated and glowing in the night, grew nearer only slowly, allowing him ample time to think. He looked up at the still-distant tower, remembering how during World War II, a P-51 pilot flew under it between the supporting arches, pursuing a fleeing German Me-109. Gauging the distance between the pillars and the height to the first deck, the Pilot decided yes, a man could fly under the Eiffel Tower in a Mustang, or a Spitfire, if he lined his pass up carefully and didn't lose his nerve. When his attempt to use the iron tower to the scrape the P-51 off of his tail failed, the panicked German had crashed into the Seine flowing nearby. The French government awarded the American Mustang pilot a medal, Le Légion d'Honneur, for his exploit. There was a lesson in that, but the Pilot couldn't pin it down and thought no more about the episode. He had other things on his mind.

His dinner interlude with the intriguing French woman had interrupted his mental debate, but now the troubling questions returned with a vengeance. Flying the new fighter would eventually lead him into more war in the air. New weapons were always used. When was war avoidable, and when was it not? He didn't fear war; a part of him thirsted after more combat. When was an individual's decision to go to war fairly based on altruistic patriotism, and when on an egotistical desire for personal glory and high adventure? What were his alternatives to more airborne killing, and could they ever be more desirable than the purity of air combat? Was fighting because you liked it and were good at it morally evil even if the cause for which you fought was just? How much did being good at killing harden your soul? Did men, and now women, fight for abstract causes or the respect of their squadron mates? Was the F-35 a vehicle to take him further into the future, or back to his past? He needed answers; his decision point was fast approaching, and he wasn't getting any closer to choosing a way forward.

Reaching the tower's immense, arched base, he slowed his pace, hesitating and pausing in the deserted, wind-swept plaza directly under it. His back was turned to the flood-lit military school glowing malevolently in the distant darkness at the end, or the beginning, of the field of war. Four massive supporting pillars leaned inward toward him, each equidistant from where he stood. A century and a quarter ago, the engineering magic of Ingénieur Gustave Eiffel suspended seven thousand tons of wrought iron in the air directly above his head.

A cold west wind blew the overcast's remaining ragged remnants past and through the spire's spidery structure. As he looked directly up, without reference to the ground, the passing wispy clouds presented the illusion that the great tower was itself eerily moving across the night sky, lit from within like a spirit ship sailing on a sea of stars, covering and uncovering those stars as it went. The Pilot, or someone he knew well, had taken in a similar scene before, long before, in another moonless night--a night seemingly without end.

CHAPTER 5

NORTHWEST THAILAND/SOUTHERN LAOS

June 1971: At twenty-two thousand feet, the stars shine as bright points of light, white and clear and hard with no twinkle. A huge, four-engine tanker plane floated above the Pilot in the night, suspended at 320 knots indicated airspeed. The black aluminum cloud partially blanked his view of the heavens passing above. Looking up from his cockpit, he saw the tanker's tail uncover star after star, as if each was born the instant it emerged from behind the trailing edge of the tanker's horizontal stabilizer. Each star was left behind in turn, bright and new. The moonless night was clear, free from the monsoon's misty stratus and devoid for once of smoke from burning rice straw on the dry paddies far below.

The Pilot wasn't there to enjoy the spectacular astronomical view; he was there to refuel his thirsty fighter. His immediate task entailed putting his F-4 Phantom in close trail behind the tanker, slightly lower, and holding it there in the dark, motionless relative to the much larger aircraft. His visual reference had to be the tanker, not the horizon, not the stars, and particularly not his flight instruments. The Phantom flew in tight relationship to the tanker. When the tanker started a gentle turn, it appeared to the Pilot the stars above the tanker's tail moved, not him. The white dots wheeled and turned when the tanker overhead banked; they resumed their march across the night sky when it didn't.

A flying hose pipe with aerodynamic control surfaces resembling small wings, the refueling boom extended down from the tanker's aft fuselage. Looking down and back at the trailing Phantom outside through a glass panel in the floor of the tanker's crew compartment, a crewman flew the boom while lying on his belly. On the Phantom's dorsal spine, behind the rear cockpit, waited an open refueling receptacle, a socket matching exactly the boom's bulbous end. The Pilot stabilized the big fighter in position; the boom operator flew the boom over the open receptacle, extended the boom's telescoping end, and inserted it into the receptacle, which locked it in place. Once coupled, the tanker pumped thousands of pounds of jet fuel down the boom and into the willing Phantom. The act's sexual imagery was both undeniable and stale. All the jokes about stiff booms thrust into willing receptacles had been told and retold decades ago. Tonight it was just another routine segment of the mission, a prelude to the action to follow.

Flying close-in formation, as the Pilot was doing with the tanker, was akin to riding a dressage horse; the same skills applied. The secret was to make tiny, imperceptible control movements to position the aircraft, or the horse, in such small increments as to give the appearance of the steed responding imperceptibly. Three feet high on the boom, the Pilot relaxed his back pressure on the control stick without letting it move, and the Phantom descended three feet at 320 knots (380 miles per hour) airspeed. One foot too far back on the boom. He added a touch of power and moved forward. The Phantom, enormous for a fighter, mounted two gaping engines side by side. The difficulty lay in translating the huge throttles with movements small enough to slide the jet smoothly forward and back only a few feet relative to the tanker. To move forward, the Pilot rotated his left hand counterclockwise, advancing the right throttle and retarding the left. The resulting differential setting added a few hundred pounds more net thrust and eased the Phantom forward. Once in place, he straightened his hand, equalizing the throttles and the engines' thrust and stabilizing his position.

Not only the throttles but everything about the Phantom was big; the control stick, the canopy, the instrument panel, and the ejection seat were all massive. The cockpit was roomy, with expansive consoles and enough space to move around. The airplane gave him a feeling of solidity, reliability, and heft, as well as raw power and speed. The Phantom represented the Harley-Davidson of fighter planes but carried a pickup truck's load.

Even at 320 knots, the Phantom was sluggish, slow in responding to the controls. Loaded with two full, external fuel tanks, six cluster bomb canisters weighing 815 pounds each, a kayak-sized electronic countermeasures pod, and two Sparrow radar-guided missiles, it was a five-fingered handful to fly smoothly behind the tanker.

At last the boom operator saw the fuel had stopped flowing, indicating the receiving tanks were full. He extracted the boom from the receptacle and stowed it stiff up against the tanker's belly.

The radio came alive in the Pilot's earphones with a transmission from the tanker's pilot. "That's all I can do for now; hope it was good for you." An old joke.

The Pilot pressed his mike button on the inboard throttle as he closed the refueling receptacle. "It's been a business doing pleasure with you. Satan's off." The call sign used his squadron's nickname, Satan's Angels.

"Roger that, Satan, good luck and good hunting."

The Pilot appreciated the encouragement from the tanker driver. *These guys are heroes,* he thought. *They're up here every night in all kinds of weather, and they never get to see the bright lights or feel the thrill of actual combat. "What did you do in the war, Daddy?"; "I passed gas all night."*

The Pilot retarded both throttles slightly to back off from the tanker, checked that the refueling receptacle had closed, and turned the Phantom eastward toward the Ho Chi Minh trail. As he pushed the airspeed to 450 knots (500+ miles per hour), he felt the jet come alive in the night--the controls were once again solid, not mushy as when flying with the tanker. The Phantom felt more alive with faster air flowing over the wings. Time to clock in at the job site.

Forty-two inches behind the Pilot were an equally spacious, rear cockpit and the Navigator, or as he liked to call himself, "Assistant Fighter Pilot." He would play a vital role in tonight's mission. Although not a rated pilot, he could fly the jet if required to do so. He would operate key weapons systems, monitor the gages, and keep track of their position.

"Steer one ten degrees, for sixty miles," The Nav. gave the Pilot a compass heading and distance to tonight's mission area.

Up front the Pilot practiced his ritual, preparing for combat. There would be hundreds of people on the ground tonight in Laos who would do their level best to kill him and the Nav.; he needed to be ready. He checked the tightness of his lap belt, stowed his flight bag with its checklists and maps, selected the weapons delivery mode, and designated wing stations for bomb release, his leather-gloved hands darting around the lower instrument panel. One last step: he raised the master arm switch to Arm.

"Pickle button is hot," he advised the Nav.

The Navigator's control stick also mounted a red "pickle button"; he could release the ordnance if required. The nickname "pickle button" carried over from World War II when bomb release switches mimicked the size and color of dill pickles.

"Roger that," the Nav. replied.

Housekeeping accomplished, the Pilot turned down the lights. At night the fighter cockpit normally blazed with glowing instruments, dials, switches, radar displays, and electronic countermeasure displays, all of which adversely affect a human's delicate night vision. He blacked it all out, took the portable map light, clipped it to the glare shield over the front instrument panel, and trained its dim red glow on the basic flight instruments. He would fly by memory and feel, looking outside into the dark Laotian night, not inside the cockpit.

Alone in the night, the two men flew through the darkness. No "gunner's moon" was up to cast shadows in the blacked-out cockpits or silhouette them against any clouds. The lone cockpit aid left illuminated, the gun sight shone dimly red on the front windscreen and was the aiming index for the ordnance.

That ordnance was cluster bombs. Each fiberglass canister was stuffed with bomblets the size and shape of baseballs but much heavier. Cluster bombs were dropped exactly as if they were conventional explosive "iron" bombs. At a preset height above the ground, a radar fuze would set off an explosive charge, splitting the canister in half and releasing the deadly bomblets. The bomblets would explode on impact with the ground, each blasting ball bearing-sized shot lethally over an area the size of a tennis court. The bomblets would arm themselves by spinning as they fell, the spin generated by ridges molded into their aluminum outer shells. The spin made each bomblet take a curving flight path instead of falling straight--the same aerodynamic principle followed by a major-league curve ball, but without the Commissioner of Baseball's signature affixed thereto. If the radar fuze functioned too high, the bent flight path of each bomblet would produce a doughnut-shaped impact pattern on the ground. It was not uncommon for a pilot to fly a perfect bomb run only to have the bomblets ring the target, leaving it relatively untouched in the doughnut's center. If the fuze opened the canister too low, the bomblets would not arm and would impact the ground, useless and safe.

The steel hail of tiny, spheroid shrapnel fired across the target area by the exploding bomblets would not be effective against anti-aircraft guns or fortified bunkers. The horizontal storm will be lethally effective against soft-skinned targets such as canvas-sided trucks or human beings, the gunners in their recessed emplacements. Each canister contained 666 bomblets--666, the Number of the Beast in the Bible's book of Revelation. Given the cluster bombs' raison d'être, the number seemed appropriate to the Pilot for Satan Flight's mission tonight.

Beneath them, the two flyers could barely make out the Mekong River's broad, silvery thread shining in the night, flanked by black banks sprinkled with the lights of fishing villages. Passing over the river's east bank now, they flew over the Laotian panhandle. As the Phantom carried them eastward, the scattered village lights quickly disappeared, leaving only inky darkness below. A dark war zone in a dark war.

The infamous Ho Chi Minh trail wasn't one trail but a spiderweb of one-lane dirt roads bladed through the Laotian panhandle's tropical jungles. They were hot and dusty in the dry season, hot and muddy under warm monsoon rains. The red dirt tracks wound, branched, and reconnected through the crumpled Anan mountain range forming the boundary between Vietnam and Laos. During daylight hours, the trails were easily seen from the air and seemed deserted. At night, they crawled with motorized and foot traffic--trucks and men hidden in the night.

Equally invisible in the night were the sheltering mountains. The steeply pitched slopes, covered with triple layers of verdant jungle canopy, appeared to the Pilot and his navigator as a featureless, pitch-black void passing beneath their Phantom. An unwary pilot could convince himself the blackness below was flat, that he could fly low and fast over the jungle with impunity--a mistake made only once with steep hillsides reaching into the night sky awaiting the unskilled or foolhardy and promising a sudden impact with instant death too quick to feel the flames of the explosion.

Laos's convoluted surface and the convoys making their slow way south with men and munitions were hidden in the night from the Phantom at fifteen thousand feet but were not invisible to Spectre. The Spectre gunship, a converted four-engine turboprop transport, was crammed with electronics, guns, and guys. Peering sensors turned night into day and displayed it on glowing scopes in the gunship. The sensor operators could find a convoy in the blackest night, using only light from the watching stars or imaging the heat signatures of the vehicles. Sometimes the operators were alerted to the trucks' passage by acoustic sensors dropped from F-4s and embedded in the damp jungle floor to listen. Alerted by the listening posts' microphones, Spectre's sensors would lock onto the convoy and pass the target's location to the guns filling the aircraft's cavernous aft cargo compartment. Spectre was named a gunship for good reason. In its belly lurked several 7.62-caliber mini-Gatling guns, 20 mm full-sized Gatling guns, 40 mm automatic pom-pom guns, and a howitzer cannon, all firing through gunports cut into the aircraft's left side. The crew of fourteen men included one brawny guy, striped to the waist in the sub-tropical heat, whose sole job was to wield a coal shovel and hurl overboard the rapidly growing piles of brass shell casings spit out by the guns. Spectre orbited in a left turn to bring the guns to bear, and once a convoy of trucks was identified and engaged, the barking guns would light up truck after truck with precision impacts and few wasted rounds.

Entering Satan Flight's assigned patrol area, the Pilot could see below him a ragged line of intermittently spaced dots--a broken skein of angry pink pearls--glowing red against the jungle's crumpled black velvet. Every minute or so, another dot blossomed after first being illuminated by sharp, white pinpoint explosions. Some dots exploded in red and orange then faded to black. Others flared, burned for a while, then dimmed to embers, barely visible in the night. Occasionally, the sparkling white pinpoints twinkled without secondary effects, signifying a rare miss or, more likely, a truck with inflammable cargo, such as rice.

"Spectre, Satan Flight's on station," he transmitted.

"Roger, Satan, we're working a convoy. No reaction yet from the Bad Guys. Call when you have us in sight," the reply came back from the gunship's copilot.

Spectre had spotted a convoy of southbound trucks, lit up the lead truck first, and then hit the last one in line. With trucks burning at each end of a convoy traversing a single-lane track cut into a steep hillside, the others were trapped, unable to pass or turn around and escape. The circling gunship was methodically picking off each truck, one by one. Each burning truck meant one less load of munitions available to kill Americans in South Vietnam. The surviving truck crews had probably fled down the steep hillside into the jungle and were frantically digging foxholes while contemplating the long walk back to North Vietnam for replacement vehicles.

The lumbering gunship proved lethal to trucks but found itself dangerously vulnerable to ground fire while it circled low and slow over the truck carnage. Discouraging the anti-aircraft gunners from shooting down Spectre was the Pilot and Nav.'s mission. The gunners defending this segment of the trail would have only a vague idea where the gunship orbited in the night; it was painted flat black and unlighted. The four turboprop engines' low-frequency drone was non-directional to the ear; the defenses would fire on a hunch.

A ghostly line of dim, green lights ran the length of the gunship's fuselage. Another line of lights intersected the first, spanning the wings. The resulting cross stood out in the night but only when seen from above. The Nav. spotted it first. "Spectre. Ten o'clock low."

The Pilot searched, saw the slowly moving green cross, and transmitted, "Spectre, Satan's got you in sight. We'll hold high." The gunship acknowledged as much and continued to methodically work over the doomed convoy.

While they orbited in a lazy left turn and scanned the empty blackness around the area for ground fire, the Pilot realized that tonight Satan Flight protected an aircraft displaying the symbol of Christianity by dropping bomblets in the Number of the Beast while the cross-bearing aircraft killed Buddhists and atheists. Was that Kosher? It was enough to over-temp a theologian's brain.

After the Phantom's third wide circle around the kill zone, the defenses awoke. Slightly east of Spectre's lower orbit, a 37 mm anti-aircraft gun jumped into action, pumping clip after clip of shells blindly up into the night sky. The gunners were firing tracer bullets at night, a career-limiting move for them. The white trails streaked up from the blackness--pinpoints of light reaching, reaching for Spectre. The 37 mm shells, identifiable by their white incandescent streaks, climbed quickly at first then gradually slowed as gravity clawed them back. At their apogee, the tracer elements burned out, the shells bursting into tiny, white-hot fireballs in quick sequence like Fourth of July fireworks brought up from Hell.

Tracers in the daytime allowed a gunner to adjust his aim while firing, much as a firefighter aims a fire hose. In bright light, the tracer elements are easily seen by only the gunner. At night, tracers worked both ways; the Pilot could follow the streaks backward toward the ground to get a rough idea of the gun emplacement's location. A rough idea was all that was needed for aiming an area weapon like the cluster bombs hanging underneath the Phantom's wings.

He fixed his gaze on an area in the night-enfolded mountains and guessed at the tracers' origin. Triangulating his aim point on the ground from the line of burning trucks, he wouldn't look elsewhere until weapons release.

"Spectre, Satan's got the guns and tally-ho on you," he transmitted. "Satan will be in from Louisiana to Michigan," meaning he would make his bomb run from south to north.

There were persistent reports of the Bad Guys monitoring USAF radio frequencies and trying to use the overheard position reports to target the Good Guys, although the Wing Intelligence Office could neither confirm nor deny the existence of this technique. Use of an improvised code between Satan Flight and Spectre assumed the Vietnamese were better at clandestine electronics than American geography.

"Satan, Spectre will hold over Arizona," the gunship replied, meaning he would hold southwest of the target area.

The unblinking stars seemed to spin, swirling over the canopy as the Pilot rolled the big Phantom up on its left wing and pulled the nose down in a shallow dive toward the target somewhere in the inky void below. He balanced several competing factors while doing so. The longer he took, the more his eyes would wander off the featureless aim point in the night. However, the quicker he yanked the nose around and down, using more Gs, the more airspeed would bleed off and the harder he would find it to control the F-4 precisely. At low airspeed and turning tightly, the Phantom transitioned into an evil-handling pig with dodgy aerodynamics. The ailerons would be ineffective; he would have to use the rudder to roll the fighter. With too much pull on the control stick and too much aileron input, the jet would violently depart from controlled flight and flip over into a spin. Recovery before impact would be doubtful. In the daytime, he could use the afterburners to maintain airspeed, but at night, their long, blue-white plumes stretching behind the aircraft would be a shining beacon in the night sky for the gunners to target.

"I'm padlocked," he told the Nav., meaning he looked at nothing but the target. As the big jet headed down, he kept the engines howling at full power but without afterburner.

"Roger that," the Nav. responded, and he began calling out altitude and airspeed information from his cockpit gages. "Eleven thousand, airspeed 350; ten thousand, airspeed building; eight thousand, airspeed is good, 450. Ready. Pickle. Now." Using the target area's approximate elevation, the Nav. had made a quick mental calculation and determined the correct altitude for weapons release.

The gun sight's dim, red reticule was in the general area identified as the target seconds ago. The Pilot pressed the red pickle button on the top of the control stick. Two slight thumps told him when one cluster bomb ejected off each wing in close succession. He ensured the Phantom's wings were level by referencing the gun sight's artificial horizon and, using five Gs, pulled the jet's nose up toward the watching, uncaring stars.

A quick look back over his left shoulder revealed two sharp, white explosions suspended in the night sky over the target. The canisters had opened, and the bomblets were twirling down unseen in the blackness. He started a left-climbing turn around the line of burning trucks just in time to see two intense circles of white light pepper the area of the anti-aircraft gun. It looked like a thousand sparklers going off at once but burned out in a second or two. The two solid circles of flashes overlapped, their common area encompassing where his gun sight had been projected on the ground. The Pilot hoped he had drawn a Venn diagram of death.

The experienced gunners weren't dumb; the dumb ones didn't live long enough to become experienced. They would know what was coming when they saw the twin flashes as the canisters opened. The Vietnamese would understand they had five seconds at the most to duck into a nearby bunker. Or they might trust the law of averages and hope a bomblet wouldn't happen to fall right into their dug-in gun pit. Who knew what went on down there in the hot jungle night? This was a battle of forces, each having only the foggiest notion of the other's location--a switchblade knife fight in a dark gym. The gunners knew Spectre was in the area; they could hear the four propellers droning, and they probably could hear and see the truck convoy's kinetic destruction. They knew from the distant jet noise that a Phantom was high overhead, but they couldn't plot with any precision where each blacked-out aircraft flew in the night sky. Once the 37 mm gun opened up, even the scant information provided by sound would fade with their impaired hearing as they were deafened by their gun's muzzle blasts.

The Pilot trusted rather than knew with any certainty that his cluster bombs had rained exploding steel balls on his target. He had few aiming references on the inky surface; the bomblets could have sprinkled themselves over the far side of a craggy ridge. But the bomblets from the Book of Revelation would silence the guns for a time. Even if the gunners survived, they couldn't be sure of a miss next time. Spectre could return to the area and resume plinking trucks.

The Nav. was the first to speak, his breathing rate returning to normal after the stress of dive-bombing an anti-aircraft gun at night. "Two canisters should cool the area down for a while."

"Yeah, halftime at the Apocalypse."

The Pilot wondered if his cluster bombs had made a difference. More importantly, had Spectre's torching of the convoy stopped supplies from reaching the south, or had the AC-130 just whacked some crude trucks and killed a few terrified drivers? Whatever the answer, all three players in this nighttime Kabuki play would return, probably tomorrow night, and the night after that.

The Pilot, the Nav., and the Phantom would remain on station over both Laos and Spectre with their four remaining canisters and make perhaps two more trips to the waiting tanker for more fuel. A long night stretched ahead of the Phantom's blunt, black nose.

CHAPTER 6

UBON RATCHATHANI

Thailand

June 1971: In dawn's fading dark, the dense air already bore the coming hot day's fetid odor. The Pilot hailed a samlor, a three-wheeled pedicab taxi, from the lineup outside the US airbase's main gate, a portal nicknamed "Check Point Charlie" by the local airmen. The samlor driver nodded when he gave the driver her address in his best broken Thai. For about a dollar's fare, the Pilot reclined on the bench seat to enjoy the ride. In front the Thai guy's butt bobbed up and down as the driver struggled to pedal across Ubon City. Samlor drivers could pedal a slight Thai passenger or two while seated on the bike seat, but a much heavier American required him to stand on the pedals.

The tropical sun rises quickly, climbing almost vertically into a soon-blazing sky. The transition from a warm, muggy night to an even hotter, more humid day is quick, with no dawn twilight to soften the thermal blow. In the dry season, the sun, once risen, bakes the flat, featureless plains of northeast Thailand. The rice paddies stretch empty to the hazy east and west horizons, and their ochre mud quickly dries into dust. The brown dust, stirred by hot winds, rises into the thick air and produces a haze that seems to dirty even the scattered puffy clouds overhead.

Promising the day's heat, the sun had just cracked the flat eastern horizon when the samlor coasted to a stop in front of her house. The Pilot gave the sweating driver forty Baht, about a buck and a half, more than expected.

"Kop koon mach kop. (Thank you.) GI, number one." Like most Thais interacting with Americans, the samlor driver spoke a strange mix of formal Thai and the English slang words for "American" and "excellent." The driver should welcome transporting GIs. They were much more weight to haul, but generous tips came with the big-spending, big-living, big Americans, whose military pay made them rich by Thai standards.

She lived on the outskirts of Ubon, the teeming regional capital--a ramshackle city choked with too many people and too little sanitation, and a foul air all its own. Her classic Thai-style house surrounded by bare, red dirt was nestled in a dense grove of dusty banana plants. Nearby, the languid Moon River drifted along behind a thin line of scrubby trees. Not the Moon River Andy Williams crooned about but the mighty Mekong River's muddy tributary.

The Pilot was physically bone tired and emotionally exhausted from the previous night's airborne adventures, but he had enough energy left to see her. Indeed, her cheery spirit somehow had the power to rejuvenate him, to wash away the mental fatigue of an endless war. Her house served as his sanctuary from combat and from the rigid military regime of the air base.

The house was all unpainted teak, or maybe mahogany, perched on short, wooden stilts to let the inevitable monsoon floods pass underneath without ill effect. True to type, it was crowned with a steep-pitched, planked roof as if to slough off snow, unknown in Thailand. No one knew why Thai houses displayed such high, pointed roofs; perhaps they warded off seasonal monsoon downpours more efficiently. Doorways with six-inch, raised sills separated the house's four small rooms, the wooden barriers a constant source of tripping. She claimed the step-over sills deterred invading snakes from easily gliding from room to room. The Pilot thought it would take a uniquely dumb-ass snake to be foiled by a six-inch step after slithering up a six-foot, open staircase to the house. But still, even folkloric precautions were welcome. The local Thai elders counseled that there were fifty-seven varieties of snakes indigenous to the Kingdom of Siam. Fifty-four were poisonous; the other three coiled around and crushed you.

The few compromises to modernization her Thai house boasted included electricity and bottled propane gas. These luxuries were rare; most of her neighbors along the sandy dirt road that linked their houses did without. The road paralleled a swampy, weed-clogged canal (*klong*) which carried sewage to the Moon River and also served as a source of bath water.

The costs of the modest comfort upgrades and the house itself were covered by her salary as the liaison officer between the regional office for the US Agency for International Development (USAID) and the local Thai government. Thais and GIs alike assumed USAID to be a front organization for the CIA, collecting intelligence and running secret operations across the wide Mekong River into Laos, as well as buying off venal Thai politicians with American dollars. This common perception of powerful but covert, perhaps dangerous, connections was one she neither addressed nor attempted to rectify. The rumors gave her immense clout with the locals.

Half-Thai and half-Caucasian, her looks combined the best of both worlds--a sort of hybrid vitality applied to womankind. Relatively tall in a society that equates height with status, beauty, and competency, she possessed all three attributes in abundance. Her eyes were round, dark, and large, accented by a western nose on a heart-shaped face. Her jet-black hair, a source of pride to her, was silky and straight, cascading nearly to her trim waist when she let it fall. Her Thai genes contributed an easy and graceful movement; she flowed when she walked like a Thai folk dancer. The Pilot could attest that every inch of her light brown skin was silky smooth. Tourist brochures pitch Thailand as "The Land of Smiles," and she did her part living up to the hype. Her radiant smile could light a room, a rainy monsoon day, or a heart hardened by combat.

Many had made the mistake of being mesmerized by her exotic beauty without considering the person within. She showed a fierce intelligence and a quick mind, which she made no attempt to conceal. Individuals from both sides of the east/west cultural divide learned to their regret not to treat her as just another pretty face and curvy body. She communicated with Thais in their indirect, vaguely circular fashion with much unsaid, using overly formal politeness. Yet in her dealings with Americans, she was direct and up front, almost blunt. Her excellent English showed little accent, and by all accounts her Thai was flawless, albeit with the softness of Bangkok's elite--another source of status--instead of the Laotian-tinged dialect of northeast Thailand.

Her background, education, and ancestry were not subjects she willingly discussed. After a few futile attempts at drawing her out, the Pilot had given up on where she came from and focused on enjoying what she had become. He didn't dwell on how she functioned so well in two very different worlds. He didn't know how she came to be where and who she was, but somehow that didn't matter, only the present did. Flying and fighting in a deadly war encouraged living for the present--the past was gone, and the future would appear in its own good time, maybe.

The Pilot stopped in the dusty courtyard, his arrival scattering scrawny chickens whose awakened scratching in the brick-colored dirt signaled the start of another steamy day in the tropics. *Why do I need her so?* he asked himself. *I should be able to fly night combat missions without seeking refuge in her arms each morning. What is it about her that soothes me even while she turns me on? Where does this flood of relief I feel come from? Some macho fighter jock I am--pussy-whipped, left breathless by a local pooh-yeng* (young woman). *But still,* he thought, *she fills a vital need. Not only a need for uninhibited sex but a need for sanity and reason, maybe a need for mutual love. Every night I fight, hanging it all out, and for what? The Vietnam War goes on and on; the losses mount and no one cares. More and more of my squadron mates disappear in fiery explosions or slam into oblivion against black Laotian mountainsides, and yet nothing changes. We don't even know what victory would be or even how to end the war without it. But, I fight nightly, and I do it well. I enjoy the action as a moth might feel warmed by a candle just before he too disappears in a ball of fire. But come the dawn, she provides sanctuary, a way to pull back from those hypnotic flames burning in the dark. She's proof to me that goodness exists even in a war zone and that there's a normal life possible outside of flying, fighting, and risking death, however addictive those pursuits appear.* He finished his thoughts with: *It's a hell of a note when your model of stability is a woman who may or may not be a CIA agent.* It was time to lose himself in her. The dusty chickens resumed cautious foraging as he walked on toward the stilted house.

He climbed the ladder-style stairs to her house, and the unmistakable floral aroma of simmering jasmine rice greeted his nose. The open, wooden window shutters left the main room in a broken pattern of early sunlight and deep shadows, dark remnants of the previous night being dispelled by the rising sun.

She hovered over a propane-fired, stamped-steel wok and stirred the thick, broken-rice soup the Thais call *jok* and the rest of Asia knows as *congee*. She had already prepared the condiments that would elevate the perfumed porridge, which was not made from Scottish oats but from rice, to another, more sublime flavor plane. Hot sesame oil, fried onions, diced scallions, minced pickled ginger, cilantro, dried shrimp, pulled pork, and chopped peanuts filled an array of small plastic bowls. Two fresh eggs, contributed involuntarily by the hens outside, waited to be cracked into the simmering soup and soft cooked therein.

As his shadow darkened the doorway, she looked up and beamed her killer smile. She was barefooted, wearing the robe he bought for her in Bangkok from the Jim Thompson Thai Silk Company. Lit by unseen fires within the coarse-weave fabric, the Thai silk shimmered with an unworldly iridescence in the slanting early morning light. The robe's bright green and deep purple stripes set off her ebony hair and light brown skin with all the radiance he had pictured when he bought it. She crossed the small room to him, and her long legs split the robe open. The robe was tied at the waist, and she let it trail behind her. He saw that the robe, his robe for her, was all she wore.

She matched beauty with grace. The Pilot always got a thrill seeing her partially in, partially out of, Thompson silk. The enigma of Jim Thompson and his precious silk fit perfectly with her personality and lent to her mysterious air. Thompson served as a key operative during World War II in Thailand for the US Office of Strategic Services--the legendary OSS, forerunner of the CIA. After the war, he left the agency, stayed in Bangkok, and single-handedly built the Thai silk industry from almost nothing. But did he really leave the intelligence business, or did he go even deeper undercover? Thompson maintained and cultivated political, military, and intelligence contacts throughout Thailand, Vietnam, and Laos, contacts far beyond those needed to produce and market Thai silk. Was the silk business a literal and figurative cover for more nefarious activities? Was the USAID another CIA front operation? Was Thompson a spook back then? Was *she* now? She represented an enigma wrapped lightly in a fiery, silk robe. The silk was also the product of a shining but murky business.

He slipped off his loafers--no one wears shoes in a Thai residence--and looked at the simmering jok with its waiting condiments. "Are you expecting someone, or are you going into the food street vendor business?" he asked.

"I'm expecting the US Air Force, and what I'm vending you can't buy on the street."

"The rest of the Air Force can't make it; they sent me instead. If I could buy what you have on the street, I couldn't afford it."

She cut short her laugh, wrapping her arms around his neck, and their lips met. He enveloped her, slid his hands down her back, and cupped her firm cheeks. He could feel her silky robe sliding across her even smoother bare skin. She backed away as he reached to untie the belt holding her robe on.

"Breakfast before dessert!" she said with an impish grin.

"Great, how soon can we eat, and how fast can we do it?"

They sat in the room's cool shadows, avoiding the early, intruding dawn. Uncharacteristically quiet and somber, she ate slowly. He could see she had something on her mind as the jok worked its taste magic on both of them. Good Thai food should feel like a war in the mouth, and the soup's disparate elements were locked in cuisine close combat.

After a long silence, she asked, "How was your night?"

"Same-O, same-O, three trips to the tanker. Spectre found a big convoy and shot it up pretty good. The Bad Guys got pissed and tried to bag Spectre. We suppressed ground fire during all our shifts."

Like an American, not a Thai, she got right to the point, looking at him with her spoon poised in midair. "Are we winning the war?"

He found the use of "we" significant; most Thais considered the war a matter between North Vietnam and the USA. Apart from a poorly supported and unpopular Communist Thai Party, the war's effect on Thailand was mainly to offer lucrative business opportunities to the elite and the common folk alike.

Sunlight crept across the room toward their seats on woven bamboo mats as he carefully constructed his answer. "We're not winning the battle for the Ho Chi Minh trail. We only make it harder for the North Vietnamese to move south. Can we win the real war, the one for South Vietnam? I don't know if we can. Probably the best we can do is to convince the North that they've lost."

Her next question dug deeper. The bright patch of sun reached and warmed their bare feet. "Is what you do very dangerous?"

"Lots of folks on the ground with lots of guns try to make it just that."

"Is it more difficult flying in the dark?"

He paused before replying. Normally he would laugh off the risks of what he did nightly with a lame joke, or he would change the subject, but something about her sincerity this morning encouraged honesty. He had to play it straight or feel like he'd betrayed her. "Ground attack at night in the mountains requires you to be on top of your game; it's a challenge. Most guys hack it; some don't."

She focused on the issue bothering her as a band of hazy brightness, cloudy in the dusty house, climbed up her shapely calves and lit up his jeans. "If it's difficult and dangerous for such an uncertain cause, why do you do it?"

He thought for a while before answering as he stirred his jok with his Thai-style ceramic spoon. The climbing sun illuminated his bowl, and the liquid rice shimmered in the harsh light, the condiments swirling. "It's difficult and dangerous; that's why I do it."

She frowned, evidently not satisfied with such a simple, shallow, safe answer. "The same is true of the job done by fishing boat captains sailing the Gulf of Mexico or the Gulf of Siam, but you're not doing that, even though their pay is probably better."

He attempted to joke with his jok, "I wouldn't have met you if I were fishing." The quick look of sadness on her face urged him to return to the seriousness of the question; he tried to explain his motivations. "Flying fighters is something few people can do. Ninety-eight percent of Americans can't even pass the physical for basic flight school. Anyone can drive a shrimp boat."

"So you do it because it marks you as one of a special breed, an exclusive elite thriving on danger."

He had to admit she was on to something. The early morning sun had enveloped them and highlighted her shining ebony hair. He took longer than necessary sprinkling more salty, roasted peanuts into his soup.

"Do you hate the North Vietnamese?" she asked.

"No, I don't. I hate what they've done to many of my buddies. I hate how their shitty war is tearing my country apart back home, but I don't hate them as men. They're trying to reunite their country, albeit on bogus terms. After the war, long after, we'll probably meet in a bar somewhere, maybe Paris--a lot of those guys speak French. We'll buy each other drinks and debrief the war. The Bad Guy fighter pilots that is. I have nothing in common with grunts, but the MiG pilots and I will speak the same language, fighter aviation, whether in English or French."

"If you believe the Americans and the South Vietnamese can't win and you're sorry the war is taking such a toll, why do you fight it? Are you in love with the danger; are you an adrenaline junky?"

The small room was now almost fully illuminated; dust motes danced in the sunlight above the bare wood floor. The raised door sills cast the few shadows left.

"Yes, I suppose that's part of why I fly. The guys in the squadron say it's a crummy war, but it's the only one we have."

"So you fly every night to kill people because it's fun and because it elevates you to a higher status."

That hurt. The Pilot tried to decide if her words stung because they were true or because she believed them to be true. He was on the defensive now. "The North Vietnamese aren't the only folks with a sense of duty. There are several hundred thousand guys fighting the war who aren't fighter pilots. They and I believe in carrying out the last known orders, even if those orders are wrong-headed. Our country called, and we saluted and stepped forward. The decisions on where, why, and how to fly are made way above my pay grade. 'Ours not to reason why, ours but to do or die.' "

"As I remember Tennyson, that episode ended badly for those who followed wrong-headed orders. What's the difference between a cavalry charge into a fortified line and flying into a mountainside in Southern Laos? When is enough enough?"

"Not yet." His eyes unaccustomed to the morning light, he looked at her and stared into those deep, dark eyes. The new day's brightness showed just how insightfully beautiful she was. His cursory reply seemed to satisfy her curiosity, at least for now. Or, he thought, she now had enough to report on to whomever she worked for. She set down her now-empty rice bowl and slowly crossed those shapely legs. The fiery silk robe slit open up to her thighs. He dropped his bowl with a clatter on the floor and reached for her as she untied the belt encircling her slender waist. The iridescent silk whispered, sliding from her body to the wood floor.

They would make love until it was time for her to dress for work. He would doze alone in her house until the arching sun and humid heat made sleep impossible. His air-conditioned Officers' Quarters, his hooch, waited at the end of another samlor ride and would allow him to catch enough cool but fitful sleep until it was time to fly and fight at night once again.

•

CHAPTER 7

LE BOURGET AIRFIELD

Paris

April 2014: On time to the minute, the RER train screeched and slowed to a stop at Le Bourget's open-air, above-ground station. The Pilot opened the sliding car doors and stepped into a gray, overcast day. Train car doors in France close automatically but require passenger action to open, the presumption being that passengers want to stay on the train. The doors closed behind him, and the train left, gathering speed as it disappeared down the tracks into the cold mist.

Would she show? Did he come on too strong at the restaurant? Why didn't she want him to know where she lived? Is there a jealous husband in the mix? Walking from the train toward the station's exit, the Pilot scanned the few people waiting at the station, looking for her and hoping for the best, but prepared for a no-show.

Some women appear to have been selectively bred to look hot in tight jeans, and she was spectacularly one of them. Crossing the damp concrete quay, she walked toward the Pilot, her hips swinging. Skin-tight, black jeans stretched over trim thighs, slender hips, and a round derrière, all apparent at first glance. A white, cowl-neck sweater showed off her breasts. High-heeled boots, a Hermès scarf, and a shoulder bag finished the outfit. Her dark hair bounced around her shoulders as she turned and strode purposefully to join him. He grinned as they greeted each other; was it too soon in the relationship to smile? She answered his internal question by returning his smile with a careful one of her own. He told himself to look her in the eye when they spoke, not to let his gaze descend to fixate on more carnal areas.

"Thanks for meeting me. It might rain; let's take a taxi to the airfield," he said. The airfield lay a wet, fifteen-minute walk away, and a threatening overcast hung low above the village of Le Bourget. They caught a taxi from the rank outside the station, and the driver was none too pleased at the short fare to the air museum. An extra Euro tip added to the meter's tab improved his mood considerably. She sat on the far side of the back seat, a respectful distance between them.

At the entry kiosk, she paid her own admission despite his protestations that he had invited her as his guest. While she dug through her leather Louis Vuitton bag for money, he caught a glimpse of a shiny black object, one she pushed hurriedly to the side of her purse with her free hand. A small pistol, probably a Beretta .25 automatic, nestled in her bag. He wasn't a gun nut. However, the Pilot was familiar with various side arms; he recognized the make and model.

That's very peculiar, he thought as they walked into the museum's colonnaded entrance hall. The cavernous area previously served as the passenger concourse for Le Bourget Airport when it still hosted commercial airline flights--when commercial air travel was a luxury not a commodity. Crossing the open, marble-floored expanse, he considered the fact that the French, particularly women, never carry a piece. The French public sees no need to pack heat in well-policed France, and the pervasive paranoia stalking the United States remains unknown in their country. Even if a civilian wanted to arm herself legally, the bureaucratic hurdles required for a concealed carry permit are insurmountable. No, honest citizens in civilian clothes are only armed when they work for the government itself. Did she?

Why would a member of France's ruling class need a piece in her purse? he asked himself as their footsteps echoed off the distant walls. Undoubtedly one of the elite, her education, sophistication, monetary means, and attitude marked her well. *As the King of Siam said in* The King and I, *it 'is a puzzlement.' I'll think about that tomorrow,* the Pilot resolved, *but not now and not today.*

The air museum featured a wide variety of military and civilian aircraft from the late 1700s to the present, but he focused on the fighters as they toured the displays. A running commentary from the Pilot followed concerning airplanes that he singled out and the importance of each example on display. They started at the rickety biplanes from World War I, flimsy contraptions of spruce, linen, and bicycle tires--little more than powered box kites fitted with machine guns. A SPAD VII fighter decorated in the livery of French ace Georges Guynemer hung inverted from the ceiling in perpetual flight, frozen in space and time. The replica of Guynemer's craft, Vieux Charles (Old Charles), displayed a white stork on its fuselage. It was the mascot of his squadron from Alsace, the famous Storks.

Looking at a Fokker D-VII, a slab-sided, blockish machine, they were somehow unable to look past it, attracted by its shear brutality, its garish red/black paint job, and its deadly purposefulness with no thought given to esthetics.

"It is hard to believe men went to war in these machines," she said.

"Many did; fewer lived to tell about it."

"Flying must have been dangerous then, no?"

"Yes, these old crates were unreliable, prone to sudden mechanical and structural failure. They killed as many of their pilots as they did the people they fought." No one back then, he went on to tell her, knew the optimum configuration for a fighter plane, hence the examples of single-winged aircraft, biplanes with stacked wings, and even triplanes whose three wings resembled a flying venetian blind.

"Were they difficult to fly?" she asked.

"Certainly, and cold, miserably cold, unbearably cold. Some, like the Sopwith Camel, could reach twenty-one thousand feet in the winter over northern Europe." He hunched his shoulders as he spoke and shoved both hands into his pockets, suppressing a shiver. With a backward glance at the planes of the Great War, he turned and quickly walked on, eager to leave the display. She tagged along behind him, trying to keep up in her stiletto heels.

The peaceful interwar years and the Great Depression slowed technical progress, but the urgencies of World War II once again accelerated the development of airborne killing machines. Next he showed her fighters whose air-cooled, radial engines necessitated jug-shaped fuselages, like wine bottles flying base first, and how the installation of liquid-cooled, in-line engines produced fighters with tapered, shark-bodied profiles.

After World War II, jets flamed across the skies. He acknowledged that the first jets appeared hilarious to the unschooled eye, their barrel-shaped bodies filled with bulbous primitive jet engines. By the 1960s, esthetics had caught up with aeronautical engineering and produced sleek feline designs, such as the French Mirages.

She seemed interested; her questions were pertinent and logical. Encouragingly, she tolerated his narratives with good humor and grace. But the restraint he noticed when they first met never melted; a well-hidden barrier remained between them.

They stopped in front of the British Supermarine Spitfire, the Royal Air Force's legendary World War II fighter. The Pilot fell uncharacteristically silent, staring toward but beyond the perfectly proportioned, propeller-driven aircraft. His gaze was focused in the middle distance or perhaps farther, into the past.

"You seem taken with this machine. Do you know it well?" she asked, tilting her head to one side, her dark hair flowing.

"In a way, I do. The old Spit brings back memories."

"Marcel Proust believed our recollections are trapped in material objects, waiting for their liberty. Are any of your memories imprisoned in this airplane?"

"Proust also wrote that the release of those locked-in memories of times past requires one to touch the object. We can't touch the Spitfire; it's behind ropes."

"It seems to me that the Spitfire has already touched you."

Without replying, he swallowed hard, taking her elbow in his hand, leading her further along the display line, and walking quickly again. For the first time, he touched her. She pressed her arm, and his hand, against her slim side. Maybe the icy blue barrier was starting to melt.

"This mini-trip into the history of fighter aviation is fascinating, but what about the art? You promised an art appreciation tour."

"Of course, I did. To see the art, we must look closer."

He led her through the cavernous, linked exhibit halls and directed her attention to the wings of selected aircraft. The leading edges of nearly all the wings on display ran straight as chalk lines, particularly those of civilian airliners. He explained that straight leading edges are cheap and easy to build, with no compound curves and little complicated metal work required. Also, the simple aerodynamics of straight wings are well understood. The jet age swept back most wings to reduce transonic aerodynamic drag, but the leading edges remained straight as a school boy's ruler.

He went on. Occasionally, designers obsessed with wringing maximum efficiency from their wings abandoned the cheap and easy, designed a wing the way the airflow wanted it, and ignored the cost. He pointed back to the Spitfire's wing. The Spitfire's trailing edge resembled a scimitar, curving into the airflow starting at the wing root then more so at the tips where the sinuous metal met the leading edge's short, symmetrical reverse curve, that metal shying away from the airflow. The resulting elliptical wing was the Spitfire's visible trademark, and its aerodynamic magic made the aircraft blindingly fast but also easy to fly well.

For the pièce de résistance, he took her to the mammoth hall housing two white, dart-shaped Concordes, the only airliner to cross the Atlantic at Mach two and above fifty thousand feet. They looked up at the leading edge of the Concorde's triangular delta wing. The aluminum displayed not a single straight line in any dimension. The sensuous leading edge curved inward then outward, up then down. When seen from below, the wing resembled the profile of a naked woman lying on her side, backlit from a distant window.

"If that isn't art, what is?" he said.

She took a step back from the exhibit, crossed her arms over her chest, and again cocked her head to one side, daring him to continue, to explain his theory of art.

"I saw a work by Jackson Pollock at the Pompidou Centre," he countered. "It consisted entirely of an unframed purple canvas. No image, no pattern, no content, just a purple rectangle. It probably took Pollock ten minutes to paint it, five if he used a spray can. That fabulous objet d'art is displayed in the Pompidou. Which would you rather look at: a nonsensical blank purple canvas or the Spitfire's scimitar shape, or maybe the Concorde's sensuous wing?"

"What I would rather do now is eat lunch."

In the culinary universe, France is a star. But in the sandwich domain, it is more of a black hole. The event horizon for French sandwiches is limited to ham, cheese, and butter on a baguette, called a Parisienne for some unknown reason. Ideally, the bread is fresh, soft, and crusty, the butter salted and rich. But without fail, the ham is always sliced thin enough to see through, and the white cheese is nondescript. The museum snack bar, L'Hélice (the Propeller), offered no sandwiches except the standard Parisienne, which they ordered with a bottle of Perrier.

While they ate, she stepped quite a bit out of the cultural norm and asked him a direct question about his profession. She was moving fast, faster than advisable in a new relationship, and he wondered why. In some ways, she was approachable, in others distant.

"You know quite a bit about aircraft design. Are you an engineer?"

"No, I'm a pilot."

"You expanded my knowledge of aircraft, mainly fighter aircraft. How did you learn all these details?"

He looked into those dark eyes for a sign of her motivation but came up empty. She was probably a good poker player. "It goes with the territory; I'm a fighter pilot. To uphold the traditions of my job, you must understand the evolution of the state of the art, how we got to where we are now. It's important to know how these machines flew, how the men who flew them did it and why. 'Those who cannot remember the past are condemned to repeat it.' "

"A quote by Santayana, no?" Are you knowledgeable about past fighter operations, as well as aircraft design?"

"As if I flew those historical missions myself."

"Does all this knowledge of history help you fly today's fighter planes?"

"I like to think so."

She pulled the thread some more before taking another bite of her sandwich. "What aircraft do you fly now?"

"Currently I fly a wooden desk left from the cold war at the American Embassy in Paris. But I have the opportunity to fly the F-35 soon if I so choose."

"You haven't accepted the assignment? Isn't the F-35 the crème de la crème of American fighters? I thought any fighter pilot worth the title would leap at the opportunity. Is there something about the F-35 that worries you?"

"No, nothing about airplanes worries me. Worry is counterproductive when there are problems to be solved." He bit off a hunk of his sandwich with more force than necessary. How did she know so much about the F-35? Who was this woman? Where did these questions come from? "I have two weeks before I report, if I do. Why do you ask?"

She dropped the subject like a laser-guided bomb. "I have another question, if you don't mind?"

"Zut alors, you are filled with questions. Only one more."

The look on her face softened, as if she had just abandoned a difficult job. "All the fighter planes we've examined today employed one pilot. Is there a reason for flying alone?"

He thought a minute over his answer and tried to craft a reply not too technical and yet not too superficial. "Yes, the increases in size and aerodynamic drag caused by adding a second man outweigh, literally, the benefits of the additional help. The F-4 Phantom was the only successful fighter with two crewmembers."

"Is there also some psychological reason you fighter pilots prefer to operate alone?"

He needed time to compose his answer. *This woman is unable to conduct small talk*, he thought. She digs ever deeper. I've got to be straight with her; she'll know if I'm bobbing and weaving. "Yes, we prefer to fight alone."

"Alone in combat with no support from your comrades."

"Yes, and we die alone."

It was her turn to pause. She looked directly at him, her sandwich poised in mid-air. "Don't we all?"

They both fell silent, staring down at the bubbles rising from their glasses of Perrier. She smiled and returned his gaze as he looked up at her. "I hope I haven't been indiscrete with my questions." She made amends for prying, using "Je ne veux pas être indiscrète," a ritual apology in France. She added a bonus "Et si on se tutoyait?" (May we use *Tu*?)

She told him the night they met that she believed the French language superior to all others in conveying meaning and unequaled in describing the world. When she wanted to be clear, she used French. Her request to use *Tu*, the familiar form, was the equivalent in English of using first names and signified friendship. But in French its use means so much more. Never again would they operate alone in conversation with each other; use of the familiar tense joined them, made them a pair. But to what end?

He took the offer of verbal familiarity as an invitation to get closer. To do so this soon in a relationship was extraordinary. The familiar verbal form signaled emotional contact between them. But had there been a spark across the gap before the contacts joined?

"Bien sûr, mon amie." (Certainly, my friend.) Rising from the table, he proposed a change of pace from engineering to literature as he helped her slide back her chair. "Come with me; let's go see an old friend," he said.

The museum featured an exhibit on the life and exploits of French writer, aviator, and bon vivant Antoine de Saint-Exupéry. Indeed, one large exhibit hall bore his name. On display, in addition to black-and-white photos, his books, and mementos, were fragments recovered from the wreckage of the P-38 fighter from his last, fatal flight in 1944.

"Do you know Saint-Exupéry?" she asked. "I am surprised; A Frenchman, he flew and wrote in the 1930s and 1940s."

"Anyone with an interest in flying knows Saint-Ex. In a time when pilots were considered to be mere technicians, chauffeurs, he showed with his writing that it's possible to be both an intellectual and an aviator."

The Pilot fished a few coins from his pocket, mostly French Euros, but one was very different: an American five cent piece, reserved for just this occasion. He flipped it with his thumb into the exhibit, the coin clattering on the cement floor, rolling randomly around like a lost soul searching for sancutary then falling over under the P-38's battered nose landing gear strut standing on display.

"Why did you do that?" she asked.

"It's a tradition from World War II. We would throw a nickel, a five-cent piece, on the patch of lawn in front of Wing Headquarters for good luck to ensure a safe return from a combat mission. Now they're thrown on fighter pilots' graves for good luck. Saint-Ex was lost over the ocean, so this will have to do. The custom comes from a drinking song. 'Throw a nickel on the grass, save a fighter pilot's ass,' the words say."

"Did throwing a particular coin on the grass always bring good luck?"

"Usually, but sometimes not. That's why we throw them on graves today."

"You said, 'we.' You could not have been there."

"In a way, I was." He took her arm again and led her away from the display, leaving the nickel on the floor. After a few steps, she stopped and looked at him, her eyes narrowed.

"A superstitious ritual for an intellectual. Interesting. A good luck offering for a pilot you never met, a man not a squadron mate."

"The nickel wasn't for Saint-Ex; he's been dead for decades. It was for me."

For the second time that day, she stopped and looked at him, carefully, her head tilted. To his great surprise, she took his hand and they hurried away, leaving the exhibit.

After a final walk-through tour of the exhibits, she elected to board the RER with him back to the city. The weather had worsened late in the day. The overcast was lower and darker, the rain harder. The train left Le Bourget station gliding on surface tracks. Nearer the city, it seemed to accelerate as it descended, diving inside the dark tunnel network under all of Paris.

He looked at her sitting across from him with her legs crossed and leaned forward toward her. "Would you be interested in joining me for dinner? The US embassy can do without my services any night this next week."

"Yes, I would. As long as we don't dine on an airplane."

"No airplane food. I'll try for a reservation at my favorite, family-run bistro on the island, near my apartment." He hoped his choice of a restaurant near his apartment would signal his ultimate intention, bed and breakfast. If successful, he would finish breaching remnants of the crumbling emotional wall still somewhat erect between them, get to know her intimately, and solve some of her mysteries. "May I call you?" he said.

"As you wish."

The train entered the massive Les Halles RER/Metro interchange and connection point, the squealing brakes echoing off the arched tile above the quay. Without warning, she rose to leave and handed him a card from her purse. "Thank you for a wonderful day and for expanding my art horizons." Then she was gone in the throng toward the exit marked "Correspondance," her high-heeled boots' staccato clicks on the polished concrete clearly audible over the crowd's shuffles.

He slipped the card into his pocket until he exited at the next station and walked toward his waiting, empty apartment. He stared at the card in the twilight, shielding it from the rain with his left hand. At first glance, it was a lady's personal card, displaying only her name, a telephone number with a Parisian prefix, and a cell phone number with a French country code. But no, the card was printed, not embossed, and on plain white stock. Her name was not in a flowery script but a more business-like font. No additional information, no address, no company title, just her name and the two phone numbers.

Her card presented a revelation; he had seen such cards several times in his dealings with certain French officials. He suspected the card in his hand was one issued to employees of the Direction Générale de la Sécurité Extérieure, the DGSE, French equivalent to the Central Intelligence Agency (CIA). This could be easily verified; he only had to compare it with known DGSE cards in his file. Or he could call the land-line number. If someone answered without formal or official greeting, no "Allô" or office identifier, and just the last four digits of the number, "27 27," his suspicions would be confirmed. But the inevitable caller ID display would reveal he called, and she would suspect why. He decided to match the cards at work instead and contact her on her cell phone.

Her mystery deepened and became more complex the closer he got to her. Was it possible she was a DGSE operations agent? A functionary or an administrator wouldn't pack heat, yet he was offered a glimpse of her pistol in her open purse. And later she gave him a DGSE-style card. Were these slips actions of poor tradecraft? No well-trained agent would commit such mistakes if she wanted to remain under cover. Maybe she made intentional mistakes, clumsy warnings. Or perhaps she had issued a covert challenge, daring him to get involved with her despite the blatant display of tri-color French caution flags. He mulled over this latest set of obscure issues in his life in the late afternoon's poor visibility and made the decision to assume the third explanation. If this was a challenge, he would take it on.

He believed flying fighters was not only a vocation but also a way of life, an attitude, an approach to problems requiring an aggressive response to a significant opportunity. He couldn't refuse a beautiful woman's challenge and betray a century of social conditioning shaping fighter pilots' behavior. Whatever the true situation, he would pick up the woman's stylish gauntlet and see where the relationship led. *Come, Watson, the game's afoot,* he thought.

Crossing the Seine, he looked upstream, the water shining in the dusk. A clearly defined gap stretched between the low overcast illuminated by the city's lights and the rippled surface of the river. He turned and stared downstream, the amber lights reflecting off the flat water stretching into the distance along where the river's straight course ran, impersonating a wet runway. It was a space where a pilot could take off, carefully. It would be difficult to fly under the overcast, staying out of the clouds, avoiding the wet ground, and ignoring the temptation to climb out to the safe sunlight. The imitation runway beckoned, taunting him, is if saying, "Can you hack it? Or would you bust your sorry ass trying?" Long ago, one of his kind, or maybe he, had accepted such a challenge. He felt the bouncing movement of hard rubber tires rolling on a concrete runway, not a watery one, and sensed a cockpit tight around him. As he felt his nerves sharpen, his reflexes whetted, honed for the flight to come, and the sky above the overcast beckoned.

CHAPTER 8

RAMSTEIN AIR BASE

Germany

December 1961: *Not a pretty day for an airplane ride*, the Pilot thought, *but duty calls. Anyway, I'd rather be up there wishing I was down here than down here wishing I was up there.* He swung the jet's needle nose onto the active runway, the ceiling a leaden overcast five hundred feet overhead with misty rain limiting horizontal visibility. Through the rain-streaked windscreen's "bulletproof" center segment, the wet runway glistened, reflecting the yellow boundary lights just off the concrete border of each side of the pavement. The strip faded into the foggy distance, the departure end out of sight in the gloom. The runway's disappearance into the mists mimicked the appearance of an infinitely long strip. It wasn't that long; it didn't need to be. A few thousand feet would suffice.

The airfield control tower radioed, "Volunteer One cleared for takeoff."

"Roger. Volunteer's rolling."

Flying the F-104 Starfighter was like riding the tip of a thrown spear. From the cockpit, the Pilot could see little of the aircraft, even if he looked back over his shoulder. The tiny wings were mounted far to the rear on the F-104's stiletto fuselage and visible only in the rearview mirrors, almost out of his sight. Spanning only 7½ feet, the wings slanted down, their square tips lower than their roots. Such pronounced anhedral increased the roll rate of the aircraft but did nothing to improve the total lift available. The sharp nose sloped away invisibly in front of the canopy. The body barely stretched wider than the canopy rails. His view of the aircraft was limited to the myriad of switches, dials, lights, indicators, and controls in the cockpit itself. With nothing but the interior in his view, the impression was one of flying a cockpit, not an entire airplane.

When F-104 images became public during the mid-1950s, the popular media christened the Starfighter the "missile with a man in it." "An engine attached to a cockpit" would have been more accurate, with an enormous, single jet engine taking up most of the fuselage. The designers, toiling away at their drafting boards in the fabled Lockheed "Skunk Works," sacrificed everything for three key performance goals: rate of climb, acceleration, and top speed. They saved precious weight and drag by shrinking any feature deemed unessential, such as wings.

The engineers defied convention in other areas, as well. The Pilot boarded the Starfighter from the aircraft's right side, not the left. Calvary horses were mounted from their left side. In the formularizing days of World War I, cavalry mentality transferred from scouting on horseback to flying scout planes, and the pilots continued mounting their now mechanical steeds on the left. But not on the Starfighter.

The Pilot barely fit in the tight cockpit. Stepping off the external boarding ladder, he had to bend his flight boots on tip-toe like a ballet dancer to clear the narrow gap between the instrument panel and the ejection seat. If he ejected, braided steel cables would reel in his heels when the seat's rocket motor fired, preventing his toes from taking out the instrument panel or vice versa. The cables snapped into aluminum sockets strapped onto the heels of his black leather flight boots--the distinctive F-104 "spurs." Tinkling like rowel spurs in the Long Branch Saloon, Starfighter spurs were a macho badge of honor worn into many a stag bar at many an Officers' Club.

The instruments almost sat in his lap, and the switch-laden consoles pressed against his thighs. In order for him to reach the throttle and control stick, his elbows had to be at his sides. With his seatbelt and shoulder harness cinched tight, his range of movement consisted solely of leaning forward about three inches. Still, the diminutive cockpit felt right; its intimate dimensions made him feel integrated into the jet, not like a detached operator. Some aircraft you sit in. This one he strapped on; it became a part of him and he of it.

Checks completed, he stood on the brakes by rocking the rudder pedals forward to hold the Starfighter motionless as he ran the single engine up to full power. The nose tilted down slightly, pushed there by the howling jet behind him. A quick glance at the gauges: rpm one hundred percent, oil and hydraulic pressures in the green, no warning lights. He punched the stopwatch on the cockpit clock to record the flight time and released the brakes. His leather-gloved left hand pushed the throttle outboard and forward into the afterburner range. A firm shove on his shoulder blades told him the afterburner had lit, and a gauge showed the exhaust nozzle open. A quick thrust pushed the throttle full forward to the maximum afterburner stop, and additional thrust came on line. The nose came up; the jet leapt forward, eager to be shed of the ground. Speed built quickly, the runway edge lights changing from individual spots to a continuous blur. He released the nose wheel steering button as the rudder became effective enough to keep the jet on the centerline. Most aircraft tell their pilots they are ready to fly by feeling lighter on the controls as the wings generate sufficient lift. Not the Starfighter. At 180 knots (210 miles per hour), he raised the nose two degrees, and the vibration from the wheels rolling on concrete ceased. The jet lifted off, barely supported by those vestigial wings.

Speed came faster now; he hurried to get flaps up and landing gear retracted before the fierce airflow damaged either. Still more acceleration as the aircraft cleaned up, free of parasite drag. The jet wanted to climb, but the Pilot fed in nose down trim to hold it on the deck. He wanted even more speed before entering the low clouds. He crossed the airfield boundary at 420 knots, waited three seconds more, and saw 450 knots (525 miles per hour) on the airspeed indicator. Time to go upstairs. He released his forward pressure on the stick ever so slightly. The jet entered the clouds instantly, nothing visible outside the canopy but dull, white nothingness.

He let the nose come up to the fifteen degrees mark on the artificial horizon at the top right of the instrument panel and pulled the throttle back, out of afterburner. The afterburner's external plume died, and the clouds around the jet dimmed to gray, the blue-hot flame no longer reflecting back into the cockpit. The jet continued to climb effortlessly.

He changed radio frequencies and contacted the Ground Controlled Intercept site. The ground-based radar would vector him around other traffic embedded in the weather and help him establish a flight path along the West German/East German border. The assistance was welcome; high-speed instrument flight was hard enough without navigating at the same time.

Around ten thousand feet, he broached free of the clouds, now a ragged under cast beneath him. The stiletto Starfighter erupted out of the solid cloud deck like a billfish leaping from a foamy wave on the Sea of Cortez. But instead of falling back with a splash, the jet continued toward the high blue sky, driven there by the relentless engine.

As the sun instantly illuminated the cockpit, the Pilot thought, *I can't believe the State of Tennessee pays me to do this; I'd gladly do it for free. Check that, our squadron has been called to active duty. Now the US government picks up the check for this flight, not the good folks in Nashville. Your federal tax dollars at work.* But still written in large, black letters along the F-104's fuselage, "Tennessee Air National Guard" showed the world where the Pilot and the Starfighter hailed from.

Hell-bent on reducing western influence in Berlin, the Russians and their East German stooges were causing international problems. In violation of the World War II peace treaty, access to the city, which was surrounded by East Germany, had been restricted by the commies. The ugly Berlin Wall grew taller daily. The westward flow of East Germans changing countries and seeking freedom was slowly choked off. To show firm national resolve, Washington scrambled the Pilot's Tennessee Air National Guard fighter squadron from their homebase near the Great Smokey Mountains outside Knoxville, Tennessee. This resolute move was calculated to tell the Russians, "Doggone it, we're peeved." At the same time, the administration hoped their saber rattling wasn't loud enough to touch off World War III.

The Tennessee Air National Guard showed the flag to the Russians, but which flag: Old Glory or the Stars and Bars? This southern squadron was from the Deep South and manned by rebels who when they said, "Back during the war" meant the War Between the States, not any more recent conflict. It wasn't clear to anyone in the squadron how much the West German civilians living around Ramstein Air Base appreciated being defended by the Confederate Air Force's ear-splitting jets.

The airspeed indicator's white needle quivered around 450 knots as he climbed. In a small window on the dial's face, a series of single-digit numbers ticked upward: 0.7; 0.8; 0.9. As he screamed through thirty thousand feet in gin-clear air, the 0.9 reading meant he was traveling at 9/10 the speed of sound, or "point nine" Mach. Now he disregarded the airspeed displayed in knots. Adjusting the nose's pitch to vary the rate of climb, he concentrated on holding 0.9 Mach. The aircraft was climbing slower now, the stratosphere's thin air robbing the engine of some of its sea-level thrust while the wispy air offered less drag in compensation.

Turning northward parallel to the West German/East German border and following the ground control radar's commands, he could relax for a few seconds. Two and a half minutes after break release, the altimeter read fifty thousand feet. The Pilot leveled off--any higher and he would need a pressure suit to stay conscious in case of a loss of cabin pressure. At maximum rpm since brake release, the engine seemed to grumble when he retarded the throttle. Even reined in, the Starfighter held 0.9 Mach effortlessly.

He was utterly alone at that extreme altitude, just he and the jet, tens of thousands of feet higher than any airliner. Overhead, the sky shone a midnight blue as it started its transition to the black of space. He looked left then right and believed he could detect the earth's curvature on the horizon. Far below, Europe was covered by the cloud deck he had quickly climbed through, a fuzzy, rumpled blanket of white. The unfiltered, fierce sunlight at fifty thousand feet bathed the cockpit with arc light radiation and cast an inky-black shadow under the instrument panel's glare shield.

He was unaccompanied by human contact, but it didn't feel that way. Fighter pilots consider themselves a team of two--a human/machine symbiotic pair, a pilot and a jet aircraft operating together. His only connection to Mother Earth came via the radar controller's disembodied voice. He referred to himself in the plural with his transmissions to the ground. "Ramstein Control, we're steady at flight level five zero zero." He and the jet were on station.

Critics, jealous of fighter pilots' bravado, classified the use of the plural tense as the "royal we." If ever notified of such carping, the Pilot would have replied as did Queen Victoria, "We are not amused."

The solitary human/jet partnership flew alone at high altitude because the MiGs never came up to play. The Russian MiG fighters always stayed well inside their border, never challenging the Starfighters. Their fearless pilots only harassed civilian airliners and lumbering military cargo planes transiting to Berlin inside the treaty-designated air corridors far below.

The Pilot often speculated what it would be like fighting a MiG in a dogfight and tried to visualize the encounter in his mind while lying in his bunk off duty. He believed that if he ran through all the likely moves and countermoves again and again in his mind, he could avoid surprises and let his reflexes take over when the graduation exercise finally came. It would be an interesting encounter. One could hardly imagine two more dissimilar fighter aircraft than the F-104 and the MiG-21, the Russians' latest model. The lighter MiG could maneuver tightly using its delta-shaped, unburdened wings and easily turn inside the F-104. The Starfighter would have much greater acceleration, climb faster, and reach its top speed sooner. It reminded him of individual combat in a circular Roman arena--one gladiator with a net and trident and the other with a sword and shield.

His plan was a simple one, the best kind. Ground control would vector him to the fight and position him behind the MiG. He would point the F-104's tapered nose directly at the MiG and hold it there, pushing the throttle into minimum afterburner. The flame of the "burner" would erase the highly visible smoke trail normally left behind by the jet engine. Seen head on, the Starfighter presented a silver circle less than five feet in diameter. The unsuspecting MiG pilot, cursed with poor sight lines to his rear, would be hard pressed to see the fast-approaching dot on the horizon until the F-104 closed inside the launch range for a Sidewinder heat-seeking missile.

The Sidewinder's name was borrowed from a snake, a pit viper native to the southwest deserts of America, which also uses heat to locate and track its prey. Within range and locked on, both the reptile and the missile are usually lethal. When the Pilot heard the guttural animal growl in his earphones, indicating his first Sidewinder had picked up the MiG's heat signature, he would squeeze the red trigger on the control stick, release, check the second missile's aural tone, and squeeze again. The MiG could out turn an F-104 limited to 7.33 Gs, but it couldn't out turn a Sidewinder and its 32-G capability.

If the missiles were suspect and the MiG pilot still hadn't picked him up visually, the Pilot would press home the attack. Once the F-104's nose-mounted radar locked on the target, the gun sight would project on the windscreen in front of him and predict the flight path of his cannon shells. The tiny, red dot in the center of the sight, the "pipper" (terminology inherited from the Royal Air Force of World War II), would show him where the projected bullet stream intersected the target. Inside three thousand feet of range, he would fly the pipper onto the MiG's canopy, squeeze the trigger, turn on the gun, and light up the MiG. Firing forward past his left leg, the Gatling gun buried in the fuselage behind him would spew 20 mm high-explosive shells at six thousand rounds per minute, one hundred rounds per second. One or two hits could torch the fragile, lightly-built MiG. At one hundred chances per second, he liked his odds in a gunfight if--and it was a big if--the MiG driver didn't see him until it was too late.

French pilot and writer Antoine de Saint-Exupéry asserted that fighter pilots don't fight fair, they murder. It is difficult to shoot down someone who spots his assailant; the intended prey can maneuver for his life, fight back, and spoil the attack. Fighter pilots find it far easier to gun down some poor bastard who never sees what hit him.

If the MiG pilot picked him up visually or was warned of the Starfighter's approach by his radar controller, a more likely occurrence, the MiG would turn into the attack. The Sidewinders wouldn't be denied, but a successful gun attack on a defending, turning MiG would present a formidable challenge. Then it would be time for Plan B. He would point his nose well behind the MiG's tail, go to full afterburner, and bug out, letting the howling engine carry him to safety. No MiG can accelerate with an F-104 in full afterburner.

By the time the MiG turned around, the Pilot and his jet would be out of Russian missile range. Thanks to good intelligence work on their part, the Russian Atoll heat-seeking missiles were carbon copies of the US Sidewinder and thus well understood by the Good Guys. Clear of the fight arena and the MiG, the Pilot would look for a minimum of 520 knots (600 miles per hour), indicated airspeed; 600 knots (700 miles per hour), would be better, his best turning velocity. Then he'd pitch his jet back up and over, into the fight, at 7 Gs and retry Plan A.

However, such an encounter remained firmly in the realm of speculation and planning. Back in East Tennessee, he had told her he didn't expect to see a MiG in this deployment, and so far his prediction was accurate. Wondering what she was doing now, part of him wished he was with her to find out. He found it funny how her soft memory popped into his consciousness at the oddest times, like now at fifty thousand feet above West Germany.

The radar controller came on the air, rudely interrupting his memory chain and bringing him back to the Starfighter's cockpit. "Volunteer One, cleared for the Mach run."

"Roger that. Let's wake up some Russians." He hoped the Bad Guys were monitoring his radio transmissions and would take note of his bravado.

This preplanned maneuver was intended to convince the Russians of the folly of their ways. Russian air defense radars inside East Germany would track the F-104 and see the Starfighter's thirst for speed luridly displayed on their glowing scopes. The Pilot advanced the thick throttle with its many buttons forward into the afterburner range and once again felt a reassuring jolt in the back as the afterburner lit. A quick check of the gauge confirmed the exhaust nozzle was fully open. At fifty thousand feet and 0.9 Mach, the Starfighter had plenty of performance yet available. The Mach meter began to count up, the airspeed and altimeter needles twitched, and the Mach readout jumped from 0.98 to 1.1; he had slipped through the so-called sound barrier without undue drama.

More and more thin but super-cold air was rammed down the engine's intake as the speed quickly built. Jet engines develop greater and greater thrust at higher speeds--the faster they go, the faster they go. The F-104 accelerated, running like a horse with the bit between its teeth. The aircraft seemed to want to go faster; it said to the team's human half, "Let me run!" Through Mach 1 now, the Pilot and his Starfighter entered a novel aerodynamic regime unknown to generations of subsonic pilots, one in which the airflow around the jet obeyed far different rules.

The effects of that supersonic airflow on the F-104 were bizarre, powerful. Responses to stick inputs became more solid, discouraging any speed-killing turns. Invisible, conical shock waves now attached to the nose, wingtips, and tail changed the airflow affecting the jet in subtle ways and made the control surfaces marginally less effective. Mach 1.5 came quickly, still accelerating. At Mach 1.8, the flight controls were still effective, enabling straight line flight on the tip of a supersonic spear. The rpm gauge read 104 percent, a mathematical impossibility, but there it was, producing even more thrust. At Mach 2, an amber light began to blink at the top of the instrument panel in the darkness under the glare shield. "SLOW, SLOW, SLOW," it flashed. If left unchecked, the maniacal engine, the Starfighter's soul, would drive itself, the airframe, and the Pilot to instantaneous fiery destruction as the engine exploded, the victim of its own excess.

The Pilot slowly pulled the throttle back out of afterburner and gently rolled the jet into a shallow turn westward. He liked the no-nonsense "SLOW" warning. Any other chief designer than Kelly Johnson, boss of the Skunk Works, would have specified something like, "Intake temperature reaching limits." Not Kelly. "SLOW" was all it read.

The mission behind the Mach 2 run was to get the attention of the East German proles far below on the earth's surface as they slopped mortar on concrete blocks, building the Berlin Wall. The unexpected impact of the sudden sonic boom produced by the Pilot's Starfighter fifty thousand feet overhead might make them reconsider. *Yeah, right*, thought the Pilot.

These shameless displays of raw speed did keep the MiGs at bay and on the ground. As he turned the now subsonic jet toward Ramstein and began a gliding descent, the Pilot and his jet were still alone in the air.

Flying against always-absent aerial opposition was like being the marshal of Tombstone, Arizona, and missing the gunfight at the OK Corral. The squadron's pilots exhibited more than a little of the gunfighter attitude. Mentally, there couldn't be much difference between loosening a Colt .45 in its holster while stepping onto dusty Main Street of Tombstone, and lighting the afterburner to go up against a MiG-21 with a 20 mm Gatling gun.

The Pilot had to remind himself that, unlike lawman Wyatt Earp and his brothers, the Tennessee Air National Guard's part-time pilots all worked civilian jobs like Wyatt's deputy, Doc Holliday, a dentist and a gambler. Instead of cleaning up the dusty desert outpost of Tombstone, the Guard prepared themselves to police the clear skies when called away from their civilian occupations. They were a school yearbook representative, farmer, airline pilot, teacher, and various other workaday professions, but none were dentists.

The squadron formed a close-knit group, united in their unique ability to fly the world's fastest interceptor. They practiced their dangerous craft often. While sitting on a tractor, teaching students, or coaching little league baseball, each F-104 jock often wondered in the back of his mind what it would be like to engage mano- a-mano, aircraft-to-aircraft, with a MiG pilot and his jet. The likely outcome of the fight was obvious: one man a hero and the other man dead, a loser. One aircraft partner would be converted into flaming wreckage; one would have a victory symbol, the enemy's flag, painted under its canopy. No one in the squadron wanted war. But they did hunger to know how they would measure up once the engagements, the dogfights they constantly trained for, played out for keeps when someone picked up their hat in the ring.

They rehearsed the hoped-for encounters endlessly, but not only to increase the chances of success and survival in combat. To its dedicated pilots, the F-104 approximated a beautiful woman, with alluring lines, passionate performance, and a welcomingly tight cockpit. She was capable of delivering intense pleasure if treated well. But she could be a hard-eyed bitch with thin lips and demand frequent attention. Leave her alone too long and your ability to handle her slowly ebbed until you were unable to cope and were judged to be inept. Then she screamed at you right before she busted your ass. The USAF official accident report would state, "failure to maintain aircraft control" or some such boilerplate jargon. The remaining pilots would know the truth, that he hadn't loved the bitch often enough and she killed him. Today the man/machine liaison was well lubricated; they slipped through the cold German sky with ease. The Pilot left the thoughts of comely women and bitches behind him and prepared for an unwelcome end to the flight.

Like it or not, he now had to leave the realm of the airman, where things are simple and clear: fly, fight, win, survive, repeat. Once again he would return to the flat earth and the two-dimensional domain which non-pilots perceive as everyday life, where things are messy and complex and problems can't be solved with a burst of 20 mm cannon fire or a well-placed heat-seeking missile.

The cloud deck came up to meet him. Soon he and the jet would be trapped in its encompassing, white blanket, committed to land by their low fuel state. Next would come a radar-controlled instrument landing to a wet, foggy runway. The final approach would be modified for the F-104, projecting a flatter than normal glide slope to cope with the stiletto Starfighter's abject inability to glide on its abbreviated wings. The Pilot would have to hold the aircraft in the air on short final with power tapped from the engine. Landing the jet in the soup wasn't in the same challenge league as fighting a MiG, but he quickly stabbed at the left consol, using a long-rehearsed move to the weapons panel, and selected "Gun" anyway, just for practice.

CHAPTER 9

PIGEON FORGE

East Tennessee

June 1961: The Little Pigeon River is not little, not a river, and the passenger pigeons for which it was named are long extinct. It is instead a meandering, broad creek where clear, shallow waters splash, burbling over slick-rounded boulders and pooling in shaded ponds. Willows lean precariously over the stream from banks thick with wild blackberry bushes. Muscatine vines, honeysuckle tangles, and poison oak bushes form a vaulting green tunnel guiding the wandering stream on its way.

Her cabin, inherited from some never-named ancestor, perched beside the river's West Fork and faced the water running twenty feet in front of the porch steps. Elevated on log pilings, the rustic cottage was immune to the creek's frequent spring floods and shaded by the surrounding second-growth forest.

The Pilot liked to wake before dawn, brew a pot of strong coffee, and drink it hot and black. The java, steaming in the cool morning air, filled the screened-in porch with the aroma of dark beans and roasted chicory. Here he waited on the tardy dawn while sitting on the porch swing's wide bench seat. Shadows of the Great Smokey Mountains to the east shade the Little Pigeon until late morning, until the sun clears the forested peaks, their rounded contours lost in the gray mists giving the mountains their name.

A sniff of sticky-sweet honeysuckle nectar wafted through the screens, mixing with the scent of hot coffee and chicory. The Pilot drank it in with a deep breath, once again remembering how delicious air could be when not expelled from an oxygen tank, expanded through a pressure regulator, then filtered by a saliva-soaked rubber mask. The metallic taste of the Starfighter's bottled, sterile oxygen was never far from his memory. Neither was the memory of the jet itself. He had to push thoughts of flying from his mind when he was with her, or else his eyes would tend to focus on the middle distance, on some tactical situation. He would mentally leave her, and she would sense his departure and be hurt.

Once during a romantic candlelight dinner in one of the finest French restaurants in Knoxville, Tennessee, he checked out, completely lost in thoughts of flying. He was jolted from his reverie by her curt question, delivered unerringly. "Where are you?" she asked. "Fifty thousand feet and Mach two? Or here with me?"

He refocused his eyes on her and apologized sincerely with a sheepish grin, "Sorry. I guess I did it again."

His squadron mates held that a fighter pilot was a guy who when flying, thinks about women, and when with women, thinks about flying--a dangerous attribute degrading the efficiency of both activities and putting the desired outcome of each engagement at serious risk. A fighter plane is a jealous mistress; if you let her, she'll destroy your relationships with the ones you love. Recognizing the trap, he would push flying away for a time, at least during this soft green morning in East Tennessee.

Also up before the sun was the local mockingbird, whose personal turf encompassed the tangled trees surrounding the cabin. The Pilot enjoyed communicating with a fellow male aviator and whistled a few notes for the listening bird. Usually after he repeated the same musical bar a few times, the mockingbird would replicate the notes by mocking the Pilot's whistle. This morning, he tried without much success to teach the bird to chirp a short sequence of notes from "Jolie Blonde," the Cajun national anthem. After half a cup of coffee and ten or twelve tries at avian musical instruction, he experienced a caffeine-driven, blinding flash of the obvious. *You moron*, he thought, *the mockingbird is the state bird of Tennessee, not Louisiana.* He switched his coaching to a signature phrase from

"The Tennessee Waltz." After a few rehearsals, the bird made real progress in mimicry.

He heard the cabin's wooden door creak and looked around to see her padding barefooted out onto the porch, holding her coffee mug in cupped hands to keep them warm in the cool mountain air. He smiled as he saw she wore one of his blue Air Force uniform shirts with only a few buttons fastened at her waist and hips. "Good morning. You'll catch your death dressed like that," he said.

"Would you rather I put on my long, flannel nightgown?"

"That's a rhetorical question with only one answer: of course not."

She was tall with honey-blond hair falling in lazy waves past her soft shoulders. Her height emphasized her curves: full breasts, flaring hips, and flat stomach. The too-large shirt whispered across her slim thighs. Trim ankles and bare feet completed his early morning vision. Not for the first time, he noticed how her green eyes and sharp nose set her apart. If eyes are windows into the soul, her soul was one to be reckoned with. She projected a keen intellect with those eyes, often accompanied by a wry smile hinting, "I've heard that before." At first glance, she could pass for arm candy. When she spoke, one immediately thought "southern belle" with all the implied negative and positive connotations. But those eyes gave her away.

Her distinctive accent was historic East Tennessee with neither the honey-dripped speech of Mississippi nor the cornpone tones of Georgia. She spoke with a mountaineer's twang, faster than the usual southern drawl and more nasal. This morning she seemed reluctant to talk at all, staring out through the screens at the babbling river. Her eyebrows were pinched over her nose. He wasn't used to her being quiet. Something must be bothering her, and it was clearly up to him to draw her out.

He slid over, and she sat beside him, careful not to rock the swing and spill either cup of coffee. She crossed her smooth legs, tucking the loose shirttail between her bare thighs with one hand.

"I'm afraid I have to report a failure; I've started the day off badly," he said.

"Nothing serious, I hope."

"No. I can't teach your mockingbird to sing your theme song."

"Which is?"

" 'Jolie Blonde,' what else? But the bird couldn't get it. So I tried plan B, to get him to greet you with 'The Tennessee Waltz.' " The joke broke the cool morning's emotional ice and produced a big smile as she leaned against him. He felt her curvy body against him through the shirt's thin oxford cloth.

They listened to the mockingbird's full repertoire of the bird world's greatest hits without interrupting the impromptu concert with human conversation. An energetic mockingbird can sing forty songs, and by the time he started his second chorus, they had finished their coffee. Clearly, they were listening to the Elvis of mockingbirds.

Finally, she broke the human silence, took a last sip of coffee, and asked, "This deployment to Germany, why are all y'all going? I understood the squadron's mission was protecting the Oak Ridge nuclear plant."

"Correct, along with providing air cover to Washington. We can be over the capitol from Knoxville in fifteen minutes in our F-104s. You've read the intelligence reports. The Russians are acting like jerks again over Berlin, and the President wants to station his best unit on the West German border. Oak Ridge and DC will have to go unguarded until we get back."

"Couldn't the regular Air Force handle this assignment?"

"Maybe, but not with the Starfighter's panache."

She smiled but with her lips pursed as she balanced her empty cup on the swing's armrest. "Won't it be dangerous, maybe fighting the MiGs?"

The pilots often discussed among themselves the possibilities of trying on a MiG or two, but he thought it wise to not get too excited about the possibility of real combat. He attempted to downplay the risk. "I doubt we'll ever see a MiG. We'll fly around in the rotten German weather for a few months, and then we'll come home."

"Penetrating German weather is dangerous in itself, never mind the MiGs. What do you think about that?"

He had to concede her point; the F-104's accident rate was sky-high, the highest of any century-series fighter. The Starfighter crashed more often than the F-100, F-101, F-102, and F-105 combined. Throw in icing, rain, and perhaps snow, and things could get dicey.

"You've obviously read the accident reports on file in the squadron. Yes, flying a single-seat, high-performance jet in the soup can be a challenge."

"If it's so dangerous, why do you do it?"

He answered her sincere question with a dollop of truth and grudgingly acknowledged his adrenaline addiction. It wasn't the first time he had heard and responded to the question. "Maybe that's why I do it. Réné Descartes said, 'Je vole, donc Je suis.' I fly, therefore I am."

"It's amazing Descartes would say that; he lived most of his life in the 1600s, well before manned flight. Are you sure that quote didn't come from Antoine de Saint-Exupéry?"

"No, Saint-Ex never wrote anything for adults that concise."

"Didn't Saint-Exupéry die in combat? He must have known the risks he took, but he ignored the danger. Why would a famous author, a student of human nature, a bon vivant, blow off the possibility of sudden death? Do you discount it as well?"

It was hard enough to discern and articulate his own motivations without reading a dead Frenchman's mind. He asked her for another cup of coffee, stalling for time to think. When she left, the mockingbird tuned up. She returned with two more steaming mugs and let the cabin door slam behind her. The bird fell silent with the sharp noise. She sat as demurely as possible wearing nothing but a shirt and peered at the Pilot from behind her coffee cup.

"He was shot down flying a P-38 fighter/photo reconnaissance plane near the end of World War II," he explained. "But his death was more suicide by Messerschmitt than a combat loss. The German after-action report stated he offered no resistance; he flew straight and level, letting bullets find the cockpit. The German fighter pilot who logged the kill was devastated when he discovered who he'd bagged; he'd read all of Saint-Ex's books. For him, it was a bitter kill, not a victory."

"I thought a kill was always a victory."

"Some guys say a kill is a kill, but there are different types of kills and different rewards to be had from each. Yes, shooting down an unarmed, old drunk is a kill but hardly qualifies as a victory. A victory would be a shoot down of another fighter pilot in a head-on fight."

"How could such an intelligent pilot let himself be killed like that?'

"At that point in his life, Saint-Ex was fat and old and sick and tired and hurting from too many crashes and too much alcohol, too many long-night dinners and too many dreams shot down by reality. He was tired of flying and tired of life, which is sometimes the same thing."

She paused, perhaps to ponder the mental image of a dissipated Saint-Ex, maybe to listen to the mockingbird caw a good imitation of a crow. "That sounded like bad Hemingway. Papa was familiar with airplane crashes, was he not?"

"You intelligence officers are certainly well read. The dividing line between bad Hemingway and good Hemingway isn't always clear and distinct. Ernie himself dabbled in bad Hemingway at times. In either case, I'll take that as a compliment. Yes, Papa lived through some prangs and suffered from them. For him dying well was as important as living well. He wanted people to believe he courted death as a lover."

"Do you worry about all that can happen with your plane? At Mach two and fifty thousand feet, I suspect a lot can go wrong. Aren't you worried about dying? Or do you, like Hemingway, court death as a lover?"

There it was, the key issue. She had blurted the question a little too loudly, then shut her mouth, her lips thin, looking away into the woods. Outside the mockingbird was quiet. She re-crossed her long legs, sat back on the swing, re-tucked the shirt tail under her taunt upper thighs with both hands, and waited for his answer.

Her body language told him she was sincere, that she cared for him. He wanted to respond truthfully, but a faithful answer carried the seeds of its own avoidance. Learning to fly had been an exercise in numbing himself to ever-increasing risks. From the first propeller-driven trainers, through low-performance jets, to the Starfighter, each successive airplane was more lethal with more ways to kill him and more opportunities to do so. To cope he mentally shoved the threats aside, ignored the consequences of an accident, and got on with the missions at hand calmly, dispassionately, professionally. If he had dwelt on the risks, the crouching beast of fear would have slipped its leash and gnawed on his ability to function accurately. Fear isn't allowed to ride along in a supersonic jet. An accurate answer to her question would surface what needed to stay deeply buried in his brain and reverse the mindset necessary to cope.

Damn it, he couldn't mislead her either. "No, I don't worry. I can't afford to. I'm not allowed to. You do what you can, as best you can. You make damn sure you don't screw up, and if something beyond your control happens, well, them's the breaks. You bury your emotions deep, so they won't betray you."

"Isn't denial of valid feelings a problem? You can't just submerge some particular emotions. What if you bury them all, the joys as well as the fears?"

"It's an occupational hazard. Flying a supersonic fighter is the most fun you can have with your clothes on, but you pay a mental price. That price is detachment and sometimes emotional separation from those you love."

She unfastened another button on her shirt with one hand and took a deep breath as he went on.

"I keep reminding myself to live fully, to enjoy life, to feel what's intense and good and real. When a man loves a woman as I love you, he's truly alive, regardless of what he experiences in an airplane."

"That's more bad Hemingway, but I'll accept the sentiment as being your truth. What about the MiGs? Do you want to see one?"

"I'll try to do more than see one. Every fighter pilot's ambition is to gun down a MiG, or even better, bag five and be anointed an ace."

"Why this crusade for personal glory? Aren't you killing people to boost your ego? What about the MiG pilots? They're human beings; don't they count for something?"

Here, he was on more familiar, comfortable ground. The fate of the losing man/machine combination in a dogfight was a subject he had considered at length. Killing someone in cold blood requires some moral justification or mental rationalization, and he had found his long ago. He looked at her, and his eyes lost all expression; his voice had a chilly, honed edge. He saw her shiver, her breasts jiggling under her loose shirt. "The MiG pilots feel the same way about us; all fighter pilots have the same mentality. We know the risks, and we welcome the challenges. Killing someone for glory is just wrong, but killing someone who is trying to kill you or one of your buddies is righteous. I'll not lose a minute's sleep after winning a dogfight. I do hope the other jock ejects and gets out. Someday we can buy each other drinks, refight the engagement, wave our hands, over-G our wristwatches. . . . If the guy doesn't survive, that's just too bad; I'll buy my own drinks then."

"Do you think MiG pilots feel the same way?"

"Of course, they do. There's probably a MiG driver and his girlfriend having this same discussion right now."

"Boris and Natasha in their dacha on the banks of the Volga discussing the coming competition. You make it sound like a blood sport."

He imagined two Russians in the same conversation, only drinking vodka not coffee. It would be dark, early evening there with the time difference. Being Russians, they would be slowly getting hammered.

"Now you're the one quoting bad Hemingway. Ernie believed there are only three sports: bullfighting, mountaineering, and auto racing; the rest are just games. He'd probably put aerial dogfights in there with auto racing. If it is a sport, each team plays for high stakes, life or death."

"You scare me when you talk like that; I feel as if I don't know you. Who is on this team, your wingmen? Are they as cold-blooded as you?"

"Wingmen sometimes, but my team is me and the aircraft. We live and fight together."

"Do you ever think of teaming up on the ground? As with a wife? Or is the Starfighter your lover?"

Her quick burst of cannon-fire questions finally found her mark, forcing him into a defensive move he had long practiced. He wanted to blow her off, avoid the subject of an emotional lifetime commitment, light the afterburner, and exit stage right; but he couldn't, not this time, not with her. He had to be honest. "Someday, when I'm done killing people with airplanes. Then there'll be room for someone else, without reservations."

"Thanks for sharing that chilling bit of yourself. Maybe I'll do more reading on your kind and get more perspective." She spoke softly and looked at him with her chin tucked in as the mockingbird ran through another avian imitation, this time of a robin. She smiled and looked outside the porch, searching for the hidden songbird. She found him at the top of a tall pine tree and sat back, relaxed, her breasts threatened to slip from the deep cleavage of her unbuttoned shirt.

"Is reading classical literature what you do in the intelligence shop, that inner sanctum where we mere pilots aren't allowed?" he asked.

"I have to do something to keep my self-respect. You might have noticed not everyone in the squadron accepts me. If the title Military Intelligence is an oxymoron, some think 'female military intelligence officer' is a double oxymoron. But all you pilots have been supportive."

"We may kid around and swagger a bit--"

"A bit? Make that a lot."

"Pilots tend to be pragmatists. If you can hack the mission, you're in." He didn't add that pilots were also not unmoved by a pretty face and an hourglass figure flaunting curves no loose-fitting uniform could disguise. "Seriously, do you have a stash of great literature in there?"

"That's classified information. You're denied access." She laughed and recrossed her legs. The shirt slipped from between her thighs and gapped open, revealing that she wore the shirt nude. "However, you are not denied access to me."

He looked at her, exposed from her narrow waist to her bare feet, his desire rising. "You're out of uniform, Lieutenant."

"More precisely, I'm out of your uniform."

She rose, turned toward him, and straddled his lap, facing him with one shapely leg on each side of his, her movement rocking the swing. The shirt's last two buttons came open, and she shrugged her shoulders, her arms at her sides. The blue cloth slipped off and floated softy to the bare wood floor. She tilted her head back, shook out her blond locks, and sighed as he entered her.

The porch swing rocked, squeaking on its rusty chains. The first rays of direct sunlight spilled onto the swirling eddy in a shallow pool against the far bank of the river. The shaft of bright light penetrated the deep shadows in the Little Pigeon River's gorge. A smallmouth bass rose to swallow a bug skating on the creek, and now high in a hickory-nut tree near the cabin, the mockingbird tried to sing "The Tennessee Waltz" in time to the porch swing's pulsed creaking.

CHAPTER 10

4TH ARRONDISSEMENT

Paris

April 2014: Dawn came slowly to the island of Saint-Louis's man-made ravines. The narrow central street running the length of the island, Rue Saint-Louis-en-Ile, boasted barely enough room for one lane of traffic. Interrupted by three boutique hotels, four- and five-story apartment houses lined the avenue, each crowding and shading the street. Running east and west, the street gathered early, direct sunlight only on the few days of the year when the rising sun aligned with its constricted course. On days like today, the street--more of a lane than a thoroughfare--remained in deep shadow until late morning and was lit only indirectly by the pale spring sun rising in the southeast.

The Pilot stood looking out his apartment's open window at the quiet scene below. His part of Paris, his quartier, was coming alive, its familiar rhythms long practiced. He had watched the scene on the street below many times but never after a night like the last one.

Wielding a long, plastic witches' broom, a street sweeper clad in blue coveralls opened water taps and washed last night's debris into the gutter. The trash must be swept away into the sewers before it found its way into the River Seine one apartment house width away. The early-morning ritual mounted another battle in the endless war between the city administration and aggressive litterers and unsupervised dogs--a war the sweepers usually won. Paris is one of the world's cleanest big cities, excepting Singapore and cities in Switzerland. The Pilot knew he would miss Paris, if indeed he ever left, not just for its cleanness but also for its energy.

Night desk clerks at the local hotels were leaving, turning over rings of keys to their daytime replacements and hurrying to catch the Metro home for some shuteye. Along the narrow street, they might stop at the patisserie, where the owner was carefully setting out the day's assortment of fresh pastries, croissants, and *pains au chocolat* and firing up the well-used espresso machine.

A delivery man riding a goofy French motor scooter with a pair of undersized front wheels slowly made his way up the one-way lane, his engine purring like a sleepy cat. Mounted on the scooter's back fender was a large perforated aluminum box stacked high with fresh-baked baguettes for delivery to the pâtisserie, local apartment house foyers, and hotels. Once, the pastries, croissants, and loaves of crusty French bread would have been baked on site, their toasty bouquet permeating the neighborhood around four in the morning. No longer. Now modern efficiency dictated they be manufactured in suburban industrial bakeries and delivered all across Paris at dawn, soaking up noxious traffic fumes on the way. From the fourth floor, he could easily detect the unmistakable aroma of fresh-baked bread wafting aloft behind the shiny box. This morning the bread smelled yeasty and raw, not with the toasted flavor of fully cooked baguettes.

The hot bread perfume drifting in the open window woke her as well. Her eyes still closed, she yawned and stretched, her arms reaching for the headboard. The Pilot looked back into the dimly-lit room to see her lying face down at the epicenter of swirled sheets. She was nude, her dark hair fanned across her pillow and her smooth back. Her buns were even cuter when not being squeezed together by sprayed-on jeans or hidden under a tight miniskirt. He couldn't help but remind himself how lovely he found her bare body, lithe and supple in the new day.

She raised her head slightly and looked over at him silhouetted darkly against the open window. "Bonjour. You are up early. Do you always rise with the sun?" she asked.

"Bonjour. Yes, I like to watch the city come alive, but today I'd rather watch you wake up instead."

She laughed and cocked her slim calves back over her thighs, crossing her ankles. Only then did they both notice she still wore her black stilettos. Each smiled, but neither knew what to say. He broke the awkward silence first. "Do you usually sleep in high heels?"

"I usually sleep in my own bed." She sat up, swung her feet to the floor, and bent over them. She unbuckled the ankle straps, stepped out of the shoes, and fell back on her side, her breasts jiggling like liquid orbs. Propping herself up on one elbow, she watched him staring off into the middle distance, out the window, and up at the slowly lightening sky.

On the back of a chair near him hung her black mini-dress, accent on the "mini". He had checked it out when he slipped quietly out of bed this morning, being careful not to wake her. The dress was the only garment on the chair. The French have a genius for lingerie, but she hadn't worn any. He found that odd. Why would a supremely sexy woman wear only a knit dress unless she were trying to advertise her sexual availability? But she hadn't hinted to him her state of dress, or rather undress, at any time during the evening. Later, back at his apartment, she had stepped out of her clothes unaided, quickly. He thought deeper, seeking a motivation. Maybe she was stating her availability to herself, going commando to work up her nerve and making a commitment she couldn't easily reverse. It would be hard for her to say no, particularly to herself, while wearing a tight mini-dress nude.

She watched him stare out for a few more minutes, the dim sunlight shadowing his face. "You are thinking about the F-35, n'est-ce pas?" The French phrase converted her direct statement into a question.

He replied without leaving the window, now brighter with the dawning sky's diffused light. He had given up on the mini-dress puzzle and returned to thinking about more important issues at hand. "Yes, you know me too well already."

"Why does it obsess you so?"

"There's no soul in that new machine." His voice fell in pitch, quiet and sad.

"I didn't know aircraft possessed souls. I'll have to ask my priest about that."

"Maybe what I'm objecting to is better described as "essence" instead of "soul." The F-35 has sold its soul to the computer. The essence of this aircraft is its software--not the engine, not the gun, not its wings, and certainly not its pilot. All the marvelous functions the F-35 is supposedly capable of performing are software driven. The software allows the jet to trade data and voice with other American fighters, with the radar command and control aircraft, the Pentagon, the President, and, for all I know, the internet." He raised his voice and turned toward her, his fists curled at his sides.

She sat up on the rumpled bed and faced him. Drawing her knees to her chin, she wrapped her arms around her legs, which she crossed at her ankles, thus hiding her womanhood behind her bare feet.

"So why is that a problem? Isn't total, constant interconnectivity the wave of the future?" Her question showed a depth of technical knowledge not expected of the average French woman. But she was way above average, and he still didn't know where she came from or who she was. She had asked the kind of leading question an intelligence agent would pose.

"If so, I can see the future, and it sucks."

"Sucks? Like extracting information from a database?"

"No, that's American slang for something bad. The F-35 software demotes the fighter pilot to a computer nerd, a slave to its digital technology. It's probably like flying a smartphone. You need a MiG shot down; there's a killer app for that. You designate the doomed MiG's icon on a flat screen display, then touch the "delete MiG" button. The radar, the software, and the long-range guided missiles do the rest . . ."

"You forgot the 'Are you sure you want to send this MiG to the recycle bin?' prompt."

"Whatever. You never see the MiG pilot, and he, or she, never sees you. All the action happens miles away. It's an antiseptic, remote way to fight, not worthy of a warrior."

"Do you consider yourself a warrior?" She veered away to a subject they both had studiously avoided during last night's dinner while laughing, eating, drinking, and flirting. When the F-35 and his pending assignment had come up inadvertently in conversation, they had quickly switched back to something trivial and more fun. In the cold, gray light of dawn, the elephant in this room, the bedroom of his flat, could no longer be ignored.

"Yes, I'm a warrior. Fighter pilots have been proud warriors for a century, fighting alone in their cockpits. But now there's someone else along for the ride. Some geeky programmers with thick glasses, hoodies, and ponytails want to insert themselves between me and the MiG pilots. The new aircraft isn't an air combat machine; it's only one airborne node in a distributed electronic network. War brought to you from the cloud by the magic of software."

"The action you describe must be less dangerous than close-in combat, a way to avoid a--what do you call it--a 'dog fight'?"

"The current term is 'fur ball' not 'dog fight.' Same analogy, different jargon. It will be safer than turning and afterburning if the MiG pilot doesn't have his own software-driven system. If he does, you could be flying along, checking your email or watching adorable cat videos on the internet when you get handed someone else's radar-guided missile. That wouldn't be safe."

"How could a MiG target you? I understood the F-35 to be stealthy, invisible to radar, no?"

"It is somewhat, but only clean, with no external stores. Ordinance or fuel tanks under the wings make it visible to radar. They also make the aircraft marginally useful."

She paused as if making a mental note of both vulnerabilities. He noticed her stopping to think, or mentally file away data, whenever he mentioned facts about the F-35, even facts that appeared in the media. She shook her head, her hair flying. "Marginal? What do you mean? I read the F-35 was very versatile. You make it sound compromised."

He was surprised again at her insight, particularly for so early in the morning, but he went on venting. He pointed his right index finger at her. "Compromised? Certainly. But the real issue is, can it do anything? The bureaucracy and Congress decreed the F-35 will replace almost every plane we fly. It's supposed to shoot down MiGs, support ground troops, bomb defended targets, land on aircraft carriers, take-off and land vertically--and spray crops, for all I know." He realized he was getting worked up, hadn't sipped his essential morning cup of coffee, and was rudely pointing at her. Dropping his hand, he returned to the open window, peered out to avoid looking at her, and wondered if he should apologize.

"I believed fighter pilots love a challenge. All those different missions certainly sound difficult to master."

He snapped his head back toward the dimly lit bedroom again, facing her verbal taunt. "We thrive on challenges, but we also love winning and hate losing. In our profession, losing often involves dying. It'll be difficult to win while flying an aircraft so fatally flawed."

"Fatally flawed? You just told me this new jet is the most advanced ever." She asked the question as if ready to note any additional F-35 deficiencies.

"Advanced in cost, no doubt. Advanced in complexity, yes. Advanced in what it can do? No. The F-35 does nothing well; it has no core mission, no soul. A corrupted essence, if you please. When we fly it into harm's way, we'll meet Bad Guys whose planes are the masters of one mission: killing us," he replied through clenched teeth.

The look on his face and even the dawn's pale light seemed to frighten her. She wrapped her arms tighter around her bare legs and pulled her ankles closer against her womanhood. His eyes no longer stared into the middle distance but focused on some target far away. She changed the subject back to something more personal but still related. "If it is so ill-suited, ill-designed, why do you want to fly it?"

"I don't know that I do. But how can I pass up the chance to pilot the 'Most Advanced Fighter Plane Ever Built,' according to the press releases? Particularly since it will be the last one built before drones take over the fighter pilot's mission. Drones are really soulless. Do I want to be part of the transition process? Why would I want to try to fly, fight, and win in a jet that can't get out of its own way when its software inevitably crashes?"

"I hear you criticize the aircraft for its connectivity. I suspect you prefer to fight alone, regardless of the aircraft you're flying. Are you--how do you say it in English--a lone wolf?"

"I fly single-seat fighters. If that makes me antisocial, so be it. Alors, why are you so curious for so early?"

She had no ready answer and channeled the conversation in an entirely new direction. "You keep staring out the window. What are you looking for? Surveillance by these Bad Guys you continually speak of, whoever they are?"

"No," he answered, grateful to leave a painful subject. He turned down the opportunity to say the "other side" might well be the French. They sold their jets to prospective buyers worldwide. Who knew where those Rafale fighters would end up? "Just checking to make sure no jealous husband waits outside."

She smiled in the knowing way of French women and released her slim legs, stretching them out across the bed with her ankles crossed and toes pointed.

"Pas de problème. (No problem.) I've never been married. But would it make any difference to you if I were burdened with a husband?"

"No, it's too late. I've gotten into you."

She laughed, "Yes, sex generally does involve penetration of some sort, somewhere."

"What I tried to say is I've begun to care for you, a lot. The existence of a husband wouldn't change anything for me now; it's too late for that."

Curiously, she didn't conversely ask him if he was, or had ever been, married. It was as if she already knew the answer, had done some homework and googled him perhaps, or maybe she had other, more covert sources of personal information.

Even if she was going to ask, he preempted her query. "I've never married either. I've come close a few times, but somehow, something always got in the way. A new assignment, a new aircraft, a new war, or a new way to avoid commitment."

That last phrase slipped out, unintended and penetratingly true. He wished he could reach out and retrieve it before it reached her ears, but it was too late. He saw the slightest hint of a wince on her face.

"Perhaps you prefer to live alone, as well as fly alone. How does being, as you say, a single-seat fighter pilot prevent you from sharing your life and yourself?"

"Maybe I never found the right woman, one worth giving all it up for, one worth changing my approach to life."

She looked at him for a moment. Slowly she swung her long legs off the bed, her knees together, and slid her bare feet onto the worn parquet floor.

Without looking back at him, one by one she stepped into her black shoes waiting perched on their stiletto heels. She buckled the thin ankle straps tight around her trim ankles and gently lay back onto his bed with one leg bent up at the knee and the other splayed out invitingly. Her dark hair was tousled across half her face, and her arms reached out to him.

Only a trapezoidal patch of blue was visible above the open apartment window; the slice was bordered on three sides by the adjacent buildings' Mansard roofs, which were steeply pitched and truncated. On their flat tops, pipe chimney pots clawed at the constrained sky like stubby clay fingers. The sky above was slowly brightening from dawn's steely light to the soft hues of a new day, not an intense indigo but a pale shade robbed of its vitality by Rue Saint-Louis en Ile's intruding buildings. The Pilot looked up one long, last time before he joined her, the old aerial memories returning once again, not summoned, not welcome, not avoidable. Perhaps for the few precious hours he would be with her this morning--loving her, losing himself in her--that faraway, long ago sky would stay safely at bay in his mind. But, buried deep in his consciousness, the shared image of the other sky shone diamond-bright and dark-burning blue, limitless, stretching to the horizon and empty, yet filled with menace--the danger all the more terrifying for being unseen.

CHAPTER 11

MiG Alley

North Korea

February 1952: The spectacular view from the F-86 SabreJet's cockpit featured un-limited visibility as far as the eye could see. All around him, the late winter sky burned an aching blue; at thirty thousand feet, the dust normally filtering the atmosphere's azure intensity was well below him. There was nothing overhead yet except the clear, indigo sky. The threat would come from above; it always did.

Two things defined the F-86 the Pilot flew: its outward visibility and its wing. He sat high in the cockpit; the bubble canopy surrounded him to below his shoulders. He enjoyed an unhindered 360-degree view. He could turn and look over his shoulder to see the Sabre's vertical tail standing proud behind him, the shark's fin the only thing at his six o'clock at the moment. Ironically, the view forward was his worst. The "bullet-proof" windshield glass was thick, slightly opaque, and bounded by a riveted metal border. The gun sight was projected on an inclined glass plate, further clouding visibility at twelve o'clock, straight ahead.

The sun, high in the west, threw an intense, circular starburst of glare and a kaleidoscope of color as its rays reflected and refracted off microscopic scratches in the surrounding canopy's apparently smooth surface. Looking into the sun produced a rainbow of optic pain even when viewed through his dark-tinted visor. The Pilot had to hold his gloved fist over the sun's disk to check for enemy fighters possibly lurking in the sun's corona. The cockpit was roomy for a fighter plane--plenty of room to move around, to turn and look left, right, up and down.

The Sabre's signature wing, a masterpiece of design, was swept back to slice through the air at transonic speed and allowed a maximum speed of 0.93 Mach, well over 9/10 the speed of sound. Thin for low drag at high altitude but with a generous span, its light loading produced tight turns at any altitude and airspeed. The wing also sported slats on its leading edge for even greater turn capability. Invented by the Germans, the slats were used to good effect on the legendary Messerschmitt Bf 109 of World War II fame. When the Sabre turned tightly, pulling Gs, the slats deployed automatically, which increased the wing's area, smoothed the turbulent airflow over the upper surface, and delayed the stall which could snap the jet over into a spin. At thirty thousand feet, no other jet could turn with a Sabre when its pilot commanded the wing to bite into the cold air. Above thirty-five thousand feet, the Sabre was betrayed by its crude engine. The limited power available caused a turning F-86 to bleed off airspeed rapidly as aerodynamic drag won the drag-versus-thrust battle. In aerial combat, speed is life--lose too much speed, lose your life.

Dogfights in the current combat arena, the Korean War, followed the precedent set in previous aerial conflicts. Victory depended on playing to the strong points of one's aircraft and avoiding scenarios where the other side enjoyed an advantage. That, along with flying skill and no small dose of luck, determined who lived and who died.

In the engagement he hoped would come soon, the Pilot's objectives were to lure the MiGs below thirty thousand feet and then turn inside them. He must avoid an extreme high altitude fight where the MiGs' higher ceiling and superior rate of climb could prove decisive for them.

Off his right wing and far beneath him flowed the shallow, muddy Yalu River, the border between North Korea and Communist China. Southward lay the parched, desolate landscape of North Korea, scarred by the ebb and flow of ground warfare. Northward stretched China, where flight by the Sabres was prohibited by a political fiat issued by Washington politicians. The Chinese could and did send hundreds of thousands of ground troops into Korea to kill American soldiers. But a handful of Sabres wasn't allowed to hunt down MiGs in China; we mustn't annoy the Chicoms. A few miles into China, the Pilot could easily see two MiG airfields at Langtao and Dadonggou, their new white concrete runways glowing pristinely up through the ground haze. The MiGs exploited the advantage of radar's all-seeing eye, as well as their political sanctuary. They could climb to high altitude, higher than the Sabres could fly, while safely inside China. All the while, their ground-based radar would track the Pilot's Sabre flight and vector the MiG pilots to attack from a position of decisive tactical advantage. The American radars were far south, useless where the Sabre pilots flew alone, unseen by friendly eyes. Not for nothing did the airspace just south of the Yalu acquire the nickname "MiG Alley," an area where sudden death comes unseen from behind, without warning.

The Pilot was on his own but not alone. On his right about five hundred feet away, trailing slightly, flew his wingman, Sabre Two. Trolling for MiGs, they followed the Yalu as it flowed southwest. On his left, looking northward into the threat as they flew formation on Sabre Lead, hovered Sabre Three and his wingman, Sabre Four. The second pair floated about twenty degrees back and a quarter of a mile out, slightly higher than their flight leader, the Pilot. All eight eyes squinted into the trackless blue--looking, searching, seeking the tell-tale dots in the distance heralding the coming of the MiGs.

The Pilot constantly scanned, looking for something that wasn't there, and simultaneously tried to ward off boredom. Too many of these MiG sweeps were nothing but sight-seeing trips--no MiGs, no action, just an airplane ride for an hour and a half. He found it strange that he waited on and looked for opponents who would do their best to kill him and his buddies, yet he had a hard time keeping mentally focused. What was her name, the cute secretary on the General's staff in Tokyo?

"Get a grip, you moron!" he yelled at himself, his voice trapped inside his tight-fitting oxygen mask, and resumed scanning the still-empty sky.

The Pilot's engine hummed at ninety-eight percent of its maximum rpm. This allowed his wingmen a two percent margin to fly formation and make adjustments in their flight paths without falling behind. They could fly higher than thirty thousand feet but not without giving away their exact location. One of the primary by-products of jet engines is water vapor. Any higher and the water vapor, a product of combustion spewed by the jets' exhausts, would instantly turn to ice crystals, leaving highly visible condensation trails or "contrails" pointing like marks on a blue chalkboard directly at the four Sabres. The Bad Guys' radar could determine their location and flight path only imprecisely, within a mile or two. If the Sabres climbed even one thousand feet they would pull contrails, called "marking," which would allow even the dumbest MiG pilot to set up a killer intercept from above the contrail layer. The MiG-15s could easily fly above the altitude band where contrails would form. The F-86s shouldn't and didn't.

There it was! He saw it! North, high in the sky at three o'clock above his right wing, he picked up a sharp glint, a reflection of the sun off an aircraft canopy. Nothing else was that brightly visible, and nothing else would be up there but a MiG-15. The glint sparkled at least five thousand feet above him and his flight. It lasted only a second or two then disappeared; the arena was as empty as before. Today's bright sky--what baseball players call a "high sky"--had no clouds the Pilot's eyes could focus on. With nothing to be seen against the burning blue, his eyes tended to focus at a range of a few dozen feet, not much help in spotting distant MiGs.

A jet's canopy is on its topside. For a glint to be visible from five thousand feet below, the glinting aircraft must turn, tilting its canopy downward. The Pilot knew MiGs lurked up there all right, but where? They were turning, but in what direction?

"Sabre Flight, tanks." As he made the radio call, he raised the red guard on the external fuel tanks jettison switch and punched off the tanks with a flip of the toggle. Beneath and behind each Sabre, two silver, empty fuel tanks spun and tumbled end over end. They fell away toward the ground far below, reflecting the sunlight as they went.

Jettisoning the tanks represented a calculated risk. It would indicate to the MiGs that they were sighted, the Sabres were prepared for battle, and the element of surprise was lost. Now the MiG leader might press his attack sooner than he wanted, before he set up the intercept from behind the Sabres. Getting rid of the tanks precluded someone from retaining their extra drag by mistake in the heat of the combat sure to come. It felt good to have the undersurface of the wing clean again; the jet responded more eagerly to his touch.

The Pilot sensed adrenaline coursing through his veins; his heartrate increased, and his breath came faster now. *Whoa, easy big fellow*, he thought. *You have to keep your cool, stay calm.* He knew the outcome of the fight depended on him making the right decisions for the four of them.

Sabre Three saw them first. "Sabre Flight, bandits at five o'clock high, coming in." Three's voice was calm, even detached, as if he was announcing an air show, which in a way, he was.

The Pilot spotted the MiGs diving through a contrail layer; each of their downward slashing contrails looked like a housecat clawing a dark blue curtain hanging behind his flight. He counted four, five, a total of six curved, white trails. Make that one of Hemingway's polydactyl mutant cats with their six claws on each front paw.

The MiG attack instantly thrust the Pilot into what athletes know as the "zone," where time slows to a crawl. In the zone, decisions taking seconds to make earlier in training were now instantly enacted. Mental processes accelerated; reflexes sharpened to a straight razor's edge.

When the Pilot played shortstop on his college team, being in the zone meant a pitcher's fastball looked like a beachball floating up to the plate, and ground balls hit to him seemed to be bouncing under water. Adrenaline and aggressiveness generated the zone. Fear had no place there. In it he made life-or-death decisions with reptilian detachment. Only later, if he survived the fight, would he realize he had lived once again in the zone.

The Pilot took a deep breath--he would need the extra oxygen soon--and rolled into a gentle turn to the right, into the attack. A phrase often used by the Royal Air Force (RAF) exchange pilot in his squadron popped into his head, "Softly, softly, catchee monkey." He had to turn Sabre flight toward the MiGs just enough. Too tight a bank and the Sabres would lose speed and energy due to the increased Gs and make the MiG leader's problems easier. Too sharp a turn would also totally screw up the MiGs' attack geometry; they might go home and try again tomorrow. The propeller-driven fighters of World War II could shoot high-deflection shots, sometimes with targets crossing ahead thirty or forty-five degrees off their flight path. Jet speeds cancelled that idea; now the shooter had to be directly behind his intended kill. He needed to sell the attack to the MiG drivers, making them commit, to press home their attack without realizing they couldn't close the deal. But too gentle a turn would allow six MiGs to drive in behind him and his buddies, also not a good decision.

Watching the MiGs approach ever closer, he operated on feel alone. Reaching into the cockpit, he made sure the gun sight and its ranging radar were on, the six fifty-caliber Colt machine guns were armed, and the control stick trigger was hot. Instead of loosening a Colt .45 in his holster on Tombstone's dusty main street, he heated up six Colts in the SabreJet's nose high in the clean air of MiG alley.

The MiG flight bored in fast from five o'clock, inside half a mile and at almost the same altitude as the four F-86s. Time to set the hook.

He pushed the radio transmit button and in as calm and cool a voice as he could muster said, "Sabre Flight, come hard right." He pushed the throttle against the stop, demanding one hundred percent thrust.

The four F-86s pivoted, banked up on their swept-back wings, and wheeled into the attack. The Pilot could see he had hooked the Bad Guys true and fair. There was no way the MiGs, diving faster than the Sabres, could round the square corner he presented them. Test pilot legend Chuck Yeager flew a captured MiG-15 and reported that at high speed, the Russian jet's ailerons were very stiff, almost frozen, and rolling the aircraft was difficult. The MiG pilots couldn't rein in their mounts fast enough nor pull enough Gs to stay behind the Sabres. While the Pilot watched over his shoulder, the MiGs slid to the outside of the F-86's turn. Their faster speed pushed them in front of the Pilot and his wingman--a massive overshoot, a rookie mistake, and usually fatal.

Now he could reverse his turn back to the left and roll in behind the MiGs. The F-86's controls remained sweet at combat speeds. *It's our time in the saddle,* he thought as he cranked his Sabre around to the left. He anticipated the MiG flight would attempt to use their higher airspeed and greater energy to zoom back to a higher altitude, safely out of the F-86's reach. He would have one chance to cut across their vertical flight path and get in a snap shot.

What the hell! The MiGs pressed on at the same altitude in a gentle right turn and made no attempt to either escape upward or turn back into the fight. Wait a minute; he counted four MiGs a half mile ahead nearly in front of him. Where were the other two?

The bubble canopy made it easy to look back behind his jet. Nothing there but his wingmen, spread in a shallow V, flying in pairs. Something up in the deeper blue caught his eye. There they were! Two silver specks, each trailing a wispy contrail. They had broken off the attack, held high, and let the other four MiGs overshoot. Re-entering the contrail layer for a few seconds, they had made a serious, possibly terminal, mistake by revealing their location and, more importantly, their identity.

His mind raced, even in the slowed-down world of the zone. Those would be the Russians. Only they would be cagey enough to pull off the maneuver trapping his flight of four Sabres. They were undoubtedly veterans of what they called The Great Patriotic War against Hitler's Germany. They flew in MiG alley to teach the Chinese how to fly and fight; their students would be the four MiGs in front of the F-86s. The Russians, the "Honchos," were good pilots and in command of the MiG formations. Their Chinese students were poorly trained, inexperienced, and inept. The Honchos' jets would have red noses and red stripes painted on their rear fuselages, signifying their status as flight leaders.

Now, too late, he saw what happened. The Russians let their Chinese students overshoot the Sabres, counting on well-known American aggressiveness to goad the Sabre pilots into fixating on the four sitting Peking ducks and losing sight of the two Russians. Once the Sabres attacked the hapless students, the Russians would dive from their rearward "perch" and bounce the F-86s. The shopworn "sandwich" tactic was a cynical play. The Russians were willing to let their erstwhile allies take the brunt of American fire, perhaps dying in the process, to set up the Honchos for an easy kill or two.

The Pilot yelled as he looked back over his shoulder at the Russians, "You're not butchering eighteen-year-old Germans now. Fill your hands, you sons-of-bitches!"

In the time this analysis took, Sabre Three also saw the Russian MiGs and called them out over the air, "Sabre Lead, we've got two high at our six, on the perch."

The Pilot recognized the Texas accent of Sabre Three and replied, "Roger that. Sabre Three, take Sabre Four and engage the high element. We'll take the low four." He fought to keep his voice calm, serene even. Perceived panic now would destroy Sabre Flight's unity; they had to fight as a team or lose and lose big.

Sabre Three came back, "Roger." The Pilot didn't know so much content could be expressed in a one-word, drawled reply. Sabre Three stretched the word "Roger" into three syllables. His answer dripped with sarcasm, in effect saying, "OK Boss, We'll take on the experts who happen to be at our six o'clock while you two shoot down the junior birdmen in front of you."

The Pilot couldn't let that go unanswered. "Busy hands are happy hands, Three."

He snapped his head around to reacquire the four MiG-15s in front of him and his wingman. The trailing two had remained a little over a half mile in front, slowly banking right, edging toward the river, and seeking sanctuary in China. He lowered his nose, dove to get more airspeed, and placed his jet below and behind his quarry. The MiGs' poor visibility rearward would keep him hidden from sight, and the two Honchos weren't about to call a break on their own radio channel for the student pilots. The four at twelve o'clock remained the Chinese food in the sandwich. At one hundred percent thrust in a shallow dive, the Pilot caught them quickly.

A circle of white dots surrounding a pipper dot, the gun sight was projected on the slanted glass in front of the Pilot. Below it on the glare shield, an angry red light glowed, indicating the ranging radar had seen the trailing MiG and was feeding distance to the target into the sight's computer. The computer performed its deadly calculations; showing where the bullets would strike, the pipper floated and moved in his view.

At twelve hundred feet behind the trailing MiG, the gun sight turned from white to red. He was in range. The Pilot raised the Sabre's nose above the distant horizon, superimposed the now-red pipper over the fast-growing outline of the MiG, and waited a second for the sight to settle and complete its calculus. He squeezed the trigger on the front of the control stick to the first stop for half a second, starting the gun camera, then nailed it full back with his aptly named trigger finger.

Six Colts chattered, spewing fifty-caliber high-explosive bullets and shaking the Sabre's airframe with their staccato vibration. Instantly, the cockpit filled with burning cordite's acrid odor, and the exhaust smoke ejected by the guns found its way into the Pilot's oxygen mask. The rank aroma had the smell of death--someone else's death. He saw bright tracers fly by on all sides of the MiG and sharp pinpoint explosions as some of the lead storm hit home. Flashes erupted all over the MiG--on the aft fuselage, the wing roots, and the rudder. A sheet of flame flared briefly, trailed black smoke, and died as he released the trigger, saving ammo for the next kill. The canopy peeled off the MiG and flashed by over the Pilot's Sabre. The bright flash of the ejection seat's explosive charge shot the MiG pilot up and out of the doomed jet's cockpit, and he too was left falling, tumbling, still strapped in his seat, behind the Sabre.

Now for number two. He tightened his right turn to cut off the dead MiG's wingman.

Without warning, a dozen white-hot, golf ball-sized fireballs streaked over his canopy. At the same time, more streaks, red tracers, came screaming by underneath the F-86. Swiveling around in the cockpit, which is difficult to do under the G loading, he looked back and saw a MiG-15 behind him. Its nose appeared to be on fire with muzzle flashes almost obscuring the red paint. These MiGs mounted two different cannon types: 37 mm and 23 mm guns whose shells flew slightly different trajectories. Luckily for the Pilot, he had been bracketed. The 37 mm bullets passed over his canopy; the 23 mm shells streamed under the jet.

With the strength of desperation, he banked hard left and pulled the control stick back into his stomach. The Sabre's wing bit into the thin air, turning the F-86 on an airborne dime. Six Gs of force slammed him into the seat cushion. His anti-G suit inflated, squeezing his legs and gut like a tube of toothpaste. This forced his blood toward his head and prevented him from blacking out. Shit! Where was Three? The Russians' sandwich tactic was working.

He heard Sabre Three's voice in his earphones. "Lead, ease off your turn. I've got this one."

The Pilot relaxed his turn to three Gs and craned his neck to look aft along the Sabre's previous flight path. He saw the red-striped MiG still behind him but climbing, nose up. Nobody's fool, the MiG pilot had zoomed to prevent an overshoot and keep from ending up in front of the Pilot. The mistake of his students was not for him.

"Sabre Lead, stay in your left turn," he heard Three drawl.

Behind the MiG, whose nose was now slicing down for another firing pass, he caught sight of an F-86. That would be Sabre Three. The sandwich-*er* was now the sandwich-*ee*, and the Pilot was dead meat in the middle. The simple Russian sandwich had become a club sandwich with multiple layers.

"Tighten your turn, Sabre Lead," Sabre Three called.

The Pilot pulled back harder on the stick, and four Gs bit again. The MiG driver was almost ready to shoot; he wouldn't make the mistake of firing out of range this time. The Pilot was presented with a view of the MiG's belly as the Russian pulled lead, aiming ahead of the turning F-86. The Pilot steeled himself for the sight of the MiG's nose once again spurting flames and for the impact of cannon shells on his F-86. *Come on Three, I don't have all day, this asshole has me cold.* He hoped when the end came, when the shells slammed into his jet, into him, that death would be mercifully quick.

An explosion rocked the MiG's left wing root, an angry flash of flame flared, and shiny bits flew off the MiG. The wing tore from the airframe and went fluttering behind the fight, fire sputtering from its jagged stump. What was left of the MiG snapped over into a tight spin and pinwheeled toward the Yalu River waiting below. The canopy remained attached. Either the Russian was already dead or he was pinned inside the cockpit by the violent spin, unable to eject.

Safe for a few more seconds, the Pilot rolled out of his turn and relaxed the G loading to gain airspeed. Breathing hard, he tried to catch his breath through the restrictive oxygen mask. He scanned left, right, and behind, looking for the second Russian Honcho. Nothing there. Rolling over, he spotted the other red-trimmed MiG-15 three thousand feet below him, nose down. The aft fuselage was enveloped in a sheet of flames, and the cockpit empty.

"Nice work, Sabre Three and Four," he transmitted. "Sabre Two, your position?"

"I've got this one over the river," Sabre Two responded, his labored breathing obvious on the radio.

The Pilot spotted another MiG below, just in front of his wing line at about twenty thousand feet. Trailing black smoke, it was running north for home on the Yalu's far side, an F-86 in hot pursuit. A quick glance down at the fuel gauge told him what he expected to see: just enough left in the tanks to get home.

"Let's go home, Sabre Flight. Lead's in a left turn to the south. Rejoin." He managed to get out the radio call with his voice in a normal register without rushing.

The Pilot felt sorry to call off Sabre Two from a sure kill, but the wreckage would fall in China, and the brass wouldn't be happy with the border violation. It was past time to get the hell out of MiG alley before the Bad Guys scrambled another flight to finish the day and Sabre Flight.

Farther south and at height, Sabre Flight flew back in formation, warily watching for MiGs. No gas left to fight now. To save precious fuel, they cruised at maximum altitude above forty thousand feet, throttled back at minimum airspeed, and floated on their thin, silver wings. The Pilot was soaked with sweat, even though the temperature outside the cockpit was far below zero. The mental zone and its slow-motion tempo faded the farther they flew from MiG alley. Exhausted, he aimed the four-ship formation toward their base at Kimpo.

The long flight home gave him time to think. Not a bad day's work; the gun camera film would score three confirmed kills and one probable. More importantly, they bagged two Russian Honchos. The Kremlin bosses wouldn't be happy about that. He smiled as he tried to picture the surviving Chinese pilots trying to explain how they returned and their instructors didn't.

That action had been close; he almost bought the farm with a MiG at his six and shooting.

How many more engagements like the one he just lived through could he expect to win, to survive? A squadron mate's favorite saying was "No guts, no glory." The Pilot's guts were not in doubt; glory would come soon, but what about simple survival? When does that happen?

Killed in a war not of their choosing, two Russians didn't survive. It was a funny thing, the Pilot thought, Americans and Russians going at it to the death, fighting for Koreans and Chinese. He had no friends among the South Koreans and doubted whether the Russian pilots were tight with their oriental students not long from the rice paddies. Who really cared who controlled the Korean peninsula? No, this was a practice war, fought by two teams preparing for the big one, World War III, when the cold war turns hot. Or being contested for sport by mercenaries. Check that, mercenaries would be better paid than his meager USAF salary. These mercenaries were paid in glory. But, if he wanted to get those five MiGs and become an ace, this was the only game in town.

Out on the horizon of the aerial playing field, he saw the Kimpo airfield coming into hazy view. Slowly, he retracted the throttle and let the nose edge downward, gliding, trading altitude for airspeed. The Pilot dipped his right wing, signaling the flight to move to an echelon off his right side, ready for the break for landing. He wanted the formation to look good over the field, with everyone watching.

After landing, Sabre Flight taxied to their parking slots over the pierced steel matting hurriedly laid down to build the airfield. The jets' noses displayed the tell-tale blackened gun ports signaling to the waiting ground crews the guns had been fired. The guys would want to hear all about it, how many red stars to paint under the canopies. Like the pilots, they lived for this moment.

The engine whistled as its rotation wound down. The Pilot removed his helmet and handed it to a grinning crew chief. He told himself it all boiled down to good flying, teamwork, luck, and decisions made without fear. Sabre Flight had displayed grace under pressure. With some self-satisfaction, he realized he had taken tough decisions quickly and well, attributes not often experienced together. Being decisive is easy; anybody can make decisions. The trick is to make the right ones.

CHAPTER 12

LA CLOSERIE DES LILAS

Montparnasse
Paris

April 2014: "Hemingway was decisive," the Pilot muttered to no one in particular. Anyone who married four wives in close succession had no problems making decisions. Whether those decisions were sound was another question, as was the issue of sticking with a choice, once made. Or not recognizing a good woman even when you hooked up with one. *Maybe Ernie wasn't a decision maker to emulate after all*, he thought.

Early that evening, a professional-class clientele packed La Closerie des Lilas, celebrating the end of another grueling thirty-five hour work week in France. The noisy crowd relaxed en masse, along with the inevitable scattering of casually dressed, slightly bemused tourists. The combination brasserie, restaurant, and bar straddled the border between the 14th and 6th Arrondissements, barely in the Montparnasse neighborhood near the Luxembourg gardens. The long-standing auberge, originally a traveler's inn, had dispensed cheer to one and sundry for well over a century and a half. Tonight the elegant good times rolled, and genteel laughter mixed with the clatter of dishes and barked orders as harried waiters darted through the throng. Instead of an artificial buzz generated by cranked-up, piped-in music, the in-house pianist struggled to be heard over the din, pounding out "La Vie en Rose," the signature song of Edith Piaf, "The Little French Sparrow."

Seated at the busy bar, the Pilot held a tulip-shaped glass of Muscadet--the good stuff, Muscadet Sèvre et Maine, not the watery plonk sometimes served to American tourists who might think they ordered Muscatel or, even worse, Muscatine wine. Watching the bartender closely, he ordered it by name and made sure the clear glass bottle displayed the correct label.

I'll bet Hemingway didn't have to worry about getting bogus wine here, he thought. The Pilot enjoyed frequenting Hemingway's old haunts in the Paris of the 1920s, and this famous brasserie was tonight's choice. Legend has it that *The Sun Also Rises* was penned here as Papa nursed a single café crème and a snifter of brandy for hours, sharing the joint in the years after the Great War with the era's other English-speaking literary folk.

Another favorite haunt of the "Lost Generation," Les Deux Magots on Boulevard St-Germain was much closer to the Pilot's apartment but didn't have a proper bar, only table seating. The Pilot's solemn mood tonight called for drinking at a bar. The earnest conversation he planned for the evening would not be as effective with a table separating him from his lover as they talked. Harry's New York Bar, over on the Right Bank, fostered a suitably serious atmosphere, but was too, well, New York. In the Pilot's considered opinion, the best Hemingway bar had occupied the Ritz Hotel on Place Vendome, but that quiet watering hole was closed for remodeling, probably into a disco. Ernie no doubt had spun up to forty-five rpm in his grave over that revolting development. Hemingway claimed he personally liberated the Ritz bar from the Nazis in 1944 to make the world safe for civilized drinking in good company. Papa hadn't intended to provide a gaudy room where idle, rich Arabs could indulge their tastes for alcohol and infidel women out of sight of their Muslim minders. The Pilot was sure of that.

He looked down at the varnished molding rimming the scarred, wood-topped bar. A worn, oblong brass plaque stood out near his half-empty wine glass. Almost scrubbed away by reverential caresses, the inscription's thin, cursive script, read, "Réservée à E. Hemingway" (Reserved for E. Hemingway). The Pilot sat at Hemingway's preferred spot at the bar, and not by accident, for he would need the moral support afforded by historic proximity.

The inconspicuous plaque presented the sole visible memento in the place, the only artifact commemorating Hemingway's frequent presence there during the Jazz Age. As he sipped his wine, the Pilot speculated on the absence of other Hemingway memorabilia. Perhaps for the French, Hemingway was just another idle American ex-pat, a minor member of the Lost Generation living in Paris then--albeit a sometimes news journalist harboring greater literary aspirations. His fame came only after he left Paris. Still, they could have at the least hung a small picture of Ernie on the wall or perhaps mounted a stuffed marlin above the bar. Americans such as himself, participating in a Hemingway Parisian pilgrimage, would appreciate the homage and tend to spend more, at least on alcohol, in remembrance. But La Closerie des Lilas radiated an aura of cool aloofness--all wood paneling, green upholstery, white tile, and formally dressed waiters. The management didn't pay overt homage to any past literary icons, particularly macho Americans.

She arrived right at the agreed hour. Stepping into the room one hip at a time and weaving through the crowd, she strutted up behind him. She drew rapt attention as she moved, putting each step down forcefully in her stilletos. Men noticed the way she wore her tight, dark green business suit accented with a white Hermès silk scarf; her suit jacket's long sleeves set off her much-abbreviated skirt, and her bare legs were showcased by her usual matching high heels. The green outfit contrasted with her dark hair, hair that bounced with each step along with her breasts under her thin silk blouse.

"Ce siége est-il disponible?" (Is this place available?), she asked rather formally, loud enough to be heard by those nearby.

"Il t'est réseveré" (It's reserved for you), he answered. "I'm only occupying Hemingway's spot until he comes in."

They exchanged two air kisses cheek-to-cheek, a mandatory greeting in France between friends and lovers, but held the embrace longer than would be the case between mere friends. The displayed affection notified other singles in the bar they were each temporarily unavailable, at least for the evening. She slid cautiously onto the leather-topped bar stool next to his and Hemingway's and quickly crossed her shapely legs. She reached down with one hand, tugging at her too-short skirt, trying without noticeable effect to cover more of her nude thighs.

"Notify me immediately if Monsieur Hemingway appears. That would be extraordinary. He has been dead fifty years, no?" She said.

She then ordered a Kir Royale from the suddenly attentive bartender. An attractive woman in a tight miniskirt, perched dangerously on a bar stool, never has to wait for service, even in jaded, seen-it-all Paris.

"I'm surprised you're familiar with Hemingway. Not many French people are." He wondered if her accurate comment signified an interest in Papa's body of work or was perhaps her acknowledgement of the Pilot's fascination with the famous author's time in Paris, an obsession he had once mentioned to her. She cleared that question up immediately.

"I have read some of his books. Why are you so taken with Hemingway, a writer proposing such sad protagonists? Do you see yourself in his writing?"

"I hope not. I'm not that morose. I am fascinated with Hemingway's exploration of the concept of grace under pressure. His heroes, always male, wrestled with how to behave when you're doomed and you know it. How to face death like a man. That's sometimes a fighter pilot's lot as well."

"He didn't always write about death."

"No, but physical death or the death of self-esteem were common themes in Hemingway's books. He often wrote of the kind of death accompanying dishonor, the damage done by failing to be true to yourself."

"So fighter pilots are preoccupied with honor. Does that not lead to overweening pride? Hubris?"

"Perhaps, but what's the alternative? It would be hard to be a humble fighter pilot."

She paused, having no answer. He tried to lighten the interchange by returning to the aura of the venue around them, literary café society. Soon he would have to broach the critical subject, avoided until tonight but no longer. He couldn't be direct; he needed to ambush her, a hateful task but the only way he could trust her reply. Until he went on the attack, they could continue to discuss the classics, the unpleasantness delayed for a bit.

"Given Hemingway's examination of difficult aspects of the human condition, why isn't he read more in France? The French literary class enjoys deep thinkers."

She pondered that for a minute, sipping her wine and staring into the mirror behind the bar. "We French prefer literature with exquisite use of our language. We revere detailed descriptions, elaborate imagery, and sophisticated vocabulary. We find Hemingway's writing too simple, too spare, perhaps too efficient. He simply reported, n'est-ce pas? Why do you like him? You still haven't answered that question."

"Ernie used simple language in the style of a journalist; none of his words will send you running to a dictionary. He enticed readers to generate imagery in their minds. That might be difficult if English isn't your native tongue. Maybe my current interest in Hemingway stems from the career decision I have to make. I ask myself, 'What would one of Papa's characters do in my place and why?' "

She had no retort for that either, so she looked away toward the nearest window, over his shoulder. She pivoted toward him on her bar stool, pointing her knees at him, re-crossing her legs as she did so and showing more thigh. He had noticed that when their conversations turned to the F-35, she re-crossed her legs often, not always remembering to adjust her miniskirt. She leaned toward him to speak, pulling her skirt farther up her bottom. He found himself speculating if she had enough skirt left under her to sit on.

She tapped her long fingertips on the polished bar. Her right hand fidgeted with her flute of Kir, grasping and letting it go. He saw her lips purse and tighten like the face of someone sent on a mission, one she was duty-bound to execute. Her left hand resting in the lap of her drum-tight skirt, she wrapped her fingers around her thumb--a clinical indication of insecurity.

He spotted the movement, took her clenched hand in both of his, and unfolded her fingers slowly, one by one. He looked in her dark eyes as he spoke. "Don't be so tense. It was Hemingway that obsessed over personal tragedy not me, and I hope not you."

Her shoulders slumped a fraction of an inch, but she went on speaking, still on that personal mission. "Your new aircraft, the F-35, has been grounded. I learned it from the news. Evidently there was an unexplained software crash.

Fortunately, the software was all that crashed. The airplane in question never left the tarmac."

That's odd, thought the Pilot. *How does she know that when the classified message announcing the grounding only arrived this afternoon at the US embassy? This news hasn't yet made it into the French media. She must've been informed through some official channel.*

"I'm sure they'll sort it out. Software bugs aren't unknown at this stage of development. The local Wi-Fi might have failed, or they lost the internet link to the Pentagon and cancelled the flight. A pilot can't fly that jet without a team supervising every action."

She asked, a note of concern ringing in her voice, "Even so, are you accepting the assignment?" Once again, she re-crossed her bare legs, leaning further forward on the bar stool, not even pretending to tug down her skirt.

The Pilot realized she had just presented him with the opportunity to get to ground truth about the woman facing him, disturbing him, and taunting him with her sexuality. He hesitated, not asking the cardinal question, knowing the answer probably to be one he didn't want to hear. In most hazardous aerial engagements, there is a moment of decision when combat can be initiated or avoided. He didn't get to be where he was or who he was by backing off, but there was more at stake here in this crowded bar than he admitted, even to himself. Still, he needed to know who she was, and now was the least bad time to find out.

"Are you asking me personally or professionally?" There was a time for subtlety, but this wasn't it. He wielded his blunt question like Robert the Bruce's battle ax to provoke an unscripted reaction from her, and the ruse succeeded.

Once again she quickly re-crossed her bare legs without adjusting her skirt, which was riding ever higher. For an instant, just a fraction of a second, a look of panicked consternation passed over her face--her eyes widening a bit, her mouth opening a fraction, and her lungs inhaling a quick breath. He continued watching closely, steeling himself to focus on her eyes, not her thighs.

Her face showed she realized she had unmasked herself. She knew her suppressed emotions had flashed momentarily into view. Her surprised expression faded, replaced by embarrassment and finally sadness, the sadness of abject failure. Slowly, she regained her composure and tried to smile without success, her eyes giving her away.

Her reaction to his lightning bolt question was one she couldn't hide. It had exposed her, peeled away her cover. She was an intelligence agent; there could be no other explanation for her fleeting expression. There couldn't be any doubt now about her motivation, as much as he didn't want it to be so.

"How long have you known?" she asked quietly, looking into his eyes.

"I suspected as much the day we visited the air museum. But I wasn't sure until now. Sorry to be so direct, but I needed to know before things got even deeper between us."

"I tried to warn you." She again uncrossed and re-crossed her legs. She ignored her skirt sliding up, approaching the tops of those shapely legs. The hem stretched between her smooth thighs, only a shadow cast in the dim bar keeping her modest, on the verge of naked exposure.

"By flashing your weapon? But why? That's not good tradecraft."

"Yes, and by giving you my official business card. I don't usually carry those cards on assignment. I knew, even then, that I was--how did you say it--getting into you, or vice versa."

"I'm honored. I've never been a directed spying assignment before, at least not by an Allied country. Are you DGSE or Military Intelligence Service?"

He reached over to the bar and put his palm over the tiny brass plaque, his fingers curved underneath the railing, but didn't receive the karma rush he expected. Perhaps Papa Hemingway's macho approach to life and women wasn't optimum in the current situation.

"DGSE. One has to be in the military to work for the MIS."

"So our first meeting wasn't an accident."

"You made your dinner reservation on your cell phone."

"Which you intercepted."

"Using techniques we learned from the Americans."

He concentrated harder on looking into her eyes and not down toward her lap. She was close to revealing herself. Her green skirt bunched in tight folds, high on her slender hips, attracting more attention in the bar from people nearby--men waiting to see what would show next, women aghast at her carelessness. She asked a key question of her own. "When you approached me that night, what were your intentions? Did you fancy me as your next conquest? Have I been a two-week affair, to be left behind when a new mistress, the F-35 whore, takes hold of you?"

"You know there's only one answer to your first two questions. We fighter pilots are never unmoved by a pretty face and a curvy figure. But no, I quickly realized as we got to know each other that you were not to be just another notch on my gun."

"That sounds painful."

She uncrossed her legs and pressed her knees together, the hem of her skirt bridging the extreme tops of her taut thighs. The other patrons leaned forward for a better view.

He leaned over to her, swept back her dark hair with one hand, and whispered in her ear, her perfume assaulting him and filling his mind. "Why don't we leave here before everyone in the room knows there's nothing under your skirt but you?"

She quickly glanced down at her legs and flashed embarrassment for the second time but for a different reason. Trying to hold her hem down in front with one hand, she slid from the stool, stood, and guided her skirt off her hips and back onto her thighs with her palms and fingertips. She took a deep breath. Her eyes returned to the cool, soft look he loved.

"How did you know?" she asked for the second time that night.

"I saw that Sharon Stone film. You should have, as well."

"Maybe I did." She smiled, her composure returning. "You are a bad influence on me; I am usually more careful about not exposing myself. But you are correct; we need to depart. Too many people in here speak English."

He threw twenty Euros on the bar in the general direction of the bartender and followed her through the disappointed crowd, out onto the street corner in front of the brasserie. The Montparnasse neighborhood was dark now and getting colder.

As they walked along the busy Boulevard de Port Royal without talking for several blocks, they were oblivious to people hurrying past them and the traffic stalled at red lights. He slowed, crossed behind her, and caught up again, staying between her and the busy street without missing a step.

"Why did you do that?" she asked.

"I was taught by my father to put myself between the traffic and a lady in case there's a runaway horse or a cart splashing through a puddle." He emphasized the word *lady*, looking across at her. "Why do you do it?" he asked.

"Are you asking why I wear nothing under my miniskirts or why I work for the DGSE?"

"Is that two questions or one? Did they tell you to tempt me with sex?" Another cruel question, but one of keen interest. He waited for an answer, knowing there could be only one, but how she spun her reply would be important to him.

"I spy for France because I am a French patriot not a French prostitute. My love life is private not public. My supervisor suggested strongly that sex might be tactically helpful, but the decision to sleep with you was left to me. A choice I did not regret on the first night we spent together or on any that followed."

"You can tell your boss, Inspector Clouseau, or whoever he or she is, that their plan worked. I'm now madly in love with you. There, you have it, that's all I can say." It was the first time he said those words to her. He had hoped to express his feelings in a more intimate setting than on a busy street deep in the 7th Arrondissement, but it was time to be as honest with her as he hoped she would be with him.

They approached the entrance to the Vavin Metro station with its black-enameled, wrought-iron light post and its shocking red oval Metro sign. The shiny belle époque filigree glistened, reflecting the lights of passing cars. The stairway to the station below was a brightly lit passageway descending from the street level.

She stopped and faced him. "Bonne nuit, mon amour" (Good night, my lover), she said and turned to go.

He caught her elbow, preventing her from leaving, holding on tightly. "You haven't answered the second question."

"Why do I wear my short skirts nude? That must remain my little secret, for now."

Her spiked heel off the pavement, she wheeled on a pointed toe and disappeared down the concrete stairs into the station, the clicks of her stilettos echoing off the white tile walls and her raven hair bouncing in the harsh light.

He turned toward Boulevard Saint-Michel, the busy thoroughfare leading to his flat on the island. The walk promised to be long and cold, followed by a lonely, sleepless night. After a tough mission, he had always internally debriefed himself, asking how he could have performed better, how he could avoid mistakes in the future. Now he knew. She was after data on the F-35. If he provided it to her, he would be a traitor, also a spy like her. If he didn't, he might lose her. Was she worth committing espionage for? No, no one was. Would she stick with him if he didn't fly the F-35 and talk about it? Probably not, how could she? Her handlers would object; she'd be reassigned.

He hated to expose her, to strip her emotionally naked, particularly in a public bar, but the forced embarrassment was necessary to get at the truth. In private she could have parried his thrust or used sex to divert him into another type of thrust. Could he have treated her more gently? No, he couldn't have trusted the outcome if he had pulled his punch. As Clint Eastwood said, "Sometimes a man's got to do what a man's got to do." That grizzled cliché, his ethical polestar acted out in numerous western films, didn't cheer him up either, so he vowed to quit using it.

With his trenchcoat collar flipped up against the coming chill, he thrust his hands deep into his pockets, elbows in, and walked on. He was alone again, despite the surrounding crowds, with only his thoughts. He chose his steps and his ideas carefully. *I felt immersed in a film noir the night we met,* he thought. *Now I'm back in that same old movie, all black and gray in the night. Is this the way it ends between us, with razor-edged truth cleaving the separation?*

The protruding terrace of a sidewalk café restricted sidewalk foot traffic, forcing a slight detour. Its light splashed onto the cold concrete, creating a semi-circular oasis of amber warmth in the gloom. A cell phone lying on a table inside rang loudly as he passed by, its tones barely audible through the glass-paneled wall facing the street. The owner had programmed it to replicate the metallic, chattering ring of an old-fashioned handset--a familiar sound that echoed down through the misty decades, emitting from a sunlit but distant and dangerous past. He was surprised, not realizing that a smart phone's simulated bell, muffled by the intervening years as much as the plate glass, could bring back such intense memories--memories from younger men, men from the past--that such a faint and ancient tone could summon a raging rush of adrenaline. But it did.

CHAPTER 13

HORNCHURCH AERODROME

England

August 1940: The phone's incessant ringing was not unexpected but still provoked a startled reaction from the eight waiting Royal Air Force pilots. All jumped involuntarily, tried to hide their twitches, and stared at the receiver in tense anticipation. Was the incoming message the midmorning tea call, a trivial administrative matter, or something far more serious?

The junior officer assigned to answer it, a fighter pilot all of nineteen years old, lunged for the handset with the impatience of youth. He paused, took a deep breath, exhaled, and raised the phone to his ear. After listening for a second, he turned and spoke to the small group of men in the alert shack. "Scramble Blue Flight," his adolescent's voice stretched an octave higher than normal, tension projected in the strained timbre. He continued listening to the muffled voice on the other end of the line, scribbling quickly on a small pad of foolscap with the stub of an eraser-less, well-chewed pencil.

The other three pilots of Blue Flight in the dispersal shack jumped to their feet, stubbed out cigarettes, and gulped one last dose of strong tea. Throwing down what would be later claimed to have been a winning card hand, they pulled on leather flying jackets and laced-up, fur-lined boots. Their actions were quick, but not hurried, efficient and purposeful from long practice; they had done this scene many times over the course of the summer—a summer that seemingly would never end for England but ended all too soon for many English people.

The Pilot donned his fleece-lined jacket as he followed the first two men out the open door. He ran past the four pilots of Red Flight reclining on colorfully striped folding canvas lawn chairs in the shade of the weather-beaten dispersal hut. Red Flight was not scrambled, yet. They watched as Blue Flight jogged toward four Spitfires. The men of Red Flight knew their call would come, probably in less than an hour; it would be their turn to instantly transition from nervous anticipation to quick action and duplicate the drill now being demonstrated by Blue Flight. Until then Red Flight would sit, smoke, and contemplate the reality that somewhere above the Home Counties, or over greater London, there would be waiting for them equally determined young German flyers who would strive to kill the members of Red Flight.

Such nervous anticipation was behind Blue Flight, who were too busy trying not to cock-up the scramble and to get airborne straightaway. As the flight commander, the Pilot parked his Spitfire closest to the hut; rank has its privileges. Blue Two and Blue Three maintained that at his advanced age, the Pilot needed a shorter course to run. Blue Four, charged with copying the intercept vector details passed on the phone from Sector Control, flew the most distant airplane. By determining the minimum time for Blue Flight to get airborne, the junior pilot with the longest path was the last one to leave the shack. Sometimes rank's privileges are counterproductive.

Ahead the Pilot could see his ground crew, Alf and Chalky, preparing to launch the cocked Spitfire. Seconds earlier they had been lying on the ground, shaded by the wings and catching some much-needed sleep after working since before dawn ministering to the mechanical needs of what they called their "kite."

At the waiting aircraft, the Pilot snatched his parachute from the ground, clambered on the left wing, and tossed the 'chute, which would double as his seat cushion, onto the metal bucket seat. Then he entered the cockpit from the left side, the side on which one mounts a thoroughbred. Settling into the tight seat, he pulled up the "car door" on the cockpit's side and latched it. Hands flying, he snapped the parachute's leg harness tight and cinched the aircraft's lap belt as Alf leaned over him to fasten the shoulder harness. Alf then handed him his leather flying helmet with the isinglass goggles, with the oxygen mask and radio cord already attached. It was but the work of a moment to plug in the radio lead and oxygen hose.

Before he jumped off the wing's trailing edge, Alf shouted over the cacophony of cranking aircraft, "Good luck, Sir. Get a Jerry for us." Unstated, but clearly implicit was Alf and Chalky's other heart-felt request: *Don't bring our precious kite back shot full of holes.*

The Pilot's final task before awakening the Spitfire was to pull a white silk scarf from his inside pocket and wrap it snugly around his neck, under his jacket's collar. The Pilot endured endless bollocks about his scarf from the squadron commander, who thought it an affectation. However, it allowed his neck to rub against his leather collar without chafing as he continually scanned left, right, and behind in combat. The Royal Flying Corps fighter pilots in their open-cockpit biplanes of the Great War had passed on the tradition of the silk scarf, a tradition he followed and found useful.

He twirled his right hand over the cockpit with his index finger pointed up, the signal for Chalky to crank the engine. He reached behind him, pulled the clear plastic canopy forward, and locked it in place. Many pilots preferred to start and take off with the canopy aft, leaving the cockpit open, all the easier to exit the aircraft in case of an emergency. Not the Pilot, he believed his mental processes were not helped by breathing the oil smoke belched on start-up by the cold engine dormant in front of him.

The three-bladed airscrew wound through a revolution. He switched the magnetos on and was rewarded with a cough from the big Merlin V-12. It hit on a few cylinders, caught, and settled into a grumbling idle. The engine puked puffs of pale blue smoke from the stubby exhaust stacks, and the oily smoke streamed over the canopy. The prop was now a whirling blur. The Spit was awake.

He performed the last cockpit checks in seconds with practiced precision: mixture full rich, carburetor heat off, prop in fine pitch, flaps up, rudder trim full right, radio on. He squeezed the bicycle-type brake lever on the control stick and gave Alf the signal to pull the wheel chocks. A glance left and right obtained him a thumbs-up from his three wingmen. He cracked the throttle open and released the brakes. The Spitfire rolled, bumping over uneven dirt. The left wheel brake swung the nose into the wind, lining up with the runway stretching west.

On his left wing, Blue Two bounced along beside him in swirling dust. Three and Four taxied off his right wing, trailing by a few yards as they bumped onto the hard-surfaced runway. A quick glance down showed the oil pressure in the green and coolant temperature off the peg. His wingmen and his Spitfire were ready to fly and fight.

He gave a vigorous nod of his head to signal to the other three, advanced the throttle, and held the stick full back. The Merlin's grumble rose to a growl, and the Spitfire accelerated, slowly at first, more rapidly as he fed in more throttle. *Careful*, he told himself. *Don't pour on the coal all at once. Let the airspeed build. Give the rudder more bite.* Too much power too soon would cause the prop to swing the nose and swerve the Spit into the wingmen, bad form indeed.

The jarring ride on the uneven pavement became more frantic. He edged the stick forward to pick up the tail, not too much or the prop blades would dig into the ground passing beneath them. The nose dropped; the rattle of the wheels across Mother Earth faded away as the Spitfire became airborne. A flick of a stubby lever beside his right knee and the undercarriage retracted with a solid thump. Another glance left and right. Two, Three, and Four were right there on his wings. *Good lads all*, he thought.

Just under a minute had passed since the phone in the dispersal hut rang.

They took off to the west. He didn't know where they would find the Jerries, but it wasn't likely they lurked west of Hornchurch Airfield; they came from France to the east. As soon as plenty of air passed under Blue Flight, he started a gentle left turn back east toward the airfield. Down below he saw Red Flight still in their lawn chairs looking up as the four Spitfires roared overhead in close formation. He wouldn't get help from them anytime soon. Red Flight would scramble to replace the Pilot's four fighters and be fed into the fight when Blue Flight exhausted their supplies of fuel, ammo, or luck. Blue Flight would have to fight on their own this morning.

The radio came alive with a crackle. "Blue Lead from Blue Four, steer one two zero degrees and climb to angels two zero, forty plus bandits," Blue Four relayed the vector he copied from the phone call. They were instructed to head southeast and climb to twenty thousand feet to intercept a large formation of Germans.

"Blue Lead here. Understood. Heads on a swivel, lads."

All of southeast England lay within the Luftwaffe's range; Blue Flight had to keep a keen watch. He stopped their turn when the gyro compass needle pointed to 120 degrees and continued to climb at almost full throttle, giving the others excess power to use in keeping formation.

It would take twelve minutes to reach twenty thousand feet. Plenty of time to contemplate the combat to come and get ready in the cockpit, and in his mind. Now within range of Sector Control radio, he transmitted, "Sector, Blue Flight airborne, on course." He didn't repeat the instructions back; German ears might listen.

"Understood, Blue Flight," came the only reply from a female voice, the sector controller.

At least she could have said, "Keep calm and carry on," he thought, a bad joke to settle his nerves. Now with the scramble's frantic action completed, they had little to do but climb, watch for the Jerries, and plan for the combat to come. He had no doubt they would tangle with Germans. The last few days, every scramble resulted in an engagement, some a right royal dust-up. Once again he would lay his life on the line, depending on his eyesight, reflexes, coordination, pluck, and marksmanship to prevail. The Pilot didn't think of survival, or even fear, but concentrated on not making a dog's breakfast of the mission, on finding the Jerries, and not getting one of his flight killed. Among fighter pilots, failure meant not only the possibility of sudden death but also the chance of being shown up. Failure was a demon more fearsome than death. While death was final, failure would chew at a live pilot as long as he lived.

His partner in the coming mêlée, his Spitfire climbed slower now in thinner air. The cockpit grew colder by the minute; it would be well below zero at angels two zero. The canopy rails overlapped his shoulders by an inch on each side; it was a small cockpit built for small men. There was no room between his legs for the control stick to be moved left and right, it could only move fore and aft for pitch control. The stick top pivoted left and right to roll the aircraft. Atop the hinged portion was a leather-wrapped ring large enough to grasp with thick gloves. A red button the size of a penny was mounted at eleven o'clock on the ring. This "tit" under his right thumb would set off the eight .303-caliber machine guns, four in each wing.

Not for the first time, he appreciated how responsive the Spit was to fly, the flight controls light and free and every movement in harmony with all others. Up front the Merlin engine continued its throaty howl, its roar muted by the airstream's torrent. The Merlin clawed with its propeller, dragging the Pilot/Spitfire team ever higher. An ever-present hum, the engine's thrum permeated the lightly-built airframe. Rolls-Royce craftsmen had lovingly assembled and balanced the engine, but twelve cylinders churning out over a thousand horsepower made their vibratory presence felt in the cockpit. Now at ten thousand feet, with oxygen on and flowing and gun heaters on, one couldn't have the guns frozen solid and impotent.

It was an uncommonly cloudless, late summer day over much of the Home Counties, but a low, light mist obscured the crazy-quilted patchwork of fields below. He could trace the brown River Thames until it merged with the Channel's much deeper blue. He had little time to enjoy the view, constantly scanning left, right, ahead, behind the tail, and into the hazy sun, looking, looking for the Jerries.

Southeast of London's dirty, gray sprawl, a line of fires burned, contributing to the ground-based haze. A block of flats was alight, or rather what was left of them spouted flames. He could make out a line of bomb craters superimposed over the devastation. Proximity to the Supermarine factory that built Spitfires proved fatal to God only knew how many people in their homes. The German bombs missed the factory by a good two hundred yards, not that the German bombers seemed to care all that much; they scattered their lethal loads over large swatches of the pristine English countryside. It had been obvious since early July that the Luftwaffe bombers' mission wasn't so much to destroy high-value targets as it was to lure RAF Spitfires and Hurricanes into the air, where they and their pilots could be killed by the Luftwaffe's prowling and expertly flown Me 109s. With Fighter Command decimated, the Channel could be crossed by an invasion fleet. From the Pilot's point of view, the German plan was working, evidenced by increasing numbers of empty seats in the Officers' Mess and by familiar faces absent from the crew room.

"Blue Flight, come left to zero nine zero degrees, due east," commanded Sector Control. The young woman's voice exhibited an upper-class English accent, icily correct with a slight nasal lisp. It wasn't *her* voice--she had a Scottish burr--but still the Pilot noted the obvious class distinction. 'Twas passing strange what a chap thought of in combat.

"Blue Flight here. Understood." The Pilot wheeled the formation of four Spitfires in a shallow left turn, still climbing, passing through eighteen thousand feet. They flew in "finger-four" formation, each Spitfire positioned like the fingertips of a hand, with the Pilot's lead aircraft the middle finger. He learned the technique from the Germans; the three-plane "Vee," or "Vic," formation favored by other RAF flight leaders proved unwieldy by comparison.

He knew a blue, wooden arrow represented Blue Flight, pushed across a horizontal map of southern England with a long wand wielded by a lady, a member of the Women's Auxiliary Air Force at Sector Control headquarters. The attacking bomber and fighter streams showed on the board as red arrows. It was Sector's job to use radar, the newest widget conjured up by the boffins, to vector Blue Flight to an intercept. The overall air action would be monitored similarly on a larger board at Fighter Command Headquarters at Bentley Priory. There the grandees of Fighter Command would watch the action and listen to the radio transmissions from a balcony overlooking the WAAF women and their blue and red arrows. He wondered if she was on duty today, carefully positioning the blue arrow representing his flight.

During a visual scan south, movement caught his eye. Something unseen moved in relation to the stationary background of the patchwork English countryside below. The Pilot peered down to his right, and there they were. The *something* was a formation of around twenty brown-green airplanes, their flight path aimed at eastern London. The formation's orderliness identified the aircraft as bombers--German fighters flew in a loose *schwarm*.

He felt the cramped tightness in his stomach that always came with imminent combat, along with a powerful urge to do something now, to get cracking. Waiting for lethal combat was worse than the actual dust-up. But he continued to climb, headed east, opposite the bomber stream's heading five thousand feet below. *Softly, softly, chatchee monkey,* he thought.

Where were the fighters? The Jerries never sent bombers over England unescorted. There, a half mile behind and slightly above the bombers, they escorted closely. A basic mistake, probably ordered by Herman Göring himself, the Luftwaffe's supreme commander. Bomber pilots of all nationalities like to see their escort fighters close by, their proximity a comfort in the war zone. Göring probably gave in to complaints from his bomber corps that the RAF was chewing them up, with no Me 109s to be seen nearby. But this order tied the German fighters to the bombers' airspeed, much slower than optimum for air combat, and locked the fighters near the bombers' altitude, depriving them of the tactical advantage of height. Göring knew better. His wing commander during the Great War, Baron Manfred Von Richthofen, adamantly gave his fighters free rein. "All else is rubbish!" the Red Baron was wont to say. But the top German's miscalculation was the RAF's gain. *Those who forget the mistakes of the past are doomed to repeat them,* he thought. The Pilot intended to make the Jerries pay for such a sophomoric error.

"Sector Control, Blue Leader here. Tally-Ho," he notified Sector he had the Jerries in sight. The terminology came from fox hunting, but the quarry was human. For the benefit of his flight, he pointed down at two o'clock with one leather-gloved hand.

"Blue Flight, understood. Good luck and good hunting," Sector replied. The WAAF woman's voice had softened and betrayed her emotions, a girl's voice doing a woman's job. The upper-crust detachment gone, a slight hitch broke into her speech from swallowing hard, perhaps signifying her acknowledgement she had just vectored and committed four Spitfires to attack at least twelve Germans.

He was released from radar control; the rest was up to the four men/machine teams of Blue Flight. The Pilot now grasped Sector Control's battle plan. She had vectored Blue Flight to a position up-sun from the German fighters. To spot the four Spits, the Jerries would have to look directly into the blinding mid-morning sun. The Hurricanes from Biggin Hill or Tangmere wings were probably lower, vectored to the bombers from the south. The slower Hurricanes would go after the lumbering bombers while Blue Flight's faster Spitfires kept the Me 109 fighters busy.

The Pilot believed the Germans must be as thick as two short planks. They didn't seem to understand what radar did for the RAF. The Jerries never twigged on to why they kept getting bounced from out of the sun. He kept his formation of four high, let the German *schwarm* pass under his right wing, and constantly checked the sun's position in relation to the fighters below. He wanted the sun directly at their backs when they rolled into the bounce. The Spitfires' slim outlines would be difficult to discern in the sun's radiant corona. They would need all the edge they could manage, four Spits against at least twelve 109s. *This could be bloody dangerous*, he thought.

At last the seconds passed and the angles were aligned; time to get stuck in. He slipped his boots into the metal loops on top of the rudder pedals so the extreme G forces wouldn't pull his feet off the controls. He confirmed the reflector gun sight was on and illuminated. It projected a white dot the pilots called the "pipper" on a small square of glass on top of the glare shield. Around the pipper shone a white ring, set to thirty-two feet, the wingspan of an Me 109. The four guns in each wing were harmonized so their bullet streams converged at three hundred yards ahead, a position in space identified by the pipper. When a 109's wings filled the sight's outer circle, the stream of hot lead would pass through the projected pipper.

"Blue Flight's on the bounce," he transmitted. " Line abreast, chaps." The Pilot wanted all four Spits evenly spaced to hit the Jerries as one. He cranked the willing Spitfire into a right wingover, pointed the nose down, and aimed well behind the last German fighter in the formation droning on below. He set up the bounce for a lagging pursuit, wanting to pull out of the dive just outside of gun range and then level out. It was hard to shoot accurately under G loading.

In the shallow dive, the Spitfire gathered speed rapidly, its slender fuselage and thin wings offering little drag to the slipstream. The Merlin in front of him howled at full throttle, and the prop whined higher and higher in pitch. With his left hand, he adjusted the trim settings, balancing the control forces fed back through the stick and rudder pedals. If the rudder wasn't trimmed to neutral, the gun sight wouldn't predict where the bullets were shot. As the airspeed indicator spun up through four hundred miles per hour, the ailerons became stiff and the Spit's roll control sluggish. The Pilot needed to set up the firing pass early; only fine corrections would be possible at this speed. One last deep breath and the four Spits were among the slower 109s; the German aircraft grew larger in their bullet-proof windscreens.

The Germans never saw them come out of the sun. The Pilot selected one of the laggard 109s at the rear of the German *schwarm* and pursued from dead behind and slightly above the unaware Jerry. At one hundred fifty miles per hour of overtake, things would happen quickly. With quick pressure on the controls, he superimposed the pipper on the 109's dirty, green fuselage and held it there until the Messerschmitt's wings grew to span the gun sight's larger circle. His right thumb pressed the firing tit on the control stick's ringed top, careful not to jab the red button and disturb the calculated flight path.

An unsynchronized vibration shook the airframe as all eight guns erupted spitting bullets at slightly different rates. The pipper jittered with the guns' staccato hammering, and he saw white tracers bracket the 109. Brilliant flashes marked the 109's aft end as shells found their target. Still he held the tit down.

Instantly, the 109 exploded in an incandescent, red-and-white fireball. The airstream flowing past the doomed aircraft shaped the fireball rearward into a tear drop shape; the intense flames encompassed all of the 109 except the wing tips, engine, and airscrew. The explosion flared for a second or two then died away, leaving the fuselage a hulk trailing black smoke from burning engine oil and the cockpit an inferno. The Pilot's Spitfire flashed by the slowing, dying wreckage already arcing down toward vertical impact with the ground.

The Me 109 mounted a gasoline tank behind and beneath the pilot. On the bulkhead behind the tank sat the pilot's breathing supply, a metal canister of highly pressurized, pure oxygen. An incendiary bullet had penetrated both the oxygen bottle and the fuel tank and mixed an ignition source, gallons of high octane aviation fuel plus pure oxygen; a conflagration resulted.

The sight of one of their own incinerated in their midst startled the remaining Germans; their formation blew up like a covey of highland grouse flushed by kilted beaters. Me 109s turned, climbed, and dove in all directions. Grouse fly to escape hunters, but the 109s turned to attack the four lone Spitfires. Each enraged Jerry tried to get on a Spit's tail and even the score.

Still with a speed advantage over the turning 109s, the Pilot singled out another Jerry in front of him, one near the front of the now chaotic German formation. They would have stationed their most senior pilots in the lead. This one was the *Jaeger* (hunter), probably with a dozen RAF kills. The Pilot wanted this bloke badly. He flew the pipper over the 109 at about four hundred yards, almost in range.

Despite the 109's poor visibility aft, the German pilot saw the Spitfire behind him, perhaps in his rearview mirror. Before the tracers could find him, the German pushed the nose of his aircraft violently over, straight down into a dive.

Sod it all, thought the Pilot, *this bugger is switched on.*

Pushing the nose down, the German would have endured two negative Gs. The negative G forces would have thrown him up against his seat belt, trying to pin him against his greenhouse style canopy. The fuel-injected Daimler-Benz V-12 engine driving the Messerschmitt continued to run under negative G, accelerating the 109 as it dove.

However, the carburetor feeding fuel into the Pilot's Merlin would cut out under negative G, stall the engine, and leave the Pilot flying a glider for a few seconds. Alternately, the Pilot could roll inverted slowly with his speed-stiffened ailerons and pull the Spitfire's nose down in pursuit of the fleeing 109. Either maneuver would increase the distance between them out of range of the Spit's guns. Word of the advantages of fuel injection over carburetors evidently spread quickly through the Luftwaffe squadrons in France, foiling the Pilot's second kill of the day.

Before he could find another target, the Pilot sensed rather than saw that he was under attack. Quick looks over both shoulders revealed three 109s turning toward his tail from three separate directions. Now the extra airspeed he carried through his two gun attacks paid off. As he pulled the stick back into his gut, the G forces built rapidly, and the nose came up into a near vertical climb. He traded airspeed for altitude, leaving the frustrated Germans falling behind below him.

The next minutes seemed like hours as time stretched in the ensuing, frantically turning, climbing, and twisting dogfight. This patch of England's sunny sky was filled with German fighters and four lone Spitfires. The Pilot threw the Spit around, built speed and energy in dives, and dissipated it in gut-wrenching five-G turns. With no time to set up firing passes, he shot at 109s when they flashed in front of the windscreen, then had to break left or right to spoil the aim of a Jerry behind him. His breath came in short gulps; he found it hard to see with fear-induced sweat trickling into his eyes. The control stick was never still as it visited the cockpit's four corners in random order. The throttle was locked full forward, demanding all the power the howling Merlin could produce. At high speed, the Spitfire's control surfaces fed aerodynamic forces back to the stick and rudder pedals. It took all the Pilot's strength to maneuver the aircraft--exertion was difficult in the cramped cockpit with no room for leverage. Pressed down by G forces, muscles ached, legs cramped, and arms grew leaden. Out of breath, the Pilot fought for his life and to end the lives of others.

He caught a glimpse of a 109 spiraling earthward, the tail shot off and the pilot struggling to get out of the fluttering wreck. A parachute flashed by his left wing. There was no time to identify the pilot. He pulled up to avoid colliding with a powerless Spitfire, its engine trailing thin, black smoke and its cockpit empty. He looked quickly at the rear fuselage; the block lettering flanking the RAF roundel identified the deserted bird as Blue Four's.

As the fight descended into denser air, the Spitfire came ever more alive, responding to his control inputs almost before he made them. At full chat, the Merlin drove the aircraft where he wanted it to go without mechanical complaint. Four Gs were but an inch of control pressure away, a flick roll could be performed without thinking, and a zoom climb was effortless. When he had a quick high-angle shot, the guns fired as commanded. Once he saw impacts on a 109 crossing left to right in front as he shot, but he had no time to follow up for a confirmed kill. That would go into his logbook as a "damaged."

No aircraft were visible in the windscreen; they must be behind him. He cranked the Spitfire around in a level 360-degree turn. No one there. He rolled wings level to gain speed and have a better look around. The sky was empty; he and the Spitfire were alone over the summer green fields of England.

"Bloody Hell!" he shouted to no one.

One minute the air was rent by aircraft climbing, diving, turning, slashing, and the next, empty, silent, void of friends and foe alike. Sometimes it happened like that, and no one knew why. He scanned the sky while he got his bearings, turned the nose toward Hornchurch Airfield, wove to check for unseen attacks from six o'clock, and tried to steady his hands that had strangely started to shake. The Pilot trimmed the aircraft to fly by itself and removed his gloved hands from the stick and throttle, but the tremors continued. He couldn't let the lass see him this way; he must gain control before they met again.

CHAPTER 14

ROYAL AIR FORCE CLUB

Piccadilly

London

September 1940: The Pilot parted the heavy blackout curtains and opened the third-floor window. His room in the Royal Air Force Club overlooked teeming Piccadilly; traffic noise penetrated the gap in the curtains and filled the small room. Green Park lay across the street behind a black wrought-iron fence, its verdant expanse scarred by sandbagged, prefabricated air raid shelters and hastily-dug slit trenches. Well-worn paths in the grass indicated frequent use of the park's bunkers and trenches during air raids by pedestrians caught too far from the entrance to the Hyde Park Corner underground station to his right. The "tube" station served as a subterranean bomb shelter, as well as a popular stop on the Piccadilly line. The expansive park languished unkempt and overgrown; the king's gardeners were busy on other duties, trying the keep the city functioning despite the ongoing airborne onslaught Prime Minister Winston Churchill had correctly identified as the Battle of Britain.

He leaned forward, trying to scan the sky above the park, but could only see an empty ribbon of deep blue directly above the street. Green Park's stately trees obscured upward vision, filtering the early fall sky through their leafy boughs and hiding from view the hard sky above.

I should be up there flying, he thought, *instead of bone idle down here*. But he wasn't offered that opportunity; orders were orders. After thirty days of continuous air combat, each Royal Air Force fighter pilot was released from duty for three days. Even with Nazi wolves straining at their leashes just across the English Channel, twelve miles from Dover, Fighter Command was of the mind that fresh pilots fought more effectively than battle-weary ones.

His restlessness eased somewhat because he knew effective air defense by rested pilots was crucial for continued survival of the British way of life. Getting himself killed through battle fatigue would accomplish nothing. If the Luftwaffe quickly established air superiority over southern England and the Channel, the first successful foreign invasion of Great Britain since AD 1066 would surely follow. The consequences of a German invasion were abundantly clear--one could look across the channel and see what life was like in Europe under the heels of Nazi jackboots. Defeated in France, the British army remained disorganized, without sufficient kit, and clueless on countering the Wehrmacht's Blitzkrieg tactics. The army troopers would fight valiantly and lose, even on home turf. The dire situation worsened daily; only Fighter Command's Spitfire and Hurricane pilots could prevent a long night of German tyranny from descending on Britain. The threat now darkened the continent, flowing from Berlin unchecked. He chafed at the forced inactivity, peered out the window, and looked in vain for the sky. He marshaled his strength for the air combat to come, waiting for him in the crystalline bowl above.

His sense of duty called him to be up there, in action. But deep down he knew a break was long overdue; he badly needed a respite on the ground. At times when airborne, he saw German aircraft far out on the horizon that weren't there. A slammed door in the smoking lounge of his home Officers' Mess so startled him that he dropped his cup of tea, a serious faux pas in an anteroom of the Royal Air Force. Then there were the nightmares. What sleep he gathered was haunted by vivid images of burning, spinning Spitfires, their cockpits aflame. His nights were almost as intense as his days, and he was fully awake long before first light. He held his hands out over the window sill, bathing them in the cool autumn air. If he concentrated, he could almost stop the shaking.

For the past thirty days, a month of constant war in the air, he had anticipated the next mission when he wasn't reliving the last. Four weeks ago, the idea
of a romantic rendezvous in London would have been dismissed as treasonous;
one couldn't be larking around when the fate of Britain as an independent country hung in the balance. But now he relished meeting her, thinking and caring
about someone else, someone not a doomed squadron mate. He needed to share
a drink, a laugh, a bed, to lose himself in her and make the war go away for a
night or two.

Few men grew as close as a fighter squadron's pilots. Each man realized his
continued existence was determined in part by the actions of others and that
the lives of those other pilots rested in his leather-gloved hands, as well. Fighter
planes flew and fought in close formation, at least until the bounce, for many
reasons. More eyes spotting the Jerries, each wingman covering his leader's tail,
and more guns--the formation provided these. Once they were wrapped up in
a dogfight, mutual support broke down, resulting in every bloke for himself, or
so it seemed when the Pilot found more Me 109s than Spitfires around him. His
squadron mates were out there somewhere in the fight, until they weren't. Each
squadron pilot's loss represented a vital piece of himself gone forever. "Ask not
for whom the bell tolls, it tolls for thee." Living, eating, joking, drinking, and
above all, fighting together forged bonds only death could sever. Often at night,
he saw their faces as he remembered them in the Mess, the crew room, the dispersal shack, and their aircraft. Only the touch of a woman, a woman he might
love, could push the images of those lost mates, those smiling men doomed
forever to be young, into the background for a time.

A discrete knock sounded on his room's varnished wooden door. "A lady
from the Women's Auxiliary Air Force here to see you in reception, sir." The
voice on the door's other side spoke in the distinctive British accent used by
generations of people proud to serve as club staff.

"Thank you very much, indeed. Please be so kind as to inform her I shall
join her straightaway."

"Very good, sir."

He straightened his black tie in his shaving mirror and donned his blue
Royal Air Force tunic with golden fabric wings sewn on the left chest. He left the

top button of his uniform coat deliberately and carefully unfastened. A glance around the room ensured all appeared in good military order.

Downstairs the tall, angular chap frowning behind the oak reception counter ruled the RAF Club with an iron fist in an immaculate, white cotton glove. The Head Concierge was fond of relating how he started with the RAF Club on its inauguration in 1922 after a stint as the Sergeant Major of the Coldstream Guards. His knowing expression gave the impression he had seen it all and dealt with it all. He booked no deviations from established protocols. As a condition of membership, each RAF officer, serving and retired, read and initialed the club's "Rules," signifying intent to comply. The Rules read in part, "Members will not entertain females to whom they are not married in the club's private areas, including the bedrooms. The Head Concierge zealously enforced this prudish Victorian policy. He had turned away amorous females, both amateur and professional, numerous times in the past when their RAF escorts attempted to take the ladies in question, and questionable ladies, upstairs.

She stood alone in the reception area as the Pilot descended the stairs. Shifting from one foot to the other, she flashed a radiant smile at his approach. The concierge immediately noticed the Pilot's top button undone; a uniform violation dared to be displayed, flaunted really as a distinguishing mark, only by fighter pilots. The older man read the signal of the open button; he certainly understood what the Pilot now meant to England. He had only to step outside and look up on any summer day in 1940 to see men like the Pilot flying, fighting, and often dying in the hard skies over Central London. Slowly the clerk turned around and concentrated on sorting the afternoon post, sliding incoming letters into the correct wooden cubbyholes behind the reception desk. Evidently, this task presented sufficient difficulty to demand the old sergeant major's undivided attention and allowed no time to turn around. His back remained resolutely to the Pilot and his WAAF friend. Where they went next apparently didn't concern the RAF Club's major domo.

As she started to speak, the Pilot quieted her with a finger across his lips, took her arm, and led her to the winding stairs beyond the foyer. She pressed his hand against her side with her elbow. After covertly mounting two flights, she couldn't remain silent any longer. "Is this visit permitted? The RAF Club does have standards, does it not?"

"We're violating several sets of rules, but not to worry. You saw the clerk in reception allow you to enter. He won't object if we're discrete."

He stepped back and took her in--taller than average with broad shoulders and sturdy hips. Her blue WAAF uniform with its calf-length skirt and loose blouse tried in vain to hide her figure. Soft auburn hair fluffed thick and shoulder length; she struggled to keep it under her service cap. Green eyes and a fair complexion gave away her heritage.

She told the Pilot when they first met that she hailed from the Isle of Skye, a windswept, mountainous island just off Scotland's west coast, but no other details of her life before the WAAF were forthcoming. Her Scots' accent retained its highlands and islands lilt; the occasional Gaelic term crept into her vocabulary. She could turn her brogue off and on at will. She sometimes sounded like a bonnie Scottish lassie and at other, more formal times she used flawless, upper-class King's English.

He swung open the door to his tiny room. She hesitated a moment, then stepped in. The sparsely decorated room boasted a bed, nightstand, clothes rack, and little else. A constant background hum, the traffic buzz from Piccadilly wafted through the open window with a slight breeze. The pilot shut the door and latched it, turning to her. "How very nice of you to come."

She turned to face him, standing closer than would a stranger, her green eyes alight. "I've brought you something from the bonnie Isle of Skye." Over her shoulder she had slung a black leather dispatch bag, the sort favored by motorcycle messengers, instead of her usual government-issued purse. She opened the top flap and reached inside.

"Could it be a haggis, that 'noble chieftain o' the puddin' race'? You must've stopped at Fortnum & Mason, just up Piccadilly." He didn't know if most English grocers sold Scottish fare, but why not guess?

"Nae, more's the pity. One has to journey north to the Highlands to procure a proper haggis sausage. However, I've brought something I expect you to enjoy even more."

"Oh, I'm quite sure you have."

She carefully lifted from the leather bag a bottle of Talisker single malt whiskey from the sole distillery on Skye. "Aged twenty years," said the faded label.

The Pilot was suitably impressed, " 'A man's a man for all that.' "

She looked at him, a twinkle now in her pale eyes and a smile playing across her red lips. "You quote Bobbie Burns rather well. Now give us some good words from your own tongue."

"I say let's open the bottle; it's waited twenty years for this very moment. It's a pity we don't have any of the water used to make it. That's what one should drink it with. What's worse, we lack proper glasses."

"What do you take me for?" she asked as she reached again into the case. She handed him two pewter drinking cups, heavy and old with Celtic characters winding in bas-relief around their circumferences. The wear of long use burnished their polished metallic surfaces. Next came a silver flask, as one would pack for a wee nip during a day at the races. She held up the flask. "Water from the spring at the base of Hawk Hill, on Skye as well, close by the distillery."

"Brilliant" was all he could say. He was truly touched at the effort she had expended for their long-dreamed-of time together. She poured two fingers' worth of the amber whiskey into each cup and added a splash of the precious water. They touched the rims of the ancient cups, and he looked into those sea-green eyes. "To us," he said. "To the king, England, and Scotland. And to victory."

It wasn't really customary to combine so many important subjects in one toast, but the Pilot cared not about defying long-established social norms. When one's life may not stretch beyond next week, arbitrary social rules become trivial. He held his cup in his steadier left hand, but to no avail. The pewter's weight damped the shaking a bit, but there it was. He saw her look down at the ripples in his drink, but she said nothing.

She replied, "To us," omitting the patriotic portions of his toast.

Each sip of the whiskey summoned the aroma of malted barley roasted over smoldering fires, along with the smoke from slow-burning peat used for those fires, added sea spray, and a hint of highland heather. The amber liquid had been melded and caramelized by long aging in oak barrels that once held sherry, bourbon, or Tennessee whiskey--barrels bought abroad and re-used by the thrifty Scots. The old Talisker fell spectacularly on the palette.

He noticed she looked again at his hands holding his drink and the quivering he couldn't halt. Taking his pewter cup in both hands to steady it, he looked into her questioning face. "Do you hear the pipes calling?" he asked, hoping to avoid the obvious subject.

"Nae, Laddie, but I can smell the gorse and the fear."

"Well spotted. I hoped to quiet down these hands before we met today. It's not fear, it's nerves," he lied, even to himself.

" 'O wad some Power the giftie gie us, to see oursels as ithers see us.' Now, it's my turn to quote Burns," she said.

He looked into those hazel eyes and saw the truth. She went on, "You're here with me now, not up there. I'm worried as well. I have my own concerns, not as serious as yours, but real all the same. On the radio, I've heard doomed pilots scream, their hands burned so terribly they're unable to open the canopy and bail out of the aircraft. I shall remember those cries all my life. Will we survive this war? If we do, what's to become of us?"

He realized that he and his mates weren't the only service members plagued with nightmares. Rather than dive into that painful subject, he turned to a more impersonal type of survival, national survival. "You, probably, unless the Jerries discover the importance of you and your sister controllers at Bentley Priory, and if their bomb aiming improves. For me, it may be a close-run thing. I have to ask you, are we winning? Surely you can see the big picture at HQ and hear comments by those in the know."

"Stuffy says--"

He interrupted her, "You call Dowding 'Stuffy'? Only his mates from the Great War can take that liberty."

"My word, no. Air Chief Marshal Sir Hugh Dowding is given all due respect by us WAAF girls, as befits the air officer commanding Fighter Command. Even Churchill addresses him as 'Sir Hugh.' But we all know his nickname and use it when he's not present."

"You've met Churchill?"

"Not met him, I've just seen him visiting the War Room during a big air battle. 'Winnie,' and no, we don't address him as such, never comments on operations; he leaves the decisions to the battle staff. Only once did he remove his cigar and ask a question."

"Which was?"

" 'Where are our reserves?' Dowding's only answer had to be, 'Prime Minister, there are no reserves.' At that moment on that day, the morning of the 15th, every fighter in the southeast was airborne."

"So, does 'Stuffy' tell you how his chicks are performing? You know he calls us fighter pilots his 'chicks.' "

"Really? He's the epitome of decorum on the balcony watching the battle unfold, watching our wooden arrows. His aim isn't to destroy the Luftwaffe, but to win by not losing, by convincing the Germans that Fighter Command isn't defeated and that you and your squadron mates can fight on until late fall. If so, we'll be secure from invasion until spring; the Germans can't cross the Channel in winter." She dropped her Scottish accent and spoke in impeccable Oxbridge English when discussing official matters. She added another dollop of whiskey and splash of water to their cups, pouring carefully as if at high tea.

"This plan of yours and Stuffy's feels like a losing hand to us chaps in the cockpits. Every day we fight outnumbered badly by the Jerries. We send four against twelve, fight outmanned twelve on forty, bounce twenty with eight. Each night we see more empty chairs in the Mess, and each day more Germans."

"On the plotting board, we see the odds. I often wonder how many of you will live out the day. We help execute Stuffy's plan: attack the Germans with penny packets of fighters and save fresh defenders for the day's next raids, and the raids of tomorrow, and the day after. The Jerries must be led to believe they can't win, that there will always be Spits and Hurries on the bounce."

"I hope to God this plan works, for it's bloody hell on the pilots in those penny packets."

Penny packets, a slang term for something small and insignificant, were named after the tiny packets of candy on offer at sweet shops for a penny or two; the nickname was the pilots' way of sarcastically protesting a tactic that was, from their view, bleeding fighter command white.

She went on, now in a Scottish brogue, the half-empty bottle of Talisker lying corked on the bed, its work nearly complete. "Aye, Laddie, it worked a charm for Sir Robert the Bruce in 1306. He secured independence for Scotland for another two hundred years. The Bruce knew he couldn't defeat you English straight up--"

He broke in, "We most certainly could defeat the Luftwaffe, given half a chance."

"You didn't in France. The Jerries are more experienced. Their pilots have won in Spain, Poland, the Low Countries, wherever they've fought. You lads learn on the run. How many hours in Spitfires did you enter combat with? Ten, twelve, fifteen?"

"Nine."

"So there you have it. Fight on as The Bruce did, and we have a chance. Otherwise, Hitler will be in Number Ten Downing Street by Yuletide. I can only imagine what you go through in the air. When one of the arrows I push originates from Hornchurch, I pray you'll return."

His hands still shook. She took his pewter cup and sat down on the bed, the only possible place to do so in the tiny room. He paced two steps to the door and two back to the foot of the bed. He was caged, not in a cramped bedroom in London town but in a battle plan offering no respite, no path to immediate victory, and only a slim chance of personal survival. She poured two more drams and added the last of the water to each cup.

"It's not as bad as all that. I've nae rung Dunvegan Castle to unfurl the Fairy Flag," she said, a forced smile playing across her face.

"A letter in the post might be more effective. I doubt Skye castles are on the phone. The flag's been used twice, hasn't it? Legend says the flag can work its magic but once more."

He stopped pacing and faced her from across the room. She crossed her legs, tightening her long service skirt around her thighs, and leaned back on the soft bed.

"Aye, Laddie, you're keen on Scottish lore. The Fairy Flag has but one more use. It's saved Clan MacLeod from total defeat twice already. Its utility in saving England is another matter entirely. Perhaps we should keep it furled until the Germans are at Hadrian's Wall."

He smiled at her Scottish nationalism, took a deep breath, and watched as she slowly removed her service cap, letting her auburn locks swing free over the down pillow.

"Sit beside me, my love," she said. She patted the coverlet next to her as she handed him his refreshed tipple. An aroma of smoky whiskey, her perfume, and his desire filled the room. The traffic noise from Piccadilly faded into the background. "I believe Churchill and Dowding are right, but I also know it's right we're here. And we need each other for what time we may have left together," she added.

He sat beside her, the slack bed throwing their hips together. With two hands he sipped the whiskey. Its fire trickled down deep inside, burning out the distress he couldn't ignore until now. No ripples sloshed in his cup.

She calmly reached for the top button of her blouse and let it slip open.

He watched her move, her slender fingers adroit with the mother of pearl button. "Only fighter pilots are allowed to unbutton a top button."

"Then ye best have a go, Laddie." She crossed her arms behind her. Her breasts pushed against the tightness of her starched, light blue blouse, her nipples standing proud against the stretched fabric.

"No one ever accused you Scots of subtlety, except maybe when referencing your revered Robert the Bruce."

"Don't slight Bobbie Burns."

"Him as well."

He downed his whiskey with a lingering final sip, carefully reached for her, and unbuttoned her blouse with steady fingers, the tremors absent for a moment. White button after button fell open revealing a long plunge of creamy skin. She was nude under her service blouse.

"Did you forget to wear something?" he asked.

"Nae. A true Scotsman wears but naught under his kilt, and the world wonders. More's the pity that no one asks what a Scots lady wears, if anything, under her frock, or uniform for all that."

"So, you're not . . ."

" 'Tis but one way you'll find out, Laddie." She reached behind her back and unbuttoned her skirt, which fell loose, sliding down around her smooth, bare hips.

The feral growl of a Merlin engine at full chat, low and fast over the city of London, reverberated into the room through the open window. The V-12's lonesome wail cut through the plebian auto traffic noise outside on Picadilly like a border collie in a herd of highland sheep. The throbbing moan echoed off the Royal Air Force Club's unadorned, smooth plaster walls. Un-noticed by the Pilot and the Lass, the Merlin's cry died away as the Spitfire it powered disappeared, unseen, into the middle distance, back into the hard sky.

CHAPTER 15

AMERICAN EMBASSY

Place de la Concorde
Paris

April 2014: Early in 1915, the second year of the Great War, French scout pilot Roland Garros became the first aviator to shoot down an enemy aircraft using a machine gun firing forward through his aircraft's propeller arc. Garros was the first fighter pilot, the founding father of a family that, while under societal pressure, is extant today. He converted a technical curiosity, the aeroplane, into a deadly, dedicated, offensive weapon system and created an original form of warfare in an untouched arena, the previously peaceful sky. For this singular feat, years later the French government named the huge international tennis center outside Paris in his honor. There is no record of Garros ever playing, or being interested in, tennis.

The office of the US Ambassador to France measured only slightly smaller than a tennis court but boasted much more tasteful decorating. Burnished mahogany paneling, indirect lighting, deep carpets, and quality Louis XIV furniture--no expense had been spared. The recent remodel included security upgrades as well. Off to one side reigned the ambassador's desk, a dark, scarred oak artifact appearing old enough to have been used by one of his predecessors, perhaps Benjamin Franklin or Thomas Jefferson. The Pilot had never heard the story of the antique desk and wasn't likely to today when he arrived for a hastily-called meeting. Rich fabric sofas and settees, grouped around a cold fireplace, occupied the expansive room's other half.

The ambassador earned his coveted posting to Paris in the usual way, raising buckets of money for the US president's re-election campaign; ten million dollars was the rumored total. His professional experience stemmed from big-money show business, a valuable source of contacts and contributions. However, being the son of American diplomats and ambassadors, he understood the world of international diplomacy well. He also spoke fluent French, always an expectation held by the French government of the US Ambassador to France, but one rarely fulfilled.

As required at many high-profile American embassies, the ambassador's private fortune funded numerous social activities hosted by the embassy. The US State Department's stingy budget for the embassy in Paris proved woefully inadequate to cover the entertaining considered customary in the traditional diplomatic domain. The ambassador made up the difference by writing large personal checks. The in-house scuttlebutt alluded to around three million dollars a year. It was not a job for anyone without substantial means and the patriotic willingness to spend those means in support of the USA.

The State Department professionals who kept the wheels of diplomacy turning at the Embassy had expected the worst: a neophyte, or a naive rich jerk, an "ambassadonor." The pros were pleasantly surprised when the new ambassador soon proved himself thoroughly adept at his assignment. His top-flight education, international experience, business sense, and language skills quickly won him the respect of his French counterparts, as well as the embassy staff. The Pilot worked directly with the ambassador only infrequently but knew and liked him.

The Pilot entered the ambassador's office confidently, with quick, long strides. The ambassador was seated behind his desk. Without looking up, he motioned to a chair positioned front and center.

"Please sit down," the ambassador said. This was strange; the ambassador usually met with his staff seated on the sofas around the coffee table. The ancient desk was reserved for unfriendly meetings with difficult official visitors and for occasions requiring protocol niceties.

The lack of pleasantries and the omission of any mention of the Pilot's name or rank set off his internal alarm bells, alerting him that this meeting, arranged only just this morning, was not intended to be enjoyable or routine. Seated, the Pilot felt as if he should be standing at military attention waiting to be chewed out by a superior officer. The ambassador had always been unfailing polite and gracious in previous encounters, but the atmosphere in the hallowed room was different this time, cold and impersonal.

The Pilot studied the man across the desk from him, looking for a hint of today's probably unpleasant subject. The ambassador was of average height with jet black hair shaped by a haircut the Pilot estimated must have cost, at the least, a hundred Euros. His bespoke, dark wool suit fitted him impeccably, accented with a blue, solid-color silk tie shimmering in the sunlight from a nearby window. His habitual manner was of one accustomed to being listened to without needing to be dictatorial, one firmly in control due to his status and expertise. However, this situation appeared to be different, uncomfortable. Without looking up at the Pilot, he continued to read a series of papers, shuffling them top to bottom. Pursing his unsmiling lips as if steeling himself for an ordeal, the United States of America's Ambassador to France and Monaco was quite obviously stalling, reluctant to proceed.

A few feet away to the Pilot's right, sat an unfamiliar, thin man with a shaved head and dark eyebrows, wearing a pair of cheap, gray slacks, an ill-fitting white shirt, and a blue navy blazer crafted from the finest polyester. The man clutched a manila folder in his lap with both hands. While still staring at the papers on his desk, the ambassador introduced him with another wave of his left hand, "This is Mr., ah, Clark, from the Office of Special Investigations."

The Pilot knew Clark was not the man's name; OSI agents on covert assignment never use their real names. He thought the OSI could have at least given him an alias not shared by a re-occurring character in Tom Clancy's spy novels. "Clark" fidgeted with his dossier, obviously not comfortable breathing the office's rarefied air. He looked left and right, trying to blend in with the background, but in the large office, the walls reached far away. Clark avoided looking directly at the Pilot.

On the Pilot's left sat a US Air Force colonel in full, blue uniform complete with silver Command Pilot's wings and a chest tiled with multiple rows of multi-colored campaign ribbons. The colonel's posture was slightly more relaxed than Clark's, but he too frowned, also not happy with the situation. Him, the Pilot recognized. A wave of the ambassador's right hand introduced the colonel. "You two officers know each other, am I not right?"

"Yes, we do, Mr. Ambassador," replied the Pilot. Turning toward the colonel, the Pilot said, "Fred, I thought you were busy hunting down and taking out Muslim fanatics with killer drones."

"Fred" wasn't the colonel's real name either, and everyone in the room knew it. Anticipating the meeting to be a rebuke for him, the Pilot fired the first shot, indicating he knew "Clark" was an alias by giving the colonel an equally ridiculous handle. Sometimes the best defense is a good offense, particularly when you don't know what the game is or how the score is being kept.

"I'm still running anti-terrorism drone operations at the agency. There's an unlimited supply of targets; the airborne assassination business is booming, literally. But I try and keep my hand in counter-intelligence operations if the Cold War should return," the colonel said.

The colonel's presence confirmed the Pilot's suspicions that the subject of today's meeting was an intelligence matter and important. The agency wouldn't have flown him from CIA Headquarters in Langley, Virginia, to Paris for a routine task. The colonel wasn't in the military chain of command leading to the Air Attaché's Office at the embassy either; he must have been sent to France because of prior personal ties with the Pilot. This was unusual, but in the intelligence world, unusual is normal.

"Mr. Clark, show us your photos," the ambassador said, finally engaging. He fixed his eyes reluctantly on the Pilot.

Clark opened his tightly-held folder and handed it to the Pilot, careful not to let the contents, a stack of photographs, escape. Each print was a clandestine photo taken of the Pilot and his DGSE lover. The shots showed them at dinner in Le Café de la Paix across from the Opera Garnier, walking down the Champs-Elysées, in the forecourt of Notre Dame Cathedral, and leaving his apartment building. The sunlight and shadows in the last picture indicated it had been taken in the early morning hours.

The Pilot glanced at each photo and handed the dossier back to Clark with his fingertips, as if the folder contained toxic contamination he didn't want rubbing off on his hands.

The ambassador spoke first, looking directly at the Pilot for only the second time. "We have reason to believe the woman you're seeing is an agent for DGSE."

"Is that so? How did you make the determination?" asked the Pilot.

"We have been notified by reliable sources that her assignment is to gather information on the F-35 Joint Strike Fighter for the French intelligence service."

"I'm shocked. Shocked to find out that espionage is happening in this city," replied the Pilot, icy sarcasm dripping from every word.

The ambassador leaned back in his chair with his hands intertwined behind his neck and his arms out to each side like the wings of an angel. He stared at the Pilot as if seeing him in a new light--no longer a subordinate, perhaps a rival.

Clark spoke for the first time. "Did you know she's a DGSE agent?"

"Of course, that's part of my job. I communicate with DGSE frequently."

On a roll, Clark continued, "Yet you didn't report contact with a foreign intelligence agent as required by the regulations."

The Pilot turned to face Clark, leaned forward, and stared at him. The OSI agent sat erect, his spine pressed against the chair's back. The Pilot replied, "The regulation requires reports of contacts by agents of organizations hostile to the United States of America. The last time I checked, France was still a NATO ally. The regulation is written so I'm not tied up reporting every conversation with DGSE, the French Military Intelligence Service, the Brits' MI6, and so forth. You're OSI; you should know that. Maybe you should put down your spy camera and read the book again."

Clark flinched. His face grew red and beads of perspiration stood out on his bare scalp. Not used to a person under investigation pushing back, he opened his mouth to speak but didn't get a chance. The ambassador leaned forward toward the Pilot, injecting himself back into the crossfire, the no man's land between the two men. "It seems your liaison with DGSE has been particularly intense and focused on one rather attractive individual."

"Yes, that's true, but our relationship is purely social, which should be no one's concern but mine and hers."

Tapping his fingers on his desktop, the ambassador leaned back again and appeared ill-at-ease. He usually encouraged constructive dissent from his minions; the resulting debates reduced the chance of policy errors. But this was pushback powered by an afterburner. The Pilot's aggressiveness seemed to unsettle the ambassador, and his fingertips drummed faster. He nodded at the colonel, passing the problem along. It was Fred's turn to face the Pilot.

"The agency suspects she targeted you personally. You know the drill; in the intelligence world there are no purely social relationships. What questions has she asked you?"

"She asked if I was married."

"What difference would the answer have made?" the colonel said.

"For me or her?"

"Ladies, Ladies," the ambassador's newly-found diplomatic skills kicked in, "let's get to the real issue here, which isn't anyone's sex life."

The colonel took a deep breath, crossed his arms across his chest, and covered his campaign ribbons. He looked up at the ornate ceiling then down at the Pilot before speaking. "We know the French have a keen interest in the F-35 program. What we don't know is exactly what data they're seeking or why."

The Pilot reached into his inside jacket pocket and slid out his phone. It was switched off as per security procedures when meeting with the ambassador. He activated it, waiting for the icons to appear. The phone signed on, announcing its awakening by chiming the first few bars of "The Wild Blue Yonder," the classic fight song of the US Air Force.

"Why don't we just call and ask what they want to know? I've got good contacts at MIS; I'll give you their numbers. Aren't our allies, the French, read into the F-35 program?"

The colonel pointed at the Pilot's phone. His voice slightly louder and more insistent, he went on, not searching for the exact words to use--the Pilot realized the Colonel had rehearsed this speech earlier and was now delivering it by rote.

"Put your phone away. No, the French don't have full access. We think they're trying to find out how the F-35 communicates automatically with other aircraft and how it shares data among formation members, with wingmen. They probably want the protocols on how the relevant data is passed and how it's displayed in the cockpit."

The instant the colonel finished, the Pilot answered, his voice also raised. "Of course, they're interested in data sharing. The French Air Force knows it will have to coordinate with US forces in the air, in combat, in the future. Look at history. The French have flown with us in every major conflict since World War One, ever since there have been airplanes. Their Mirages and Rafales practice with us yearly in the big air combat war game in Nevada to perfect our mutual support tactics. If they can talk to us electronically, the more effective we'll both be in the next fight."

His voice a few notches calmer and lower in register than the two officers', the ambassador interjected, "I'm told the F-35's ability to pass tons of data is a key selling point. The embassy's Defense Sales Organization doesn't want to share that competitive edge with the French. Their Rafale jets compete with US aircraft manufacturers for sales around the world. I'm further told that DGSE routinely passes trade secrets to French industry.

"So, the issue isn't cooperation with a trusted ally, providing fighter pilots of both countries with an edge, but it's all about the financial well-being of the American companies building the F-35, and oh, by the way, running up big cost overruns. Those marketing people in defense sales will never go to war hampered by a French wingman they can't communicate with because we didn't share the password."

The Pilot thought, *Holy shit, I'm defending the F-35's connectivity. How did I get sucked into this game? I'm arguing for what I object to. Yikes!*

"The viability of the US aerospace industry is of key interest to the US Air Force," added the colonel.

"How is that different from the relationship DGSE has with Avions Marcel Dassault?" asked the Pilot. "I'm getting the message here that money trumps combat effectiveness between close allies. Isn't that what we're discussing? We could get pilots of both countries killed by maintaining sales quotas. Their intelligence agents help their industry, and our USAF officers pimp for ours. Do you have a sweetheart postretirement job lined up, Fred?"

The Pilot's intense gaze fixed on the colonel, his fists clenched at his sides. He hadn't realized he could get so emotional about a military/industrial relationship. Colonel Fred took a deep breath and held it, then exhaled slowly.

"I don't pimp for anybody. Today's subject is what you've told your girlfriend. You know I can have your security clearance yanked tomorrow, maybe later this afternoon. Without a clearance, you can't fly the F-35. You'll finish your career running the Officers' Club in Omaha. You need to decide what your goals are, my old squadron mate."

"The only goals I have are the same ones I set as a teenager: to put an end to poverty, achieve world peace, and hook up with Dolly Parton," the Pilot replied, anxious to quit the jousting lists and stop defending the F-35.

"And to shoot down five MiGs," colonel Fred added.

"Thanks for reminding me."

Fred's eyebrows narrowed, and Clark looked around seeking a rock to crawl under. The ambassador covered his mouth with his right hand but not quickly enough to hide his wide smile. He stood and put his palms on his desk to lean forward. Looking back and forth between the colonel to the Pilot, fixing his gaze on each in turn, he spoke.

"In the late 1700s, my predecessors would've suggested that you two settle this at dawn with pistols for two and breakfast for one in the Bois de Boulogne. Being of a more modern inclination, I believe we can work this out like the civilized gentlemen we aspire to be."

"I haven't told her squat about the F-35 that hasn't been in the papers or the trade journals."

"We want to know what she asked," said the colonel.

"She can't understand why I want to fly the jet."

"No technical details, no data, no insight into program issues?" Clark re-entered the fray.

"No, none of that. What do you want me to do, dump her?" The Pilot looked directly at the ambassador with his question, pointedly ignoring Fred and Clark. The ambassador, the Pilot's direct supervisor, suddenly found a verbal hand grenade rolled onto his historic desk, with the pin pulled. The colonel spoke anyway.

"We want you to continue your contacts and report on her questions. When we've figured out what she's after, we'll give you some bogus data to share to keep the queries coming. Or, you could dump her. In that case, we'll forget this conversation ever occurred and Clark will hit 'delete all' on his memory stick."

The pilot stood, walked behind his chair, and leaned on its back. He addressed the three seated men in turn, his vision locking onto each like a Sidewinder missile tracking an afterburner plume. "Let me get this straight. You're blackmailing me, using pictures of me dating another single person, threatening to end my career unless I shovel dysfunctional bullshit to a close ally to boost export sales for a company already extracting a mint from American taxpayers. And oh, by the way, you want me to avoid enhancing combat effectiveness of both our air forces."

It suddenly occurred to the Pilot that his impassioned speech to his immediate boss might have pre-empted the colonel and just ended the Pilot's career then and there. Ambassadors rarely enjoy being told off by subordinates. All to defend an overpriced turkey of an aircraft. *Nice morning's work,* he thought.

The large room was quiet, the traffic noise from the nearby Place de la Concorde barely audible through the bomb-resistant windows. The colonel broke the silence first. "Let the ambassador know what you decide. You have three days."

"Will that be all?" asked the Pilot.

The ambassador nodded yes; the Pilot turned to go but paused and looked back at the colonel. "Good luck flying those drones, Fred."

After the Pilot left the room and closed the door with a deep thump, the ambassador sat back slowly, his leather chair with its tall, bullet-proof back creaking, and looked at the other two men. "Well, this meeting didn't go exactly as we planned. I never expected that reaction. What should we have done better?"

The colonel thought for a moment, looked toward the Pilot's empty chair, which wasn't bullet-proof, and replied, "He responded about as I expected. The man who just left is what Tom Wolfe called a "single-combat warrior." He trained and honed as a fighter pilot, willing to go canopy-to-canopy--"

"Canopy-to-canopy? What's that?" the ambassador broke in.

"That's slang for homme-à-homme, man-versus-man. Close combat, a short-range dogfight. It's a game of full court one-on-one, first basket wins, the loser gets torched."

"So we've had a meeting with a single-combat warrior who has been working in the embassy all along, who knew?" the ambassador asked.

Meanwhile, "Clark" fidgeted with his dossier, glancing at the door as if he feared the return of the Pilot or was looking to make his escape.

Colonel Fred went on, "He's mentally prepared to go against the best the other side, whoever they are at the time, can put up. Pressure will always be taken as a challenge to people like our friend. I would've been deeply disappointed if he'd responded otherwise. We need guys like him; they win wars for us if we can keep them from self-destructing during peacetime. If it's any consolation to you, Mr. Ambassador, he was even harder to deal with when he was a captain."

"You seem to know his type well. What do you think he'll do?" asked the ambassador.

"We told him to keep banging his hot French squeeze with US government approval. We'll be lucky if he doesn't submit extravagant expense account reimbursement requests for candlelight dinners and condoms."

⟟

The Pilot swung closed the heavy, armored door to the ambassador's office and took the wide stairs down to the embassy's main entrance. He returned the salute of the US Marine stationed in the bullet-proof guard kiosk outside and turned left at the gate onto Avenue Gabriel for the few steps toward the Place de la Concorde. He needed to think, and he always thought more effectively with the sky above him. His absolute best thinking occurred with sky above and air beneath, but that wasn't possible now.

At the street corner at the Champs-Elysées, one of Paris's few remaining green circular billboards advertised the upcoming French Open tennis tournament with a poster plastered on its central column. The yearly event would soon take place at La Stade Roland Garros. Waiting for a break in the traffic, the Pilot flashed on the name "Roland Garros."

Roland Garros, he thought. *Now there was a man you could learn from, you moron. Regardless of the political and industrial espionage issues, I still have to strap myself into the F-35, fly, fight, win, and survive.* He recalled that shortly after Garros invented the fighter plane, engine failure forced him to land behind German lines, and he was taken prisoner. In 1918 he escaped and rejoined the French Air Force. But in the intervening three years, air fighting tactics had evolved rapidly. Garros's lone-wolf approach was sadly outdated, leaving him at the mercy of the squadron-sized German formations, whose pilots had learned to fly and fight as a team. Garros was soon hunted, shot down, and killed--murdered by a future he was unable to anticipate, or was unwilling to accept. *That could happen to me*, the Pilot considered, quickly looking away from the tell-tale tragic name glaring at him from the billboard.

He rapidly crossed the broad Place de la Concorde. The transit, as always, was an adventure in avoiding the swirling traffic. The French don't waste paint on pavement by marking traffic lanes as such regimentation would be totally ignored. When driving in Paris, it's "every man for himself."

The Pilot entered the Tuileries Jardines (the Gardens of the Tile Makers) at the gate by La Musée de l'Orangerie. He walked quickly toward the distant Louvre, his feet crunching the broad, tan gravel path. The day was not yet clear. A pale blue sky devoid of clouds formed a featureless, inverted bowl over the Pilot's head. Random thoughts chased themselves in Lufbery circles through his mind, refusing to roll out on a firm heading.

My options are limited. Who do I betray? My sexy lover, my country, a trusted ally, the USAF, or a hundred years of fighter pilot traditions? What about betraying all of the above? All I have to do is lie to a woman who is keeping her full identify secret, swallow my pride, and press on with the business of being a double agent. I can fly the new jet, keep my lover, at least for a time, and my career. The F-35 contractors might even name a tennis court after me. Or, I could dump her and still fly the F-35, unencumbered. But, flying the F-35 will entail ethical compromises and betrayals of past fighter pilots' hard-earned values. Maybe I should draw up a decision matrix, assign weights to the various options, run the numbers, and determine the least bad choice. Or, maybe I should just pull up my big boy pants and decide. He looked up at the hazy, indistinct sky, swallowed hard, took out his phone, and rang her number.

CHAPTER 16

L'Ile Saint-Louis

Paris

May 2014: The Pilot's island residence remained one of few in the city still retaining the services of a concierge. In the past, every apartment building in Paris employed such a building manager, usually an older couple or widow living in a tiny ground floor flat just off the foyer. The concierges let tradespeople in, did routine maintenance, kept an eye on things, and made it their business to know the tenants' affairs. Lately the gossipy concierges had been frequently replaced by younger couples called *gardiens*, who tended to take less interest in the occupants' private lives. But not in his building. The elderly concierge took a liking to the Pilot and treated him like a long-lost relative, a naive American who needed her guidance. She told him she was sorry to be losing him as a client and friend when he gave notice of his departure.

For the imminent move, most of the Pilot's personal gear was boxed and ready for removal, the cartons piled in the center of the salon. He looked at the dozen or so rough wooden crates and wondered how a lifetime of action could have resulted in such a modest stash of worldly goods. Like all US military officers, he knew moving well, every two years on the average. Long practice hadn't made the process any easier; the packing and forced emotional separation pained him, as always. He would miss Paris more than any of his many other stops; in

Paris he felt at home. The most difficult aspect would be leaving her behind. Already he experienced a sense of loss and saw an approaching dark cloud of aloneness. Once again he would be leaving unaccompanied, his lack of baggage mirroring his dearth of lasting relationships with the women who had passed through his life.

His small flat was in the process of changing its ambiance from his home to someone else's, or to nobody's. With his aviation art down from the walls, his clothes out of the armoire, his military mementoes packed, and his wine collection already shipped, the apartment returned to the slightly shabby, nondescript look of furnished rental property everywhere. Only a hint of her perfume lingered, a faint reminder of the good times, the sexy times, the intimate times they spent together there. The sense of smell is the most evocative at recalling the past, and Chanel No5 worked its magic on the Pilot. Soon the faint bouquet would fade. The moving company would come tomorrow, and that would be that.

The tinny speaker beside the door squeaked and then growled.

"Monsieur Américan, votre petite ami est là pour vous voir" (Your girlfriend is here to see you), the Concierge announced.

"Je vais descendre immédiatement" (I will come down now), he answered. He was reluctant for her to see the state of his flat with its emptiness or its depressing effect on him.

She greeted him in the foyer with a forced smile, dressed almost totally in black. Her skin-tight slacks, high-heeled boots, and soft leather jacket all mimicked her raven hair but were set off by a purple scarf and white sweater.

"Shall we grab a bite up the street?" he asked after the obligatory cheek-to-cheek air kisses.

"As you wish," she answered as she took his hand in hers.

The bistro Le Flore en l'Isle was on the island's upstream side at the end of the street, a short walk away. On the corner, stone bridges crossed the river to the bank on the right and to the larger island, Ile de la Cité, on the left. Despite the longer days of late spring, a cold breeze swept down the narrow street as they hurried along.

Twilight, is the time of day the French call *Le temps entre chien et loup* (the time between dog and wolf)--the time between daylight, the domain of the dog, and night, the realm of the wolf. It came early to the building-shaded island, throwing the sidewalk into deep shadow and hinting of the night to come.

The resident busker, seated on a folding stool on the bridge to the Ile de la Cité, pumped out "Petite Fleur" on his worn accordion. His crumpled black beret lay on the pavement in front of him, containing but a few coins, the loose change barely holding the hat down against the brisk wind. With no contributing tourists apparent in the gathering dusk, the street musician's business was slack.

The Pilot left her standing at the entrance to the bistro, crossed the narrow intersection, and placed a five Euro note into the old man's upturned iconic hat, arranging the coins to secure the note. "Jouez-le encore, Sam". (Play it again, Sam), he said to the aged accordion player. The Pilot looked back at her waiting on the corner. The busker ceased squeezing his ancient instrument and followed the Pilot's gaze. She stood there smiling, naturally now, unforced.

"Vous avez joué pour elle, maintenant jouez-le pour moi." (You played it for her, now play it for me.) The Pilot grinned as he made the request. The old man immediately launched into another rendition of "Petite Fleur," louder this time, mashing the stained keys with vigor and pumping the accordion harder. If he didn't understand the cinematic references to *Casablanca* within the Pilot's request, the musician readily grasped the significance of the five Euro tip. Holding open the door of the bistro for her, the Pilot could still hear the song's notes cascading down the lane.

"The theme song of Paris," she said.

"Yes, written by a Creole musician from New Orleans, who came to Paris and fell in love."

"Did the songwriter fall in love with Paris or a woman?"

"Both. Sidney Bechet never went home again."

The modest bistro's interior glowed warm, even overly so; establishments in cold climates tend to overcompensate for a chill outside with too much heat inside.

They took a table in the back, away from the door and its drafts of cool air. She sat on a padded bench seat with her back to the black-paneled wall.

Quickly shedding her jacket in the warm air, she revealed a tight, white, turtle-neck sweater, braless.

The pilot sat down across from her at the white-tiled table, looking left, then right, then left again as he slid onto a bentwood chair. No one in the restaurant sported a bald head or an obvious wig. But why should Clark be there, he thought. What additional information would more pictures provide?

She asked, "Are you uncomfortable sitting with your back to the room? Would you prefer to trade places?"

"It didn't work out too well for Wild Bill Hickok, but I'll chance it. Merci bien anyway."

"Was Wild Bill a squadron mate of yours? What happened to him?"

"No, he was a gunfighter and lawman of the old American west, not a friend. Hickok always had his back to the wall while playing cards; his game was poker. In a big game one night in Deadwood, South Dakota, he broke his own rule, sat with his back to the door, and got shot in the head. I would've liked to meet him."

"Sacrebleu, I'll warn you if an armed cowboy approaches." She laughed after she said it but then continued in a more serious vein, "We French are perplexed about this American fascination with cowboys. Here calling an individual a 'cowboy' is not a compliment. It refers to a person who acts impetuously, who doesn't plan ahead. Maybe even someone out of control."

"Who solves most problems with gunfire? Maybe that's something we Americans need to address--proposing a kinetic solution to every issue."

"A strange thing to say by someone prepared to shoot down other pilots with gunfire."

"There are also missiles; cowboys didn't have them."

"We can be thankful for that," she said as the server appeared, standing over their table.

They ordered *moules-frites*, mussels steamed in white wine, garlic, and butter; with twice-fried potatoes, bread, and a bottle of Sancerre. The Loire valley white wine's crisp acidity would cut through the mussels' richness; the baguette would beg to be torn and dipped in the large serving bowl, absorbing the rich broth bathing the shells.

She got right to the point as they waited for their meal, leaning over the table to speak softly. "Have you made a decision on flying this new aircraft? What are you to do?"

"Yes, I'm reporting to the training base in Florida and trying to cope."

"Cope? You don't sound enthusiastic. I still don't understand your reluctance; everything I read about the F-35 says it is the most advanced fighter jet in the world. Why would you not jump at the opportunity? Is there doubt in your mind you can fly it? If so, that would not be like the fighter pilot I know."

"No, flying the jet would come naturally. What I would have to endure is the electronic baggage attached to the F-35."

"Tell me about that. Not the details; I would have to report those to DGSE. I'm sorry to pry, but by now you know I'm in love with you. I'm concerned for you and this hard choice you have made. What truly bothers you? The prospect of combat? The killing involved? Or the danger?"

"It's my turn to say sacrebleu. So many questions, each deeper than the last. I'll try to answer them without arousing your professional curiosity."

The waiter brought the wine, pulled the cork, and half-filled their glasses with a quick splash. The Pilot took a sip of his, nodded to the server, and looked back at her into those deep, dark eyes. The bistro was becoming crowded with more customers showing up at the work day's end. The noise level rose as more chairs filled. The Pilot traded confidentiality for clarity and raised his voice more than he wanted to in order to be heard.

"Is it the danger? No. From the first day of pilot training, you're conditioned to ignore the fatal possibilities of your profession. By the time you graduate to flying fighters, you've been totally desensitized; fear isn't allowed to affect your performance."

"But surely you must think about it?"

"No, you can't let your mind go there. You're aware of the danger; you deal with it. Danger is a whetstone sharpening your reactions, making you perform at the top of your game. Anyway, the F-35 is so god-awful expensive it isn't allowed to crash."

Two young men at a nearby table discussed the latest scintillating zero-zero score on the local soccer pitch, oblivious to the Pilot and his lover. In the close quarters of a Parisian bistro, it is *de rigueur* to not eavesdrop on the adjacent table, even if one understands the language.

"As for combat, that's what you live for, prepare for, volunteer for. Training as a fighter pilot and not flying in combat would be like practicing for the football team and never getting on the field for a game."

The waiter brought their dinner--the bowl of mussels steaming of garlic, the French fries piping hot, no ketchup in sight. She waited until the server laid a long baguette on the table and departed before she spoke.

"The comrades you've lost in combat, what about them?"

"I see their faces at night . . ."

"I know you do," she interrupted.

"How do you know that?"

She hesitated for an instant. Tearing off a piece of bread, she dipped it into the broth and ate the damp bread with a mussel pried from its shell. Taking another sip of wine, she looked into his eyes. "I see it in your eyes in the morning, and I wonder who you have been dreaming about. I know it's not another woman; you're too sad. . . . You're avoiding the final subject, the killing." Her answer satisfied him, but her last question was troubling.

He refilled their glasses, and the scent of new-mown hay and fresh citrus rose from the wine. The young couple beside them heatedly discussed which candidate for Mayor of Paris would be less dangerous to the bourgeoisie. If the pair heard the Pilot and his lover, they gave no indication of recognition. Evidently a conversation about using airplanes to kill people fit into the local buzz; soccer, politics, air combat, why not?

"The killing? I try not to lose sleep over the folks who get sent off. They would have done the same to me and slept just as well."

"You don't sound very at ease about the killing."

"I have to be, or I couldn't do my job. The killing isn't the problem; it's the growing numbness to the killing. When you don't care, part of your humanity dies with the people you kill. A bigger issue is trying to live a normal life between episodes of killing. You can't let it affect you."

At the table beside them, the two football fans were of the opinion that the French national team, Les Bleus, had an excellent chance to tie Italy on Saturday. The couple on the other side despaired of Paris ever being run honestly.

"So, what is it?" She finished her wine with the last of the mussels and sopped up more garlic-laced broth. He refilled her glass and leaned back in his chair, holding his own glass in both hands.

"To answer I'll have to tell you something I've never told anyone who isn't a fighter pilot. And I haven't told any of them because they already know."

"So why are you telling me?"

"Because I'm in love with you. I want you to know what makes me tick."

"Tick as in a time bomb?"

"No, I don't think so. The problem I have with the F-35 is the electronic connectivity you are supposed to be asking me about." He spoke softly, almost in a whisper. Her face showed a moment of surprise when he mentioned her assignment, but she recovered quickly. Her dark eyebrows arched in anticipation.

"Isn't this ability to communicate with everyone a big advantage?"

"To the control bureaucracy it is. Not if you're a fighter pilot. Since World War I, we've bonded with our planes. We've always been a team, my aircraft and me. We live and sometimes die on our ability to outmaneuver, outshoot, outthink the Bad Guys. See the enemy first and defeat him, or now her. In this marvelous F-35 everything is supervised by others far away, through a data link. You can't even see the Bad Guys behind you; there's a tall metal bulkhead sticking up behind the cockpit. It's as if they made it necessary to use the electronics instead of your eyes. For decades we pressed the engineers for the ability to see behind us, for big clear canopies. Now that's gone. In the F-35, you peer out a porthole." His voice rose louder now, too loud, and he fell silent. Another drink of wine and a hunk of bread dunked into the mussel bowl punctuated the sudden quiet at their table. On each side, the conversations continued. He stabbed at the bread with three fingers.

"This ability to understand the whole picture, we call 'situational awareness.' Now we're spoonfed situational awareness through some ethernet along with instructions. The orders are generated by the aircraft software or handed down from a command post manned by people who will live out the day no matter what happens to us in the air."

"So, you want to fight on your own without help or interference from the ground or the bosses, the way it used to be, no?" she asked, holding her wine glass by the base and looking over it to him. He couldn't avoid thinking how lovely she was.

"Yeah, something like that."

"Are you in search of lost times? Marcel Proust wrote you can't go back."

"Do you believe that?"

"I'm French. I had to believe Proust to pass my baccalauréat exam. But isn't this new technology progress? If we can't go back, we must go forward."

He picked up the uneaten half-baguette, skinny and tubular with a rounded tip. "Look at this bread. It's not one of Proust's invocative madeleine pastries but a good example all the same. It's pale white, only a thin ridge of brown crust on top. When you rub it, it slides in your hand; it doesn't squeak and crumble. The inside is chewy, soft, flabby. This is what you get for a baguette in Paris today. Is this progress?"

"Most Parisians think so. This new style of bread takes less energy to bake, it doesn't stay in the oven long enough to fully toast. It lasts longer, doesn't get stale in a few hours. One can receive it in the morning and sell it that night, or even the next day, for less waste."

"But what does it taste like? Nothing, that's what. You have to dunk it into buttered broth with white wine to perceive any flavor. It's new, it's more profitable, it's politically and evironmentaly correct, but it's not progress." He let the pointed half loaf fall off his fingers into the mussel bowl where it lay flaccid atop the empty shells.

"We talk about fighter planes, not boulangeries," she said.

"Fighter planes, yes, but the real issue is the way humans interact. Look around you; what do you see people doing?"

He turned to survey the twenty or so customers in the dimly lit bistro. The sickly-blue glow of phones illuminated half the faces. Three couples sat across from each other, oblivious to the other's presence. Staring at electronic displays cradled in their hands, each stroked their phone with their fingertips, like lovers.

The *Mâtre'd* punched a computer monitor with his index fingers, ignoring the customers. The bartender, who usually needed no excuse to disregard customers, tapped on his own terminal glowing behind the bar. The expected clamor of chattering patrons was diluted by silence as cell phones were consulted continuously. Even the two tables on either side of them now fell quiet, the diners reading their phones.

"This joint looks like the crew room of an F-35 squadron," he said. He knew she observed the same scene but wondered if she saw the same things. "Total electronic connectivity, all the time. No individual situational awareness. No personal interaction. Electronic zombies," he added.

"This connectivity is what interests DGSE, as you have guessed."

"I haven't told you how it works. Aren't they demanding hard intelligence data? What do they want to know?"

"They expect me to pass along information from you when you are in training. They'll have specific questions then."

"Isn't this when you offer me a hundred Euros for some trivial data, like an internal embassy phone book? I sign for the C-note, and I'm hooked as an agent by the incriminating receipt."

She sighed and replied, "Your counterintelligence training needs updating. That technique is passée; we do it electronically now. The ancient plan you describe targets an acclimatization engineer, not an officer, and I certainly wouldn't be sleeping with him."

"A maintenance man makes a better spy than a fighter pilot. I'm crushed."

"Yes, they can go anywhere invisibly in the embassy."

"I can go anywhere, as well."

"In the ladies' toilette? . . . I'm surprised you are taking the assignment; you feel so strongly about what the F-35 might do to you. Thank you for sharing your thoughts with me. That's enough business for tonight. When do you leave?"

"I'm on the last Eurostar train from Gare du Nord to London tomorrow night. I have to get a flight physical at a USAF base near there. I hoped we could share one last special dinner in Paris." He didn't mention the day-long meeting scheduled with the CIA in the US embassy in London. The agency would give him instructions on how to handle future contacts with her. "Where would you like to dine, assuming you're free? La Tour d'Argent, Taillevent, Le Coup Chou?" Price was not a factor; he intended to charge the bill to the ambassador's account.

"Why not Fouquet's? It will be romantic on the Champs-Elysées."

"Fouquet's? 'No one goes there anymore. It's too crowded.' "

"That sounds like something the yogi you are fond of quoting would say. You never told me, is he an Indian yogi?"

"That's because he did say it, and he's more of a Yankee Yogi. Fouquet's it is. We can discuss how to keep in touch and when we can see each other again."

"Aren't you playing poker with your back to the door? Come and sit by me," she said, patting the padded bench seat with her hand.

He ignored her last question and slid onto the bench seat next to her, facing the door. She took his right hand and placed it between her thighs, high up against her crotch, and slipped her left hand between his legs, both motions out of sight beneath the table. He curled his fingers around her taut thigh, feeling the silkiness of her legs and her lady part's softness through her thin slacks, only a single layer of gossamer fabric between his fingers and her skin.

"Is this when you seduce me?" he asked.

"I've already done that; I can feel it. This is when we go back to your flat."

He paid the bill, and they left hand in hand, walking purposefully toward his place. Dark now, the island was almost deserted. The street was barren of moving cars and the old man with his accordion were long gone. The short bridge to Notre Dame was empty, and only a few people were visible, each hurrying home. The omnipresent quiet was an almost physical presence between the banks of the Seine. The apartment buildings hugging both sides of the narrow way funneled and accelerated the west wind, the breeze colder now and blowing constantly. The airstream chilled their faces, sending a few discarded scraps of newspaper, missed by the street sweepers, scuttling along the sidewalk like berserk albino crabs.

Excessive heat is easily forgotten once dissipated. As they quickly left the overly warm bistro behind, no thermal memories lingered. But the body never forgets cold; past discomforts are always lurking in deep memory, easily summoned by a random stimulus, a familiar sight, or the intruding sensation of present-day cold. The numbness of an earlier, icy time, a time before his birth, surfaced in his consciousness. The freezing feeling resident in his mind was a collective, painful memory of an artic-like wind, a ninety mile an hour slip-stream. A cold that could etch snow swirls on one's very soul. Familiar in its intensity and recognizable in its frigid flow, it brought back memories passed down by others--all of the recollections freezing cold, all of them unforgettable. The Parisian wind sent an uncontrollable shiver up the Pilot's spine. It was a familiar sensation, one he had endured before and would again, soon.

CHAPTER 17

THE WESTERN FRONT

France

March 1918: At eighty knots airspeed (ninety miles an hour), the Sopwith Camel's cockpit was cold, biting cold fed by the winds of flight. Cold penetrated the Pilot's dirty cotton Burberry trench coat and his fleece-lined boots, stung through his thick leather gloves, ignored his leather flying helmet, and frosted his goggles. The air at twelve thousand feet was gaspingly thin, and the thinness allowed the cold access down to his very core, sluicing through him like a wispy, icy river. With his left hand, he tugged his white silk scarf farther up over his mouth, tightening it around his neck snuggly. The rough-woven silk afforded little protection from the freezing wind stream, but it filtered out the worst of the oil fumes from the engine.

The Gnome rotary engine whirling away under its tight aluminum cowling in front of him kept all its combustion heat for itself, emitting only the occasional whiff of castor oil. The Pilot's silk scarf strained some of the sickening odor and also reminded him not to lick his lips, however cold and chapped they might get. An inadvertent dose of castor oil would have serious repercussions in his bowels, probably before he could land. During the two-hour flight, his face, goggles, and scarf would accumulate a grimy misting of used, black lubricating oil.

At least now he wouldn't have to endure the coating of whale blubber applied to every exposed inch of bare skin on his face, an attempt to prevent frostbite when flight at very high altitude was planned. Before his squadron transitioned into the Camel, they often flew above 20,000 feet in the Camel's predecessor, the Sopwith Pup.

The Camel's cockpit was comprised of nothing more than a cramped plywood box fitted with a padded wicker seat and a few flight instruments in round brass cases painted black to eliminate sun glint. There was no parachute; senior British officers, none of whom were aviators, in their infinite wisdom believed the provision of parachutes would induce cowardice among the pilots. Perhaps this misconception stemmed from the actions of crewmembers of observation balloons who abandoned their hydrogen-filled, explosive gas bags frequently, taking to their parachutes at the first sign of air attack. The generals evidently equated fighter pilots with balloonists, another indication of rank incompetence in the higher echelons.

A varnished oak control stick and pivoting rudder bar constituted the flight controls. The thin, wooden structure made no attempt at providing any pilot comfort whatsoever. It was incapable of keeping out cold air, much less German bullets.

Outside the cockpit, on top of the fuselage and directly in front of his face were the circular butts of two Vickers machine guns. They were mounted under a sheet metal fairing humped on top of the fuselage, hence the aircraft's nickname. The dromedary housing represented an attempt to keep the guns somewhat warm and the lubricant in them unfrozen. The Pilot was on his own in keeping warm. The top of the oak control stick mounted a leather-wrapped ring, easy to grasp with thick leather gloves. At the base of the ring were two small paddle levers falling readily to his right thumb. Pushing either or both levers pulled on wires connected to the guns' triggers. A quick stab at the paddles woke up the guns, chattering with smoke, muzzle flashes, vibration, and a stream of lead. The guns fired unevenly, out of rhythm, as the interrupter gear momentarily suspended individual shells from firing, allowing bullets to pass without interference through moving gaps in the spinning propeller disk. The guns, if not the Pilot, were unfrozen, ready.

As cold as he was, the Pilot had no time to dwell on his discomfort. His Sopwith Camel was a sonofabitch to fly, requiring constant attention to the stick and rudder. Nearly all airplanes are aerodynamically stable; they want to fly straight and level. Dip a wing, and that wing wants to come back up. Raise the nose, and the nose will fall back to the horizon on its own. A pilot can take his hands from the stick, and the aircraft will continue flying straight and level for a few moments. Not the Camel. It was unstable, even divergent, in all three axes: roll, pitch, and yaw. Dip a wing, and the aircraft wanted to bank tighter. Raise the nose, and it wanted to keep coming up. The location of the biplane's mass made matters worse. The engine, the fuel tank, the pilot, and, most importantly, the guns, its *raisons d'être*, were concentrated in one tight section of the airframe. The upper and lower wings, tail, and rudder, lightly built of dry spruce covered with muslin cloth and thick paint, offered little weight to offset the heft of mass in the middle of the fuselage. The inherent instability and concentration of mass gave the little airplane ferocious maneuverability. Light on the controls, it could flit, turn, and loop, responding instantly. The Camel was smaller than its contemporaries, aiding its agility, but like them was little more than a feather-built, wooden frame covered with lacquered cloth and held taut by tense guy wires. The flying wires' tension hinted of stored energy, like an English longbow, all bent yew wood and stretched linen bowstring.

The Camel's engine affected its flight path when turning. The Gnome rotary's nine cylinders and crankcase, the heaviest parts, were bolted to the propeller and spun with it. The pistons and crankshaft, much lighter components, didn't move relative to the firewall at the rear of the engine. This heavy, rotating mass spinning at twelve hundred rpm generated a gyroscopic effect, a precession, which could not be mitigated, only dealt with. When turning to the right, the Gnome gyro would gladly push the nose down. Turning left against the gyro's precession, the engine would try to raise the nose. A steep right turn tended to get even steeper as the gyroscopic precession pulled the nose farther and farther down. Conversely, a left turn saw the nose wanting to come up, slowing the aircraft and risking a stall. Skillful use of the rudder was required to extract maximum performance, countering the spinning engine. Instead of being a willing steed, ever obedient to the Pilot, its rider, the Camel had a mind of its own.

One didn't merely command the Camel; each maneuver involved a rudder-based negotiation with its headstrong engine.

One simplicity the Sopwith Camel offered the Pilot was freedom from worrying about the throttle setting; there was no throttle. The engine either ran at full power or not at all. On the control stick sat a thumb button with two wires leading to it. Pressing the button cut power to some of the spinning engine's spark plugs, causing the engine to sputter and miss and reducing the power output a second or two--a feature useful for adjusting a landing glide slope. But if the switch were pressed for too long or at too high an altitude, the plugs would foul with castor oil, and the engine would die. This on/off power delivery made airspeed control difficult--too slow and the Camel would stall, then the whirling engine would wind it up into a particularly nasty spin. Recovery was problematic. Otherwise, it was full speed ahead at all times, making formation flying difficult as each aircraft liked to fly at a slightly different speed.

Lofty and Paddy, the RAF mechanics assigned to tend to this Camel's needs, once asked the Pilot what it was like flying their "kite." Without a word, the Pilot picked up a broom from the squadron workshop's oily floor and balanced it vertically, upside down, in the palm of his hand. He had to jockey constantly and quickly to keep the broom balanced. Eventually, it fell, landing on the floor with a clatter. As he walked toward the Officers' Mess, he looked back and saw Paddy trying to balance the Sopwith Camel broom.

Fighting the relentless cold while continually re-balancing the airplane, the Pilot flew between ragged cloud layers. A few thousand feet overhead, a solid deck of gray diffused the weak spring sun, its pale orb discernible only as a fuzzy, white glow. Passing five hundred feet below the Camel, a layer of broken scud occupied half the sky. The ragged clouds made navigation difficult with familiar landmarks intermittently hidden; only sections of the Great War's trenches were constantly visible. The trench lines ran in jagged courses northwest and southeast to both horizons, taking random paths across the war-blasted earth with no plan obvious from above. The land of northwestern France was forsaken by God and abused by man--gray, barren, and desolate, dusted with broken patches of dirty snow. No fields were left un-churned by artillery fire. The few trees remaining upright were only twisted sticks. Ruined villages everywhere, no one living there to work those cursed fields. Between the two wandering ranks of trenches, the no-man's-land appeared even more hideously tortured. A miasma of mud festered with shell craters half-filled with brown water, the landscape was dotted with the hulks of wrecked tanks, their crews moldering inside.

Its engine droning, the little biplane floated on alone high above the stench of modern warfare, immune from the effects of drifting wisps of poison gas. With gray clouds and frozen mist streaming by the cockpit, the cold air at altitude was clean with no olfactory traces of the rotting carnage slowly passing far beneath. The skies seemed empty of life but not benign. German aircraft could be lurking in the dark scud off to the east or waiting to dive with the wan sun at their backs, their malign presence fouling the air they flew through. The Pilot and his Camel were just as lethal to German flyers, equally eager to snuff out their lives given half a chance and a clear shot. The two sides' aircraft and their pilots operated in the antiseptic, atmospheric domain of airborne war but were themselves the dirtiest things in the air--smoking, leaking oil, spewing hot lead, and promising each other fiery deaths.

Unsure of where he flew, the Pilot knew if he kept the westernmost trench lines under his left lower wing as he flew northward, he could be assured of gliding into friendly territory in the not uncommon occurrence of an engine failure. To score a kill, he would have to venture farther east over German lines. The Germans rarely flew west; they tended to patrol over their own troops. The Royal Air Force squadron's intelligence officer reported that the Huns were forbidden to fight above the Allies. German High Command had seen too many irreplaceable pilots, like the Red Baron, shot down by ground fire. Live, downed pilots would be captured and lost to the war effort. Plus, the Germans seemed to know their enemies--only the RAF would come to them. The French and the Americans tended to stay to the west, over friendly trenches.

The Pilot sensed the weather urging him to patrol farther over the German lines. A strong west wind was blowing the broken clouds relentlessly, taking his Camel along with them to the east. He began a gentle right turn toward the far trench lines and watched his projected track across the twisted ground directly below. He and his aircraft were accelerated eastward by the frigid wind. It would be a good day for solo hunting, alone in the air with no junior pilots to watch out for. As the commander of his RAF fighter squadron, he had the authority to pick his missions, flying solo when the weather was marginal, like today. Lone-wolf hunting was becoming a thing of the past; both the Allies and the Huns were mounting larger and larger formations of aircraft. Many-versus-many dogfights had become common, and the squadron formations could, and did, gang up on solo flyers. The Pilot only occasionally left the routine patrols and boring escort missions in good weather to his less-experienced subordinates. He would fight alone today, hoping to avoid the fate of French ace Roland Garros, who was jumped by a whole Hun squadron, hunted down, and killed easily and quickly.

Turning the aircraft south, the Pilot passed over the German lines, crabbing into the wind, then banked right, paralleling the zigzagging trenches. His constant scanning of the skies around him finally paid off. Something caught his eye just behind his lower right wing--a speck of bright color moving faster than the background of tattered gray clouds. Quickly he checked the position of the sun; it was well above the horizon and behind his upper left wing. Perfect! He was up-sun from the unidentified aircraft below him. He made another search of the air around him, left and right, forward and aft, up and down. Nothing there at any distance, he could safely focus on the mystery craft for a short time. Remembering the lesson he constantly hammered into the junior pilots of his squadron, "Watch out for the Hun in the sun," he checked up-sun once again. Still nothing. No one there, the sky was empty yet still menacing. He banked right, letting the nose fall and diving for more airspeed. With his engine singing a higher-pitched note, he closed in on the stranger.

Weaving through the deck of broken clouds, between layers, and sometimes tearing through the ragged sheet of scud, flew a Fokker Triplane painted in a garish pattern of red and yellow, with black Maltese crosses outlined in white displayed on the rudder and top wings.

Bloody hell, thought the Pilot. This solo Hun had to be a member of Von Richthofen's *Jasta 11*, the Flying Circus. No other aircraft would sport such an outlandish paint scheme. The Red Baron was dead, of course. They were all dead now--Voss, Boelcke, Immelmann, Böhme--so who could this lone airman be? Göring? Now the wing commander of the Circus, he needed the protection provided by his subordinates while he killed. He wanted witnesses to validate his ever-mounting scores; his victories were not shared with his subordinates. Göring was not known to fly alone. It could be Göring separated from the rest of the Circus by the rotten weather. Whoever this chap was, he was good. The Huns only issued three-winged Fokkers to their aces. Perhaps this solitary Hun was a decoy, bait for the unwary or over-aggressive. If he dove on the singleton, would the rest of the Circus be above and behind him? Another quick look above and behind the Camel showed no enemy in easy sight.

The Pilot's mind raced, considering alternatives and making choices. He could turn back west and fly safely home; the slower triplane couldn't run down a Camel. No one would know he had avoided combat. No one but him, that is. But he didn't get airborne alone to refuse battle, particularly when he held the tactical advantage. No, that just wasn't on; fight he would. To win he would have to be at the top of his game. If the lone German was indeed Göring, the Pilot had to act quickly before the supporting Circus found and rejoined their boss.

The German still hadn't seen him. Perhaps he was intent on his mission, too focused on finding an easy kill and not watching the airspace around him--a possibly fatal mistake. *Maybe he's looking for the RAF photo ship known to be working the area*, the Pilot quickly concluded. A slow, droning, two-man camera bird would be easy prey for the Hun. The other British pilot would be vulnerable, busy navigating with precision. His pictures were of little use if the photo interpreters didn't know the exact locations of the subjects. The observer would be distracted, operating his heavy view camera and shuffling delicate glass negatives. Preoccupied, he would be unlikely to keep a keen watch around his lumbering craft. Their defensive machine gun stowed out of the way, useless, both crewmembers would be unaware of the predatory Fokker stalking them, hiding and lurking above them in the frozen mist. The reconnaissance bird would be below the clouds for maximum visibility and better photography, but the triplane could hide in the scud until the final, deadly attack, a falcon floating in the gray nothingness and eyeing a hapless pigeon. The sure fate of the reconnaissance crew cemented the Pilot's resolve; he must kill this German now or two more friendly lives would be snuffed out straightaway.

The cloud deck hiding the German also prevented him from picking up the Pilot's Camel floating above the triplane. *This has to be good, and it has to be quick, and it has to be now, before he sees me,* thought the Pilot. The triplane employed an Oberusel rotary engine similar in concept to the Camel's Gnome but copied from the French Le Rhône mill. Both aircraft liked to turn right, pitching downward as they turned. Under attack, the Hun would try to lure the Pilot into a right-turning, circular fight. The triplane could turn tighter than the Camel, and the German would soon be on the Pilot's tail in the circle. No, he had to avoid the descending spiral the French called a "Lufbery," named for unknown reasons after a French-American ace, Raoul Lufbery. Likewise, a vertical, looping engagement would be fatal; the triplane could out-climb the Camel. The Pilot had to employ his airplane's strengths if they were to fight and win together. He possessed speed, height, and the blurry sun on his side; those would have to do, along with a good plan and better shooting.

Stalking the stalker, he closed the gap between them. Following the triplane winding through the clouds, he watched the Camel's blurry shadow projected on the clouds below him. He wanted to be in the sun but without his telltale shadow falling on the German pilot and alerting him. Five hundred yards, four hundred yards, three hundred yards, almost there, surely he would be spotted soon. Just ahead he could see an opening in the clouds, a ragged gap of a mile or so in diameter. The clearer air would be their gladiators' arena. But he had to shape the fight before they reached it. Once the German left the clouds, he would spot the Camel trailing him.

At one hundred fifty yards' range between them, the triplane emerged from under the protective cloud deck. The Pilot banked sharply right and down, blending firm inputs from the control stick. His feet were held tightly by the leather straps on the rudder bar, allowing him to push the nose to the right. Letting the spinning engine take the Camel where he wanted it to go, he sensed the aircraft come alive with the blood lust of the hunt. Now the German sensed, or more likely heard, the Camel in its dive. The Pilot saw his quarry twist in the cockpit, looking back and up over his left shoulder. With a left foot jab at the rudder and a control stick shift of the left aileron, the Pilot stopped the Camel's nose in its turning dive. Peering through the Aldis gun sight, an oil-smeared glass ring firmly mounted on the cowling in front of him, he pointed the etched cross ahead and to the right of the German. The next move was the Hun's. If he turned into the attack, as all junior pilots were taught to do, the Pilot's gun pass would be spoiled; he would not be able to reverse his turn against the triplane quickly enough to bring the guns to bear. In that case, the Pilot intended to continue his dive, blow through the aborted fight, and run west, leaving the slower triplane behind in his wake. Without a clear tactical advantage, there was no sense in engaging an enemy ace.

The German proved as experienced as his choice of mount suggested; he turned right and down, trying to suck the Pilot into a Lufbery spiral. Had he made the decision to turn left, the fight would have been over, a draw, but his aggressiveness, his thirst for another kill, wouldn't let the German break it off. The instant the Pilot saw the key indicator he was looking for, the triplane's wings rolling into a right bank, the thumb of his right hand pushed both mechanical trigger tabs hard. The guns barked a cacophony of noise, smoke, and vibration, their pounding vibrating the Camel's light airframe from nose to tail, wingtip to wingtip. White-hot tracer bullets streaked past harmlessly in front of the triplane, their ballistic paths curving slightly downward. The German saw the tracers ahead of him and tried to reverse his turn, but too late. He flew right into the bullet stream. Ignoring the shaking of his aircraft, the cordite fumes' acrid smell filling his nostrils, and the rapidly decreasing range between the two machines, the Pilot held down the triggers. He turned with the German, right then left, keeping the rudimentary gun sight over the Fokker until the red and black aircraft filled his field of view.

As the Pilot watched, his chattering machine guns destroyed the Fokker as a flyable aircraft. Splinters of wood were blasted loose and left behind spinning in the air. Shards of metal sparkled as they flew off the doomed scout. Several square panels of scarlet and yellow cloth tore loose from the wings, flapping in the slipstream, still attached to the trailing edges. The delicate, naked, wooden ribs were revealed beneath. Angry, jagged holes sprouted everywhere. Still he pressed the triggers, the guns barking like the whore hounds of hell. There came a flash, then three more, then a spark, and a sheet of flame burst from the fuel tank. Streaming back toward the cockpit, the fire ignited the flammable paint-soaked covering, as it flared and consumed the aircraft that bore it.

The German made his last decision. He preferred spending his last sixty seconds of life falling rather than burning. He stood, shielding his face from the licking flames with both arms folded, and let the airstream tear him from the cockpit. He fell behind the flaming Fokker, end over end, his brown leather greatcoat fluttering in the cold air until he disappeared, a tiny speck falling, falling into the hazy air until the disappearing dot was indistinguishable from the dun-colored earth far below. The Pilot released the triggers, his guns falling silent; only the drone of his engine and the rush of the slipstream could be heard.

The Pilot quickly scanned the horizon and checked behind his tail for any wingmen accompanying the Hun and found nothing; the mile-wide hole in the clouds and the air above and below it were empty and silent. To the south, just under the cloud layer, two Englishmen in their slow photo bird toiled on taking photographs, blissfully unaware of how close they came to oblivion.

The Pilot turned the Camel southwest toward his home aerodrome and pushed the nose down in a gradual descent. He saw in his mind's eye the Hun tumbling down, down, down, still alive, but not for long. Except for one bad decision made by the German, it could have been the Pilot dead. His body was soaked with sweat, and the cold returned, gripping and freezing him. It was a cold not only of temperature but also of the spirit, the aftermath of the cold-blooded killing of another human being. Shivering, he leaned his head out over the leather-rimmed side of the cockpit, vomiting violently. The discharge smeared along the fuselage, freezing in place quickly at this altitude. Cleaning it off would earn Lofty and Paddy a bottle of "liberated" French brandy, not for the first time. He would tell them it was due to breathing the castor oil fumes. They might even believe him this time.

The long glide back to base gave him time to think, time to contemplate what he had just done, all the while scanning the sky for dangerous opponents, like the Circus, or further opportunities, like other isolated, vulnerable pilots of the Circus available for the taking. Who was the Hun he had just killed? Perhaps it was Göring. If so, it would be in all the Berlin newspapers, and British spies would pick it up, reporting the news to his squadron's intelligence officer. Ordinarily he took no pleasure in killing a fellow aviator, even one who would have most certainly killed him were their roles reversed. But he would sleep easier in the future if it were indeed Göring whom he saw falling end over end down to the freezing mud waiting far below. It is a rare wing commander who is loathed by his men, as Göring was rumored to be for his ego and selfishness, for sacrificing his men for his personal glory, using them as bait, and assigning them to fly behind him and soak up bullets. The intelligence reports were clear on that point. Göring, if it was him, was well-served by death, not because he was the enemy, an agent of imperial German aggression, but because he habitually violated the fighter pilot's code of conduct. He flew dishonorably. Not like Von Richthofen and Böhme, who were buried with full military honors in ceremonies befitting worthy adversaries and laid to rest by the Royal Flying Corps, as the RAF was then known. The Pilot hoped it was Göring who plunged to his death. From all accounts, the war effort and the world after the war would be better off without that rotter.

CHAPTER 18

LE COUP CHOU RESTAURANT

5th Arrondissement

Paris

November 1918: An august assembly of generals and politicians had signed the armistice in a railway carriage beside the River Oise in northeastern France; the Great War was at long last over. The Allies won, and the Central Powers lost. Starvation stalked a prostrate Germany, with rioting in its cities and remnants of the Imperial Navy in open mutiny. The Austro/Hungarian Empire existed no more, swept away by the icy winds of war. Eastern Europe and the Balkans lay open, up for grabs.

Victory had come at a terrible price. When the guns finally fell silent on the eleventh hour of the eleventh day of the eleventh month, men no longer died at a rate of three thousand souls per day, every day, for four appalling years. The Allies forced the Kaiser to abdicate his throne; the demoralized German armed forces surrendered with scarcely a whimper. Like punch-drunk fighters in the fifteenth round, the two sides clinched, exhausted, trying not to collapse from the relentless pounding they had both adsorbed. Peace had come just in time; units of the French infantry had openly rebelled, refusing to fight on. One army remained mired in the mud of defeat; the other tried in vain to enjoy the victory. The Allies' general staff prepared for a grand victory parade down the

Champs-Elysées, ignoring the wishes of their men and not for the first time. The soldiers of both armies were too tired, too numb, and too familiar with senseless slaughter to care much about anything other than returning to wherever home was for them.

The surviving officers of the Pilot's fighter squadron had boarded a train together, destination Paris, when it became obvious further combat flying would not be required. The weather was too dreadful for scouting--rainy, cold, and overcast. More importantly, why should they climb again into their war machines when the war they fought had finally ended? The Pilot forbad any celebratory flying and gave the enlisted ground crew a week off duty. The forced stand-down probably saved a few more lives. Half the squadron's fatalities were due to accidents induced by the Camel's tricky handling or mechanical breakdowns, or they were caused by structural failures of the flimsy craft. Committing aviation in the Sopwith Camel rivaled an engagement with the Hun in lethality. With the pilots grounded, the number of empty chairs at the Officers' Mess for once did not increase nightly. The Camel assigned to the Pilot and wearing his heraldry proved unserviceable from a lack of maintenance. The "Hun Hunter" would fly no more. Lofty and Paddy were last seen mounting a serious assault on the Sergeants' Mess's cache of warm British beer.

Upon arrival at La Gare de Nord, the squadron booked a private room at Le Coup Chou Restaurant, paid for in advance with large bank overdrafts presented in anticipation of substantial mustering-out bonuses from a grateful nation. Le Coup Chou's venue was comprised of a maze of interconnected dark rooms scattered through the ground floors of several of the oldest buildings in one of the oldest neighborhoods in Paris, deep in the 5th Arrondissement. It claimed to be the oldest restaurant in Paris and looked it, but other eating establishments disputed the boast so the title remained unproven.

The thirsty pilots engaged the services of a bartender and instructed him to keep his wrists limber by pouring. Despite the Frenchman's rudimentary grasp of the King's English, he showed considerable skill in mixing the latest fashionable cocktail, the French Seventy-Five. The concoction was named after a potent French artillery piece, the famous Soixante-Quinze, which was also widely employed as a lethal anti-aircraft gun. The irony of getting blasted by a drink inspired by "Archie," as ground-based fire was called, was not lost on the Camel pilots, and they made the most of the oppotunity. The libation's provenance was particularly poignant since the French Seventy-Five had been invented by Raoul Lufbery of the Escadrille Lafayette of the French Air Force, and later of the American 94th Aero Squadron. The 94th was the famed "Hat in the Ring" outfit, so-named due to its emblem, Uncle Sam's hat thrown into a prize fighting ring, offering combat to anyone brave enough to pick it up. Evidently, the late Major Lufbery was as accomplished with a cocktail shaker as he was with a Nieuport 17 biplane fighter.

As if the post-war festivities needed more encouragement, the enterprising *Maître D'Hotel* of Le Coup Chou summoned a local piano player, offering him free drinks and ample opportunity for tips from the celebrating pilots. The neighborhood musician claimed to know numerous British drinking songs but pounded out only those favored by the infantry. But no matter, the squadron's men resolutely set about toasting the war's end, which few of them expected to live to see.

The cigarette smoke, clamor, and closeness in the hired room buried in the historic restaurant's sub-basement got to be a bit much. The Pilot, seeking fresh air, headed upstairs for the cobblestone sidewalk in front of the ancient building. Its green awning would provide cover from the pouring rain, and the brisk fall breeze would clear his lungs. Rounding the corner at the top of the half-flight of rickety steps with no two treads the same height, he heard then saw an animated conversation in French between the Maître D'Hôtel and a lone French woman. The subject under vigorous discussion apparently concerned a dispute over a past bill. The Pilot stopped, quite taken aback by the vision of French womanhood in front of him.

She was stunning--tall, elegant, and slender with ebony hair piled on top of her head in the popular "Gibson Girl" style. It had been many, long months since the Pilot last experienced the soft touch of a woman, a condition boosting her attractiveness to him even more. She had the sharp face common in France with a thin nose, small mouth, and large dark eyes softening her visage. Her ankle-length, cream-colored silk dress, cinched tightly around her narrow waist, managed to be simultaneously loose and clinging, modestly hiding her curves yet displaying them graphically to the determined observer. He found it very odd that she was not wearing a hat.

Everyone in Paris, and London for that matter, wore hats, men and women alike. Even street whores wore hats, trying to project some last shred of respectability. Appearing in public bare-headed was unheard of. The Pilot's mind raced, churning with the quick thought processes he recently exercised in air combat. He considered and discarded in turn various classifications for the mysterious woman he now watched with keen interest. Some gentleman's wife and/or high-born mistress? No, a kept lady would not venture into a public house alone at night. A professional, a prostitute? Certainly not, they all exhibited a certain beaten-down look and jaded, world-weary expressions not the bright, intelligent manner of the woman in question. A Bohemian from the hill of Montmartre overlooking Paris? That rebellious cult delighted in violating convention, even going bare-headed at times. No, Bohemian women tended to be plain and simply dressed, imitating what they took to be sturdy peasant stock. This lovely creature exuded class, breeding, and sophistication. If the Pilot hadn't been attracted by the woman's sexual allure, and he surely was, he would have been totally fascinated by the challenge of unraveling the mystery of her background, along with her shining dark hair. He mentally pictured himself slowly removing her hair pins, one by one, letting her raven tresses cascade in waves down her smooth, bare back to her nude, trim waist, and suddenly it didn't matter anymore to him where she came from, only that she was here now.

Clasping his hands behind his back and leaning forward, he approached the arguing pair with long, confident strides and announced in his best schoolboy French, "Peut-être pourrais-je être d'une certain utilité." (Perhaps I could be of some assistance.)

The contentious pair half-turned and looked at him in surprise, the mystery woman more so than the restaurant manager. He had dealt with the Pilot earlier that evening; she had not. The Pilot gave the slightly-built Frenchman a look worthy of a quick burst from twin Vickers machine guns. Out of the woman's sight, the Pilot rubbed the fingertips of his right hand with his thumb, the universal sign of payment. Whatever the dispute, he would make it good.

The Maître D'Hôtel turned back to the woman. "Je suis desolé. Vous avez raison, Mademoiselle. Je vais changer l'addition." (I am sorry. You are correct, Miss. I will change the bill.) The host, satisfied and victorious, wheeled on a heel and quickly disappeared into the restaurant's dim warren of rooms. The use of the unmarried form of address in French, *Mademoiselle*, rather than *Madame* for a wife was duly noted and much welcomed by the Pilot.

"Thank you," said the lady in French-accented English, turning toward the Pilot. "Have we been introduced?" she went on.

"I think not, Mademoiselle, for surely I would remember such intense pleasure. Whom have I the pleasure of addressing?"

The woman told him her name with a wry smile and extended her right hand to him, palm down, long slender fingers slightly bent, wrist drooped. Bending at the waist, he took her lily-white offering in his left palm, raised it slightly, and whispered his lips over the back of her hand. He caught the barest, heady whiff of her perfume as he straightened up while clicking his booted heels together. Identifying himself, he released his light grip and added, "At your service."

She let her hand fall and pressed it against her upper leg, her fingers spread in back, her thumb wrapped in front, outlining her slim right thigh against her thin silk dress and discretely showing off her figure. Her head nodded down then up as she took in his clean khaki uniform, Sam Browne belt, polished leather riding boots without spurs, and gold, embroidered pilot's wings on his left chest. "I see you are an officer of the Royal Flying Corps."

"Actually, we're now the Royal Air Force."

"Bravo! I assume this represents an upgrade in status. Did the War Department mandarins in the corridors of Whitehall welcome your unit's promotion?" She surprised him greatly with her knowledge of the British Forces' pecking order. Most French people found the United Kingdom's military organizational charts incoherent and illogical, not compatible with the bedrock principles laid down by Napoleon.

"Much more so than the Royal Navy's admirals. They resent sharing the limelight with an upstart service, not six months old. Nonetheless, we're not bothered. Those are my men you hear in the lower room, anticipating the coming victory celebrations."

As he spoke, another enthusiastic, if thoroughly slurred, chorus of "Mademoiselle from Armentières," accompanied by the tinkling of an upright piano, rang out from the restaurant's cave. The following verse graphically extolled the physical attributes of the lusty barmaid from Armentières.

"We are, or were, scout pilots."

"Indeed you are; that much is obvious."

He turned toward the rear stairs as the noisy singing grew louder and more boisterous, the piano playing even worse. "I'll just have a quick word with the lads; they're a bit out of hand."

She stopped him by gently raising her right hand, fingers up and spread. "Please do let them carry on. They undoubtedly feel the need to release the tensions of the last terrible four years."

"Quite so. It has been a long, tough slog. Thank you for not being offended by the coarse lyrics. I'm in your debt."

"You are not singing tonight. Whatever do you do to release your own tensions?" She looked him in the eyes with her question. Her gaze was not wavering, demure, or shy, but intelligent and open. She fell silent waiting on his answer.

A grammar schoolmaster's image from long ago flashed into the Pilot's memory. The old man had often quoted Shakespeare, once saying, "There is a tide in the affairs of men, when taken at the flood, which leads on to fortune" from *The Tragedy of Julius Caesar.* In boarding school, the Pilot thought the study of The Bard, with his many clichés, to be a waste of time. Now he had to admit that Ol' William had been right once. The Pilot sensed this to be one of those oft-mentioned, classic opportunities not to be missed or mucked up. Indeed, the tide of his life was changing. For the past months, he had done nothing but fly and fight, trying to keep his men alive so they all could see the next day, and maybe the one after that. With the next week too far in the future to think about, the next month was an unknown concept, outside the realm of possibilities. It had been a simple life, one focused on survival and killing.

Now a safer prospect beckoned after the war. Could this lovely woman before him be part of that? Was his personal tide rising with his desire for her or ebbing with the absence of any war to fight, a lack of a role to play, and a loss of his identity? This strange French woman had an air of timelessness, permanence, stability. She was in no hurry, as if time meant nothing to her as she stood waiting patiently on his response. All this he discovered in the previous five minutes, transmitted with locked gazes and the touch of her hand. His mind racing, he took a chance, a calculated risk, as he had many times in combat, going for the ultimate goal with one lightning move. "May I call on you? Perhaps on the morrow?" he asked.

"Should you not be with your men? They may require your careful supervision later; the course they are on intersects with that of the Gendarmes," she said, a slight smile playing around her thin red lips.

"The men may welcome my absence, be more relaxed, without their squadron commander watching over them like an anxious mother hen. In any case, they'll all be civilians again by Yuletide. Running completely amuck in Paris will be very old news, indeed, by then."

"If they are to be discharged soon, what of you? What will you be doing after the war, pray tell?"

"I shall be flying some fighter plane, somewhere, sometime."

Her dark eyes glistening, she continued looking into his face, a bold move for a single woman. If she felt embarrassed to be so forward, it wasn't at all obvious to the Pilot. "Very well then, as you wish. Entertaining a gentleman caller may prove amusing. You are a gentleman, are you not?"

"That is for you to decide, m'lady."

She reached into a tiny, beaded purse clutched in her left hand and handed him her calling card. Surrounded by an embossed border on stiff, cream-colored paper, her name was engraved in black script sufficiently elaborate to render reading it difficult. A note of her perfume clung to the stationary. Below her name was an address in the fashionable, chic 8th Arrondissement. "Shall we say around fifteen hundred? Be so kind as to present your card to the concierge at the entrance way. She will announce you."

She turned to go, opening the heavy wooden door with its multiple panes of leaded glass before he could reach for it. Just inside the foyer stood a carved, wooden stand holding the wet personal umbrellas of restaurant patrons. In it leaned several umbrellas, dripping into a tin tray at the bottom. He selected the largest, with a carved ivory grip, and opened it as he followed her out to the narrow, rainy side street. The borrowed bumbershoot bridged the gap between the dripping canvas awning and her waiting car, sheltering her bare head from the drizzle and drips. A large, square Renault town car sat idling at the curb, the rain coursing in streaks down its vertical windows. Its engine was ticking over, barely heard.

He opened the rear-hinged car door, holding the umbrella over her as she entered. When she sat down in the padded leatherback seat, the frilly hem of her long dress slowly slid up as if caught on some projecting corner of the car. She revealed her left leg, nearly to her knee. The Pilot was treated to a quick view of a small patent leather shoe, a trim ankle, and a shapely calf, all bare skin instead of being clad in the expected black silk stocking. The shocking revelation was not an accident but was quickly reversed, her dress sliding with a whisper down her nude calf.

What kind of woman was this? thought the Pilot. Hatless in public, naked legs without stockings. Forward and unafraid, a fascinating prize worthy of pursuit, however long the chase took.

"A demain" (Until tomorrow), she said as he swung the car door closed.

Trailing smoke, the Renault clattered off on its skinny tires down the lane paved with Belgian blocks and disappeared into the wet night.

The Pilot collapsed and returned the purloined umbrella, wetter now, to the stand, turned, and stood in the open doorway, looking out into the dark neighborhood. The uncouth noise emanating from the lower room seemed even louder now, clearly audible at the door; laughter, singing, and the clink of fast-emptying glasses rang out. The cacophony represented the final chorus of an era in the RAF officers' lives. They never expected to, never wanted to, live through such a murderous time again. The Pilot hesitated and glanced for a moment back into the dimly lit restaurant, into his past. His military greatcoat and wheel-shaped military hat hung from a nearby wall peg. He pulled them on slowly. Cocking his billed hat at a jaunty angle tipped toward his right ear, he turned his coat collar up against the Parisian cold, the French wind, and the coming European deluge. The Pilot stepped out of Paris's oldest restaurant into the rain, into the night, into the future.

CHAPTER 19

FOUQUET'S CAFÉ

Champs-Elysées
Paris

May 2014: Yogi Berra's prophecy proved to be prescient; Fouquet's Café was crowded, far too crowded. The Pilot had asked her to book a table on the terrace, facing the Champs-Elysées. Her request in native French would prevent their being exiled to the Anglophone ghetto in another, more distant section of the café. The Maître D'Hôtel notoriously concentrated English-speaking diners there, better to be served by multi-lingual servers, but also as not to annoy local Parisian patrons with their uncouth English babbling. On the terrace, the crowd noise generated from the packed tables would mingle with the hum radiating from the nonstop traffic on the wide boulevard just outside. The din would hinder anyone from recording a conversation. Even eavesdropping would be difficult in the buzz despite the tiny tables being close side-by-side, each almost touching its neighbor. He thought she had chosen Fouquet's Café for its communication security.

At first her choice of restaurants surprised and disappointed the Pilot, but he changed his mind after further contemplation. A quiet, romantic dinner, their last together in Paris, would make leaving her even more difficult, and it would be harder to deceive her as instructed by the CIA. Perhaps the lack of intimacy was her objective, as well.

They met on the bustling sidewalk in front of the café. She wore a kelly green business suit, having come directly from work, with her usual tight miniskirt and a silk blouse with more buttons undone for a personal dinner than was permissible in the office. The outfit emphasized her soft hair and accented her hips and legs. As he sat there, it hurt the Pilot to look at her across the table, knowing he would not be able to do so again for some time, if ever. When DGSE realized the information she was relaying from the Pilot was worthless, their relationship, by then under distance pressure as well, would explode like a Maverick missile warhead and with the same finality.

Wedged in among the crowd, they strained to make conversation, each fumbling with personal, profound uncertainty about the future. Both agreed they were not hungry and ordered bowls of traditional *Soupe à l'Oignon Gratinée* (French onion soup) with a basket of bread. The loaves arrived brown and toasty for a change. A flask of Perrier and a bottle of Gigandas completed this most French of meals. The richness of the Rhone Valley red wine complemented well the hot soup's earthiness, the brown broth topped with floating islands of croutons and stringy melted cheese.

She put down her soup spoon and broke a short, awkward silence, looking directly at him, her gaze solid, unwavering. "I have been thinking about your lack of enthusiasm for the F-35. France has nothing to compete with it; the aircraft will surely sell in quantity to friendly air forces. I believe Stalin once said that quantity is a kind of quality. Won't the large numbers of aircraft in service overcome the limitations you're worried about? You might not have to fight outnumbered."

"Perhaps, but the jet's exorbitant price tag won't allow us, or anyone else, to buy anything like the projected numbers. The development community knows this program will be the last for at least a generation, maybe forever. They stuffed as much expensive gear into it as they could and will keep on working on the development endlessly; they have no alternative jobs in the pipeline. It's either milk the F-35 for all the dollars or go out of business, hence the stratospheric price, resulting in a scarcity of wingmen."

"So your objection is to the actions of, what is it called, the military-industrial complex?"

"Yes, and the paper pushers in the Pentagon and Congress with their private agendas having nothing to do with winning wars or even keeping pilots alive. But that's not why I'm so cold on the idea. I can cope with all of that; I have before."

"So what is it then? I must ask again."

He paused, looked past her into the middle distance, and took a deep breath, returning to those dark eyes once more. He had often rehearsed this speech looking in his shaving mirror, intending to give it to her at the right time. If this wasn't that time, when would be? "I'm much more than the frustrated fighter pilot you see in front of you here and now. I carry with me the long traditions, vivid memories, and hard-earned values of many fighter pilots stretching into the past. I represent those pilot, as best I can. For a century, my squadron mates and I have tried to fly and fight and win in the right ways. We've always struggled to prevent men's lives from being thrown away in inept aircraft, and we've fought against our superiors when they tried to impose unworkable, stupid tactics."

"You sound like the ghost of Christmas present," she said with a wry smile and a sip of the Gigondas.

"For a hundred years, we've demanded reliable aircraft, guns that don't freeze, missiles that work, cockpits you can see out of. But most of all, we've strived for, as Baron Von Richthofen said, the freedom to roam our assigned areas and engage the enemy as we see fit. He said it in German, adding that 'anything else is rubbish,' but he spoke for all of us, for all time. With the F-35, we've lost some of that. Pilots have been forced to take a giant step backward by the bureaucrats, who always prosper between wars. You can't see out of the F-35; some models don't even have a gun. The gun we do have is inoperative and only carries one hundred eighty-two rounds; the F-104 carried seven hundred fifty, the F-4, six hundred forty. Hell, even the Sopwith Camel toted seven hundred rounds. The aircraft doesn't work without programming, and the software, like all software, crashes incessantly. When everything works, which is seldom, we won't be able to roam our areas as we see fit. We'll be under the electronic orders of folks miles or continents away, people who are more comfortable operating drones. We'll be like the folks you see around us, enslaved by their always connected, always on, always intrusive electronic devices."

She listened, staring at him as if she saw him for the first time, but didn't reply. The chatter around them continued along with the banging of plates and the traffic noise. Every minute, another cell phone rang somewhere in the café.

She spoke, breaking the noisy silence. "My love, this is a battle you cannot win. You are not fighting another pilot in another aircraft; you are trying to shoot down the future. Yes, I can see around us many people tied to their electronics. The other, younger pilots you will be flying with will be just as dependent on their devices as our fellow diners. They will not feel confined by connectivity; they would feel naked and alone without it, vulnerable and abandoned. Constant communication is the wave of the future. The lone-wolf fighter pilot belongs to the past. Your days are numbered as--how do you say it in English--an apex predator. That is the right word, n'est pas? The time of the airborne apex predator is over. Trying to change this will be, I am afraid, your *Beau Geste* and this airbase in Florida your Fort Zinderneuf."

"If you mean a fight against long odds, ending with a grand gesture, then I prefer the Alamo analogy. Davy Crockett and Jim Bowie were actual men; they came from Tennessee and Louisiana."

"As you wish, but the fact remains the Geste brothers, as well as Bowie and Crockett, died in vain, overwhelmed by mindless multitudes whose alien culture they did not understand."

If in wine there is truth, the Gigondas was delivering the goods. He refilled their glasses himself, the waiter nowhere in sight. He hadn't expected her to try and talk him out of the assignment when her professional success depended on him climbing into the F-35 and reporting back to her and DGSE.

"I'm not afraid to risk my life, even in a lost cause. My mates and I have done that before."

She put her soup spoon on the table, carefully pushed her wine glass out of the way, gripped the small table with both hands, and leaned across to him. It wasn't clear whether she was trying not to be overheard or wanted to hammer her next point home. She engaged his eyes without blinking, her blouse gaping open in a long V, the insides of her breasts touching each other. "Yes, but are you comfortable with risking your soul, your manhood? If you fly the F-35, you will have to adopt its philosophy. You will become one of them, tied to the omnipresent electronic net, emotionally and tactically dependent on a data link. You will not be the man I now love, the man you have been all this time."

"I can endure all that if I have a chance to get a MiG or two, preferably five, making me an ace."

"How many MiGs have been shot down in recent conflicts?"

"You've done your homework well; you know the answer is very few. It seems that we've shot up the breeding stock."

"So why are you doing this?"

Stripped naked of his rationalizations, he realized his motivation was driven in large part by his orders from the CIA to feed her bogus data. They both fell silent as the truth and logic of what she said sunk in.

She reached into her purse and handed him an envelope, cream-colored, from heavy stock, with his name hand-written in bold cursive on the front. "I have for you a petite bon-voyage present." Her face gave no indication of her emotions beneath the surface.

The Pilot opened the envelope and took out a thin stack of playing cards, face down, four in all. One by one he turned them over. Ace of Hearts, Ace of Spades, Eight of Clubs, Eight of Diamonds. "It's the--"

"--dead man's hand," she finished his sentence, speaking softly. "The one the cowboy Hickok held when he was assassinated."

"I see DGSE has people who can do research on pop culture and have access to the internet as well," he said.

"Exactement." (Exactly.)

He looked at her long and hard, their soups growing cold, the little remaining wine un-poured, still in the bottle, and most of the crusty bread untouched. "Are you predicting I'll buy the farm in the F-35?"

"Buy the farm? What does that mean?"

"It's a euphemism for getting killed, calling it retirement to a non-existent farm."

"No, mon amour. I am making a point with my little gift. There is more to life than merely staying alive. One can die in spirit, as well as in the flesh.

Compromising your ideals, giving in to the bureaucrats and politicians, not being true to what you have fought for, is a kind of death. Hemingway knew that. Monsieur Wild Bill let his standards slip, and he paid the price. But the gunfighter never filled his hand; he died holding only those four cards you now have in your own hand. However, one additional card is available to you. You have missed the last one."

He slipped a fifth card, different from the rest, out of the envelope and turned it over. In his palm lay an elegant calling card, heavily embossed on the same thick, cream-colored paper as the envelope. The paper he had seen before. Her name was engraved in a black flowery font, hard to read. At the lower right was an unfamiliar landline phone number with a Parisian prefix, her private line, probably tapped along with all the other numbers in Paris. The lower left listed an address in the tony 8th Arrondissement, strangely familiar. It was the first time she shared with him her home's location. She had never volunteered it, and he hadn't pressed the matter. She spoke first.

"Tell me about this base you are going to. It is on Florida's Gulf of Mexico coast, no? What is it like there? Will I like it?"

He started to answer, relieved to lighten the conversation and stop the thoughts swirling around in a Luftbery inside his brain. "All you need to know about the Florida panhandle, the redneck Riviera--"

"Pardon, but what does "red neck" mean?" she interrupted.

"A redneck, un cous-rouge, is a paysan, a country person, usually from the southern states. Rednecks adore the Gulf Coast; it's their Riviera. They visit in the thousands. The defining words for that region of America are: sun, sea, sand, and slackers. The ocean beaches there are the color and consistency of granulated sugar . . ." He fell silent in midsentence. Instead of elaborating further, he abruptly stopped talking and stared at her as she sat back in her chair, her arms folded under her breasts. Waiting, but for what?

Sometimes the unforeseen truth drifts into our consciousness like soft fog enveloping an airfield at night--quiet, silent, relentless. Un-noticed, the stealthy new truth gradually displaces previous ideas until one day we realize our older beliefs were false or incomplete, and they have been slowly replaced by a new reality. In other, more dramatic times, hard truth and penetrating insight arrive with all the delicate subtlety of a Three Stooges dope slap, rattling our teeth and shaking our preconceived perceptions. This moment was one of those second cases for the Pilot.

She was suddenly revealed in the misty images of his inherited memories, backlit by an unexpected but familiar light, a light that had shone many times in his and many other pilots' eyes. He saw her as she would have appeared, lovely and naked, under harsh government-issue lights in various Officers' Quarters around the world. He could easily picture her warmed by a hazy Thai dawn, in the cool morning shade of the Great Smokey Mountains, and yes, in the dark, blurry drizzle of long-ago, nighttime Paris. She and her antecedents were known well by the Pilot and his kind.

She continued to sit back in her bentwood café chair, her miniskirted, bare legs crossed and the hem of her skirt riding higher. Her arms lifted her breasts up into the open V of her silk blouse. She obviously read the consternation playing across his face. Slightly closed, her eyes were softer now, reflecting those various lights of times past. Waiting on the inevitable question, she drew back her trim shoulders, gaping open her blouse even deeper between her breasts.

The Pilot drew a deep breath and spoke at long last. "Will you be there with me?" he asked, already knowing the answer.

"I always have been there. In your mind. In your memories. In your thoughts. In your fantasies. As you have been in mine."

"I see that now."

He laid the four playing cards in his hand face up on the table and held the fifth. In a voice infused with more yearning than direction, he looked at the now-familiar woman across from him and extended a completely unnecessary invitation, "The last Eurostar tonight from La Gare du Nord. Carriage number three. Will you be working for DGSE?"

"You know there is only one answer to that. Before we go, I must share more wisdom from the yogi you are so fond of. I found the quote online. 'You better know where you're going, or you'll end up somewhere else,' " she said.

"Good advice for both of us."

He put her calling card in his shirt pocket and signaled a passing waiter for *l'addition* (the check). He paid the exorbitant bill with the ambassador's embassy credit card and added a substantial tip, even though service was included, as always. Before walking away, the Pilot retrieved a single coin from his pants pocket and laid it carefully on the table. The restaurant's white noise receded into the background as the glass door closed behind them.

They turned right down the Champs-Elysées toward the Avenue George V Metro station. As they walked, he looked over a low hedge into the terrace's window at the place they just vacated. The waiter and busboy were looking with quizzical expressions at the aces and eights lying face up in the breadcrumbs on the cluttered table. Holding the cards down wasn't the expected small-change of Euros, but an American five-cent coin, a nickel.

CHAPTER 20

THE EUROSTAR

Northwest France

May 2014: The Eurostar TGV, *Train à Grande Vitesse* (Train of Great Speed), seemed intent on deserving its name. At 300 kilometers per hour (185 miles per hour), it streamed through the early morning darkness on seamless tracks, flowing relentlessly like a steel river across the flat plains of northwestern France, a landscape with horrendous tales to tell if one would only listen.

Nearly a century earlier, millions of men fought to advance their respective armies' lines yard by yard over the same ground. The soldiers of the Great War suffered horrific losses in human-sea attacks, dying for scant stretches of muddy ground gained, losing back those precious gains, and suffering even more. Both sides had expected a quick victory, with mounted cavalry prancing down the Champs-Elysées, Pall Mall in London, or the Boulevard Unter Den Linden in Berlin. The appalling reality they soon discovered was more prosaic--one of machine guns, barbed wire, poison gas, and new technology--catching them un-prepared. The region's sticky clay claimed their bodies, swallowed their gear, and absorbed thousands of tons of unexploded ordnance.

Pilots fell to their deaths from great heights, claimed by the battlefield mire along with their smashed planes. The piles of debris--mounds of broken wood and burnt cloth, junked engines, and mangled human bodies--were drenched, subsumed by the snow and the rain and the mud. Many are still there today, like beloved French ace Georges Guynemer. Generations of French school children were told their hero flew so high that he couldn't come down again. The reality of the first modern war was far less romantic. He was shot down, and his body was never found, sunk in the no-man's land morass along with the crumpled wreckage of his SPAD XIII aircraft. Both the man and Vieux Charles, his steed, were unrecoverable between the two lines of trenches.

The speeding TGV passed over the old killing fields, unseen and unheard by the men sleeping forever in their tens of thousands beneath the now-green countryside. Without acknowledgement of what lay beneath, the smooth, welded rails stretched over the awful remains of World War I and the many unmarked graves, representing a technological future far beyond the ken of the lost soldiers and pilots of the Great War.

The lights of small French towns flitted by the tinted windows of carriage three, anonymous villages passing quickly, silently in the night. The TGV track ran level and straight, caring neither of topography nor the habitations alongside its path. A cluster of lights would appear in the window and flash by in a blur of pale illumination tinted blue by the window glass, the hamlet set well back from the tracks and gone in seconds. The speeding train bypassed stations and towns alike, fast and remote on its dedicated and separate right-of-way.

People in the passed farm houses ate, drank, watched TV, made love, and slept, but mostly ignored the train hurtling by. If they bothered to look across the moonlit fields, they saw a blue-silver streak in the distance and a dancing stream of lighted carriage windows. They heard an eerie whoosh of displaced air and tingled to the ring of steel wheels rolling on steel rails. The passing Eurostar made no difference in their rural lives, which changed slowly, if at all. The people on the high-speed train were moving, leaving the deeply buried battlefields of the Great War behind and going somewhere else, perhaps into the future, leaving both oblivious country folk and the subterranean past behind.

They sat across from each other in the nearly empty car, taking turns looking out the dark window beside them. The Pilot sensed rather than perceived the train's speed. Even at 185 miles per hour the ride felt quiet and serene, and the carriage seemed motionless although traveling through space and time. It seemed to him the train had rapidly left something behind in the night. Paris was already fading into his memories, bright and vibrant now, but the City of Light would began soon to dim in his mind as had all the other cities until all that remained would be the highlights of his life there. Hemingway believed Paris was a moveable feast--one you could take with you when you left the city, one you could snack on later, and one that never left you. The Pilot found himself disagreeing with Ernie, once a rare occurrence but now more common. For example, Papa's macho approach to womankind was perhaps not the best for the modern world or for modern women demanding equal partnership not patronization and deserving equality. *The feast of the senses Paris provides*, the Pilot thought, *should be consumed fresh to be meaningful.* He knew he would return to the city someday, perhaps often, but it would never again be home.

He also wondered about the woman sitting uneasily across from him and their future together, if any. Would she last? There had been many other women-- or was it her--who entered his life, shared it for a brief sojourn, maybe only a single night, and disappeared into the dark distance, left behind by life's uncaring silver train. But they hadn't totally disappeared; they showed themselves again and again in his memories. Each encounter left its image, some indistinct, others vivid. Somehow they were all the same person, only in different guises. He saw that now. The French woman facing him seemed strangely familiar at their first meeting, a perception he couldn't shake at the time. It should have been hard to get to know someone so well in the three weeks they had been together, particularly hard to get into a woman from a different, French culture. Still, it happened, both slipping into easy familiarity, and love, but for how long?

"I always have been there," she had said, those words a revelation. She was there in his collective memory and in the memories of his predecessors--in Saudi Arabia, beside the Moon River, along the banks of the Little Pigeon, in London, and far, far earlier, in Paris itself. It was almost time to test her commitment, for he had to be sure.

"I've booked us a room at the Royal Air Force Club in London," he said softly, looking at her.

"Brilliant. I understand it is quite nice, with interesting ceilings. I hope to enjoy looking up at those again. Sadly, I brought nothing for us to share. None of the Scotch single malt or Tennessee sour mash whiskey I know you like."

"We don't need anything to break the ice. We already know each other and have for a long time."

He took his laptop from its case under the table between them and booted it up, pulled up a particular page, then turned the computer around and slid it toward her. A draft message was displayed on the blue-lit screen in his official email account. It was addressed to his commander in Washington and read:

With this message, I hereby resign my commission in the United States Air Force and request immediate processing for retirement and transfer to the Inactive Reserve. I will be available for out-processing and debriefing at Mildenhall AFB, UK on 15 May 2014. Please notify Air Training Command I have declined assignment to the F-35 program.

After reading it, she stared at him for a long time without speaking, not handing back the computer. Time was suspended in the rail car. "Are you sure you want to do this?"

"Yes. Dead, solid certain. You were right. Sometimes you can't compromise; you can't give in to a future hell-bent on changing you for the worst and making you an emotional slave to electronics, particularly while airborne. Also, there comes a time to do something else besides using airplanes to kill people. For me the gap between living a normal life on the ground and fighting to the death in the air has grown too wide. What that new life will be I don't know, but it'll be fun finding out. As Yogi said, 'It's hard to make predictions, particularly about the future.' "

At that she glanced up at the baggage rack overhead, a curious smile on her face, as if to say, "Why me?"

"Whatever our future together brings, I am certain your yogi and his sayings will be part of it," she interrupted him.

Undaunted, he went on, "My only desire is you'll be there with me. I wanted to tell you in time for you to back out, if that's what you want."

This was the test; it would show the depth of her commitment. In their hoped-for new life together, there could be no covert reports to DGSE. Could she change, as well, and leave the murky world of military intelligence behind?

She reached into her carry-on bag, removed her notebook computer, booted it up, and typed for several minutes as the train streamed on its direct path to London.

Instantly, the distant countryside lights disappeared, replaced by black nothingness. They had entered the Chunnel, the railway tunnel beneath the English Channel (La Manche). With nothing visible outside, all they could see was the inside of the carriage, dimly lit and seemingly suspended now in space and time. There was no perception of movement, sense of speed, or change in the subdued ambient noise; it was a well-appointed time machine. Destination: the future.

Finished, she handed the notebook to the Pilot to read what she had composed. It was addressed to someone at the director level of DGSE and read in French:

This message serves to notify you of my intention to resign my position with DGSE, effective immediately. In my desk and files are all the government information I currently have in my possession, as well as my personal weapon. In accordance with my oath, I will, of course, not disclose any privileged information, with two possible exceptions noted below. Please prepare all the necessary forms, and I will send for them in the near future. I will notify you of my mailing address shortly. Please close my email account.

The two possible exceptions are as follows. In my apartment's kitchen is a flour canister. In this you will find a plastic bag containing two flash drives. On one drive is a dossier I have compiled of the extra-judicial activities conducted by our department and approved by you. The second drive contains a similar dossier of certain potentially embarrassing, if not illegal, actions taken by our department chief. I will retain the original dossiers and have entrusted a friend with encoded copies, as well.

The email finished with the usual formal salutations and best wishes, along with her name and job title, Special Agent.

"Now it's my turn to ask, are you sure you want to do this? And what is it with these dossiers?"

"Yes, I am sure and have been since the night we first made love. When one leaves an intelligence service, it is always wise to have an insurance policy."

"Life insurance?"

"Probably not, we French don't execute retired agents. This little ploy is to prevent them from calling on me in the future, asking for more information. When they go to my apartment, they will find the entry lock forced and the door ajar. On my kitchen table, they will see a pile of flour and on top an empty plastic bag."

"So they'll assume someone else has beaten them to the dossiers."

"Yes, and they won't know who has them or exactly what the files contain."

"What do they contain?"

"Nothing, there are no files. I fabricated the whole story."

"But what of these illegal activities you referenced?"

"There are always some in the intelligence world. No one knows the whole story, but we do know there are always things that have happened that the bosses would rather not see exposed to the light of day."

It was his turn to say, "Brilliant."

He reached toward his laptop and with a dramatic flourish, pressed "Send," closed the cover, and sat back watching her. Without a moment's hesitation, she extended a slender, feminine finger and sent away her resignation with a single tap on her laptop. Both machines were deposited back under the table and promptly forgotten.

The Pilot folded the table down between them; she moved across to his side and laid her head on his shoulder. He spoke softly, "There is one last question before our new life begins."

"Why I wear my shortest skirts nude?"

"Exactement."

"It started in my Lycée, high school to you, with my official school uniform . . ."

As she continued her explanation, the train climbed a gradual incline. Rolling slower now, it emerged from the Chunnel's mouth, into the future. Meeting a misty dawn as it greeted England's home counties, the Eurostar cruised toward London, flowing and unstoppable. Visible from the windows, the sky ranged from bright sunlight in the northeast to light haze high overhead. A low, dark-gray fog covered the English Channel behind them, but horizon to horizon ahead, the blue, inverted sky-bowl was empty, silent, and peaceful.

THE END

ACKNOWLEDGEMENTS

The following long-suffering people were instrumental in the writing of *The Pilot* Doris Badger helped me break out of my Luftbery with punctuation. Dr. Brooke Landon of the University of Iowa taught me it's not how long you make sentences, it's how you make them long. Mary Barker kindled my passion for English at Chattanooga High School. Alexandrea Wallace helped me not write in French "Comme une Vache Espagnole." Dominique and Bernard Christophe were my private investigators in Paris. Group Captain Mark Heffron, Royal Air Force, sorted out my chapter set in the RAF Club, London. Quentin Gombaud of the Musée de l'Air et de l''Espace at Le Bourget, France, was a big help. Colonel Norm Fogg, ex-Tennessee Air National Guard, cross-checked the chapter on the F-104 Starfighter. Javier Arango and Chuck Wentworth provided first-hand knowledge of the Sopwith Camel. Special thanks to my beta readers, Heidi Cobleigh, Carolyn Berndt, Lisa Fisher, Jeff Koligian, Memory Seaman, and particularly, Ben Lambeth. Admiral Sir Frank ("Skip") Bowman, USN(Ret), opened publishing doors. Former US Ambassador to France, Charles Rivkin, added insight on the workings of the US Embassy, Paris. Special thanks to Irene Chambers, without her editing, the book would not be what it is.

I apologize if I didn't include your favorite cliché, stereotyped character, shopworn quote, or familiar Parisian scene. I did the best I could.

Ed "Fast Eddie" Cobleigh, Lt/Col, USAF(Ret)

82675171R00128

Made in the USA
Middletown, DE
05 August 2018